THE BOY FROM ALEPPO WHO PAINTED THE WAR

A NOVEL OF SYRIA

by Sumia Sukkar

EYEWEAR FICTION

For my precious family,
with love.

Sumia Sukkar
is a British writer
of Syrian and Algerian ancestry,
brought up in London.
This is her debut novel.

My blood has travellers in it: a Damascene moon,
nightingales, domes and grains. From Damascus
Jasmine begin to send whiteness across the air
so fragrance itself is perfumed by their scent.

— *from* Nizar Qabbani's 'A Damascene Moon'
Translated by Sumia Sukkar & Todd Swift

Characters

Adam — The boy from Aleppo who painted the war
Ali — Adam's neighbour/ friend
Amira — Adam's cousin
Aunt Suha — Adam's aunt
Baba — Adam's father
Isa — Adam's brother
Khalid — Adam's brother
Khanjar — Famous mercenary
Liquorice — Adam's cat
Maha — Mama - Adam's mother
Miss Basma — Adam's teacher
Nabil — Adam's friend
Tariq — Adam's brother
Uncle Shady — Adam's uncle
Walid — Khalid's friend
Wisam — Yasmine's lover
Yasmine — Adam's sister

Chapter One

ORANGE

'I can't draw! There's too much noise outside!' I shout to Yasmine.

'Adam, calm down and just continue Habibi!'

'Yasmine, tell the kids to yes, yes, yes, stop making noise! They listen to you.'

Yasmine lowers her head. She does that when things are difficult to explain. I don't like it.

'Adam Habibi, you're old enough to understand this is the beginning of a war.'

Mama never used to shout at me. It's at times like these that I miss her the most. Yasmine's fingers ruffle through her hair, her fingers look frail, just like the number one. I feel sorry for the number one, it seems lonely. So I think I feel sorry for Yasmine too. Yasmine lifts her head up now. That means she is not upset. Her eyes look like the number eight, friendly and sad.

'Yes I'm 14, does that make you happy Yasmine? What do you mean a war? Do you mean like in Dighton's paintings? But I can't see that from the window. Look here Yasmine, kids are just running around. No one is wearing uniforms.'

Yasmine closes her eyes. She looks green. She is usually ruby. That's my favourite colour. I use it in most of my paintings. I remember when mama used to say I should never stop painting. She promised she would keep my paintings with her.

But now they have to stay with me.

'It's okay Yasmine, I'll just paint with the noise.'

Yasmine blows me a kiss. We do this to show our love. Before she died, mama told her that she should blow me a kiss every time she is proud or happy with me. Mama used to do that to me because she understood I don't like people touching me.

'Yasmine, do you like my painting?'

'It's lovely Adam, but why not try painting something new for a change?'

Yasmine always says this. She thinks I paint the same picture. I don't. No two pictures are ever the same. It's hard to explain that to her. She starts walking away, so I don't need to explain anything. The colours are always different. I sometimes use pastel colours and at other times harsh bright colours. All the paintings have different feelings behind them. I wish Yasmine would understand this like mama used to. I feel content now so I use a lot of turquoise. I continue painting until it is time for Baba to come back home.

Baba comes back home every day at 4:48 p.m. He doesn't even need to ring the bell any more. He knows I'll be waiting to open the door for him at that exact minute. It has been like this for three years, ever since mama died. He looks more tired every passing day. The bags under his eyes are clearer now. I blow a kiss onto them every night hoping they will go away. I don't like seeing him tired. Yasmine has the hot water ready for Baba to soak his feet as soon as I open the door. He is never a minute late and is always holding a bag full of papers to mark. When he is not too tired he even stamps them with colourful words like 'well done' and 'excellent'. I like to help him when he uses the stamps. They're fun to play with. Baba sometimes complains about me playing with the elastic band around my wrist. He says the sound annoys him, but I can't let go of it. It has to always be on my wrist. It helps me think.

Yasmine has made stuffed vegetables. It is the 26th of January and mama isn't looking down on us today. I love stuffed vegetables: they are like a bowl of emotions because they are very colourful. I sometimes imagine the peppers arguing with each other because they all feel differently. 'I feel melancholy in this bowl of food', the red pepper would say. 'Oh red pepper, how can you feel that way? You should be so angry that we are going to be eaten,' the aubergine would frown. My imagination sometimes takes hold of me and I get louder.

Yasmine always brings me back, reminding me that we shouldn't be too loud because Baba is tired. When Yasmine cooks six peppers, I know that mama is watching over us, because mama always made six stuffed peppers. Today there are five on the plate. This makes me sad, but it's okay, mama is probably resting. She is ill and needs some rest. I sometimes wonder if mama eats stuffed vegetables and baklawa in heaven. I know they have a lot of yummy food up there but this is her favourite dish. Yasmine sometimes sighs and smiles a weak yellow smile when I tell her about how I know when mama is watching over us. I can't explain why some things are true. But I am sure this is true. I don't lie. The definition of a lie is an intentional false statement. It confuses me. Why do people lie? They say one thing, but it didn't actually happen and so that means something else happened. So two things happened according to them but that doesn't make sense either. Why can't they just say the one thing that actually happened? My brain hurts when I think about it. I don't understand some people.

Mama died when I was 11. I miss her. She always told me I should be good and go to university to show people my paintings. I can't wait to go to university. My classmates say I belong to the special needs class and not university. They are stupid and wrong, says Yasmine. I don't like meeting new people, so I won't speak to anyone in class at university. So many people like to create small talk. I don't see the need for it. It's silly and a waste of time. I don't know why people don't realise this.

Khalid, Tariq and Isa come in and join the table. They are all the same age and at university. They are triplets. Even though they look alike they all have different colours. Khalid is orange, Tariq is teal and Isa is green. That's how I tell them apart. Orange brother always smiles and looks cheerful, he is the one who makes all the jokes in the house. Teal brother always gets me chocolate and comes home the latest. Green Isa is the quietest. He doesn't study architecture like the other two, he studies Arabic literature instead. Hardly anyone notices his presence, but it's hard for me to overlook his aura.

'Yasmine, can I get up from the table please?'

'You didn't even finish your food Adam.'

Everyone is sharing from a plate in the middle of the table but I always need a plate of my own. I don't like my food touching anybody else's. So Yasmine can tell I hardly ate. I don't get up from the table but keep fidgeting and start banging my feet on the ground. Yasmine ignores me. I don't like it when she does that but if I say anything she'll make me eat and I don't want to. I wait until everyone else excuses themselves from the table. Yasmine is upset I think. Her face looks long. When her face is round she is happy. I have a long face when I think of mama. My heart feels bloody and black, I can't smile at anything. I try not to think of mama much because I don't like the feeling. I don't know why I feel that way when I think of her but I am too scared to ask too many questions about it. I just try to forget. Now that I am trying to forget about thinking of mama I can't stop. I hate it when this happens.

The violet colour of her death that came out of her coffin is now stuck in my mind. I can sometimes go days without thinking about it, but when I start, it is hard to stop. She looked like snow. Not made of snow, but just a pile of snow in a box, messy and about to melt and turn into water. I wanted to touch mama and see if she felt as cold as snow but Yasmine said it would be better not to. Mama's hair looked like a pigeon sitting on the snow. It is scary to remember it. I feel sick now. I'm scared.

I leave the sitting room and run to my room since it's not my turn to help in the kitchen today. I always open my door, count to three, take a step back and jump onto my bed from the door. I never step on the carpet between the door and the bed. If I do it means I won't have a good day. Even when I am too tired to jump I have to. Being in my room makes me feel warm and brown. I love the feeling, the feeling means home. My window is dusty and it hurts my eyes. I need to clean it, now. I jump to the window and try to blow the dust away. It's from the outside. It doesn't usually get this dusty. Maybe a sandstorm is coming. I can still see through the window but if I let the dust grow it will slide into my room and turn into a big weird creature that will eat me when I am not looking. It always happens in the horror movies that Yasmine doesn't like me watching. There are no children running outside like usual. The café opposite my window has the chairs on the tables. The name 'Al-Sham' is full of dust and the café seems like it is abandoned and empty.

Chapter Two

VIOLET

I SOMETIMES PRETEND I'm a dinosaur who is complaining about being the last one left here, not having anyone to play with and who eats humans who don't want to play with him. Sometimes I even pretend I'm living in the Stone Age and hunting for food, like in *The Flintstones*. It's so much fun to pretend I am someone else. I am good at playing games like that. When I am in bed and the lights are off I imagine I am a firefly glowing in the dark looking for a mate like in *Grave of the Fireflies*, but I never imagine I am a scary insect because then I won't be able to sleep.

The sun just came out. I always wake up as soon as there's light. I just can't sleep with light outside and I don't like closing the curtains because I feel trapped. I was once playing hide-and-seek with Khalid and I hid under the bed and he couldn't find me. Mama then called him and he forgot about the game. I waited for hours. After that I hated small and dark spaces. They're scary.

I can look outside my window when I sit up on my bed. The street outside is still empty and now even dustier. The café is still not open and I can see posters all over the walls. It must really be a sandstorm or maybe a war like Yasmine said. I jump up to the window to read what the posters say but I can't read them from this far. I look at my watch. It's Saturday. I don't have school today so I can't go outside. I only go out when I have school. I don't have any other reason to go outside otherwise. I will have to wait to read what the posters say. I can smell coffee from the kitchen. I hate the taste but I love waking up to the smell. I can hear the sound of the television from the sitting room. No one is usually up this early on Saturday apart from Yasmine and me. I jump back on my bed and then to my door to see who is watching television. I want to watch my morning show about modern art but I guess today I won't be able to. I walk five steps then turn one foot to the right and put the other foot down and count three steps to the sitting room.

The sitting room looks like a messy art canvas with bright colours. My eyes squint. It's too colourful for me in the morning. The whole family is sitting around the television. Everyone has their duvets on them. I wonder how long they have been there for. The breakfast is still on the table: red and yellow peppers cut up on a plate and five coffees with labna in a bowl. I miss mama's labna, she made the best.

Nobody turns around to see me come into the sitting room. I wonder what is going on. I guess it is because of the sandstorm. It can't really be a war. No one is dressed in army clothes. On the screen, there are huge groups of people on the streets protesting with banners but I can't read them from here.

'The revolution in the Arab world has been going on for nearly nine months and now Syria is facing upheaval,' says the voice-over in a tone almost as if a vicious array of metallic pins were rushing out of her mouth. I can't watch any more.

Yasmine gets up to go to the kitchen and sees me standing there.

'Adam, go wash up and I'll make you breakfast.'

'What's going on Yasmine? Are we protesting as well? I thought there was a sandstorm.'

'Sandstorm? Oh Adam, just go wash up.'

'Yasmine, why don't you tell me?'

'Adam, there is no sandstorm. There is going to be a war. A real war, we are going to go and protest tomorrow.'

'I have school tomorrow Yasmine, I can't go protesting.'

'You can't go to school Habibi, you can stay home with Isa.'

'But I have to go to school, I can't miss any classes.'

'Oh Adam… Habibi because of the war, there is no school. Everyone is out protesting. School will start again soon, I promise.'

'Okay Isa and I will stay home Miss,' I say and run towards the bathroom, through the kitchen, without stepping on any black tiles and then jump into the bathroom from three steps back. I brush my teeth with a perfect pea-sized amount of toothpaste. I have a pea I keep in my cupboard to compare the size. I brush three strokes to the right, then three strokes to the left. I then brush three strokes up and down and spit in the middle of the sink.

In the shower I think about school. There is only one boy I like in class, Nabil. He is the only one who is nice and doesn't make fun of me. He even buys me lunch sometimes, but he is usually out of money. I don't mind sharing my lunch with him, but I don't let him touch the part I am going to eat.

'I have a surprise for you,' he once said as he rushed into the room and sat next to me.

I moved my chair a little away from him, he was too close and his breath was in my face. It smelled of coffee and chewing gum. I love the smell of coffee, but not on someone's breath.

'Hello Mister. How are you today?'

'Fine Adam, guess what? I got the "Guild Wars"!'

'Really Mister! That is fantastic! Can I play with you?'

'Of course, that's why I came to you. Do you want to come over and play with me?'

'Come over where?'

'Do you want to come to my house?'

'I don't know where your house is Mister.'

The shampoo is about to get into my eyes. But my super fingers stop it just in time. If they hadn't I wouldn't have spoken to anyone today. It's bad luck to speak when it happens. I have ten minutes to wash up and change because it was so close to getting into my eyes. I finish in exactly ten minutes.

'Yasmine, I've finished.'

'Yes Habibi, I can see. You smell lovely.' She blows me a kiss.

'I'm as hungry as a lion!'

'Did you learn that at school?'

'No, I was watching a documentary on TV about lions. The man said that lions get very hungry.'

Yasmine laughs so I start to laugh too. Her laugh is funny; it's like scraping an apple on a shiny wet surface.

'What would you like for breakfast Mr Cheeky?'

'Tea and labna please Miss Pretty.'

'How do you say tea in Japanese Adam?'

'Why do you want to know? Nobody ever asks me about my Japanese.'

'Well nobody speaks Japanese here. So tell me how do you say tea?'

'Ocha.'

'Ota?' She laughs with her head facing upwards. I don't know why people tilt their head back when they laugh loudly. I think the pharynx needs more space for so much laughter. 'Ota? Like a cat in Egyptian? Would you like to drink a cat?' Her laughter is so squeaky.

'No Yasmine! O-CH-A!'

'Ocha? Oh, it's not funny any more, would you like some OTA?' she slowly mouths to tease me.

'Ocha o hitotsu kudasai!'

I quickly run off while laughing at Yasmine. I love Yasmine, she makes me happy. When we play like this, she becomes my favourite and most vibrant colour, my colour ruby.

'What? Come back here! What does that mean? Come back you cheeky boy! I'll throw my slipper at you!'

I keep running without stepping on any yellow design on the carpet. When I reach the sitting room I hide behind Baba.

'Shh Adam, we are watching the news!'

I don't say another word and try to keep my laughter inside. Everyone looks so tired and upset. Maybe it's because they miss mama. It can't be because of the war. A war is a state of armed conflict between different nations or states or different groups within a nation or state. There is no conflict in Syria for there to be a war. The dictionary doesn't lie, so if that's what it says, that's what I believe.

The day is going by slowly. I finish breakfast and leave the sitting room. It is too boring to sit around, watch the news and listen to the family talk about politics. I walk to my room and think about what book to read today. I have just borrowed *Death in Venice* by Thomas Mann from the library. I think I will start reading it.

The main character's name looks grey, which means I won't like him. Gustave Aschenbach is a very dark name; he must be bad. I don't want to finish the book in case it upsets me. Thinking about it forms hexagons in my mind with bees roaming around the shape, stinging. He certainly is a bad character then. Just the thought of reading on scares me.

The dark image I have in my head from just the first page of the book makes me want to paint. I walk over to the corner of my room and open all the lids of the colours on the table as I sit up on the chair. My paintbrush darts for the grey colour. I have a better idea though. I pick up the bottle of grey paint and splash it on the white paper. The paint runs down and before it dries I dip my paintbrush in orange. I draw a thin outline of tired looking eyes that reflects a flame in the pupils. I draw as delicately as possible so the details are fine and noticeable. I pick up a thinner brush and dip it into a midnight blue colour and trace a fine line around the pupils so the orange and blue simultaneously show the fear in the eyes. The grey in the background has mixed with orange and dried now. All together it looks like the aftermath of a war.

I move my chair back to see the picture from afar. I feel it reach out to talk to me, telling me something is missing. I re-evaluate the three colours. The unexpected clash of grey and orange shows the dark results of the war but also reflects a thin glimmer of hope. The midnight blue around the pupils speaks to me and tells me of the horrors it has witnessed. A lighter colour is missing: white. The sky should be painted white to mock the supposed ending of the war and show the naivety that still remains.

I pick up my white paint and carefully spill it at the top of the canvas. I put a piece of paper under it so there is a perfect line and so it doesn't interfere with the other colours. I then wait five minutes for it to dry before removing the paper.

I can hear weird sounds coming from outside all of a sudden. They sound like the howls of angry wolves. I never knew we had wolves in Aleppo. It is exciting to hear them but I am scared. Why would wolves be howling like this? I run out of my room quickly and look for Yasmine.

'Yasmine! I can hear wolves! Yasmine!'

'Come in Adam, what's wrong Habibi?'

'Yasmine, can you hear the wolves outside? Come, I'll show you!'

I lead Yasmine to the front of the house and keep my eyes on her face. Her eyes look so small. I think she is scared. I have never seen her eyes this small apart from at mama's funeral. She must be scared or upset, but why should she be upset because of the wolves?

'Yasmine what's wrong?'

'The protests have started darling, they're coming down our street.'

'Is this what you meant by the start of the war?'

'Yes, the boys and I have to join the crowd Adam, you stay home with Isa.'

'I thought you were going tomorrow? You can't go today, it's not time yet.'

'I thought we would be going tomorrow too but I have to go today.'

Yasmine runs to the sitting room and calls out to Khalid and Tariq to get dressed and ready. I don't feel too good, maybe it's because I am scared. What if something happens to them? Things always happen in wars. There's always blood in war paintings, all of them. What if they come home covered in blood?

The loud sounds come closer and now they sound like a huge crowd of angry people shouting. I can't make out what they're saying. I go to the front door and open it to get a closer look. The crowd is still in the distance but they are so loud I can hear them from here. They look like a huge army of ants approaching. In one of William Hogarth's paintings there is a crowd of people who look like they are protesting as well, he paints the picture with splashes of red to portray the forecast of the bloody war. I would do the same. I see blood coming.

Yasmine, Tariq and Khalid leave. I walk them to the door and hope I don't see anything yellow today because that means they won't come back safe.

'Want to watch TV with me Adam?' Isa walks behind me.

'Yes, let's watch an art show.'

We flip through the TV channels and settle on MBC1, which has an art show. It's 1:00 p.m. I had lost track of time. Of course, my art show is on repeat at 1:00 p.m.

The episode today is about the death of art. The TV presenter is talking about how true art of expression and depth has died and simplicity has taken its place. It is disappointing to hear this. Real art should never die if it is real, it is just hidden behind the layers of ignorance. This show is sending the wrong message out to people. So many people are listening to this and believing it.

'Believe in this?' Isa asks me.

'Of course not, real art still exists, some people just want to create new art so they forget about the origins and truth of it.'

'Very clever of you, I would have never thought that. Why don't you show me some of your paintings?'

'I only show mama and Yasmine.'

'Why don't you try showing me? I'll be honest.'

I don't know whether I should show him or not. What if he laughs? I only trust mama and Yasmine. He said he'd give me an honest opinion so maybe I should.

'Don't tell anyone I showed you okay?'

I lead him into my room. He doesn't jump over the threshold so I'm not sure if I feel comfortable with him being here.

'Wow Adam, there are paintings everywhere, that's amazing!'

'Do you like them?'

'Amazing, I never knew you were this good, I always just saw you go into your room and come out hours later, but I didn't think you did such good paintings.'

'Thank you Mr. Isa.'

'Why do you always paint war?'

'Because it's filled with endless painting possibilities, and the range of colours is so wide.'

'Why don't you try making sculptures?'

'I like using colours.'

'But you're good with faces.'

'Thank you Isa…'

Before I am able to finish my sentence I hear a loud shriek, gun shots and an ambulance siren. I freeze in my place. Yasmine is all I can think about.

'Yasmine… Yasmine… Yasmine!'

'Calm down Adam, let's go out and see what's going on. Don't worry it won't be Yasmine.'

'I can't go out, I can't.'

I run to the door and open it clumsily, the lock isn't unlocking. Isa pushes me aside gently and unlocks it. I stretch my neck out of the door to see if I can see what happened. All I can see from here is a group of people with banners marching on, and an ambulance in the far distance. The fear of something happening to my sister burns inside me. My fingers start to tremble and twitch. I back away from the door and sit in the corner of the corridor towards the wall. I grind my teeth trying to ignore all the dark thoughts that start clouding my mind. I can't see the wall in front of me any more; I can only see grey triangles covering my vision. My body starts rocking involuntarily. I try to stop it, but it rocks more violently as I count in my head.

Chapter Three

NAVY

Isa pulls out another cigarette. He has been smoking every ten minutes for all the hours that have passed. It doesn't smell nice. I guess it's his way of worrying about Yasmine, Khalid and Tariq. The smell is giving me a headache. I push my head onto my knees to block the smell from reaching me. Mama always said it is like burning yourself and I should never smoke. Why would I want to burn myself? Mama was always right. Isa should have listened to her more often. When mama was alive, Isa hardly spoke to her. She used to always be upset because of how he treated her. I love mama. I didn't like Isa making her sad.

My heart feels like a nest of crows hatching. It's so heavy and dark. Baba is still asleep in mama's room. I want to wake him up and tell him to go and look for Yasmine, but I don't want him to shout at me. He is very tired. It suddenly becomes silent outside. I can't hear a single person. Isa rushes to the door and opens it. His cigarette is on the ground, still lit. I run behind him and put it out. Our street looks abandoned. Ripped banners lie on the ground tracing the protesters' march and stones fill the road with dust. I can't wait for Yasmine to come home. Isa shuts the door. I head back to my corner.

'Do you want me to make you something to eat?' Isa asks. I am really hungry but I don't think Isa knows how to set my plate.

'It's okay, I'll do it myself thank you.'

I take seven steps to the kitchen and take out my plate from the fridge. Yasmine has already put some mashed potato and gravy on it. I put it in the microwave and pour myself a drink. I miss Yasmine already.

'We are home!' I can hear Yasmine shout. I start to run to her but knock my drink over and it spills on the floor. The glass crashes; I feel it pierce my eardrum. I hear blue and purple screeches in my mind. I don't know what to do. I kneel down on the floor and rock myself so the sound disappears. I don't know if I should run to Yasmine.

'Are you okay dear?' Yasmine comes into the kitchen; I look up at her and smile.

'Are you okay Yasmine? What happened?'

'We just went marching darling. Get up, I'll clean the glass.'

'I heard a gunshot.'

'Someone got hurt, but we are all fine, I promise.'

'I was scared.'

'Sorry we left all of a sudden, but you have to try to get used to it. It's only just started…'

'But I don't want to, you'll get hurt.'

'Adam Habibi I'll be all right, I promise. Do you want me to pour you another glass of juice?'

'Yes please.'

Yasmine clears the broken glass from the floor and I help her clean up the juice. She looks different. Something has changed. It looks like she's bruised from the inside, purple. It feels wrong. Yasmine puts my plate of food on the dining table with my juice. She adjusts her upper body in an uncomfortable manner like something is irritating her posture. Something is pointing out of her stomach area like it is wedged into her waist.

'Yasmine, what's that?' I ask pointing at her waist.

'Nothing, chop chop and eat while I go change.'

I am confused. I see something pointing out and she fixes herself, so how is it nothing? Why did she say it was nothing? She knows lying confuses me and I don't understand it. My brain feels like a wire track with burning fuses. I can't see straight. People are enigmas. Now, even Yasmine is one of them.

She starts to walk away. I have a bad hunch. I stop eating and just move my food around the plate. The meal doesn't speak to me today. The mashed potato looks grey. It is in an odd mood like me. It's in the corner away from the gravy. Yasmine comes back into the kitchen wearing her pyjamas. I know how she dresses in different clothes depending on her mood; today she is dressed in her navy-blue silk pyjamas. She usually only brings them out on occasions, like when cousins come over to sleep. Something seems amiss and my heart feels tight and heavy thinking about it. I feel like hot black smoke is being pumped out of my heart. I feel like I am sitting on top of a falling chair. Navy-blue smoke colours my sight. I close my eyes.

'Why aren't you eating Adam?' I open my eyes to Yasmine standing close to me.

'I am not hungry any more.'

I pick up my plate, cover it in plastic film and put it back in the fridge. I sneak a look at Yasmine through the corner of my eye. She is not paying attention to what I am doing. Something is wrong; she usually pressures me to eat. I can't read her face. I want to know what happened outside. The boys have gone to sleep so I can't ask them. I don't know how to approach them anyway. I can only speak to Yasmine and Baba, and sometimes Isa.

'Let's sleep Adam, I'm tired.'

Yasmine gets up and smiles at me. She leaves to go to her room. I take three steps outside the kitchen and five to my room and jump over the carpet onto my bed. I get under the covers but I can't sleep. What if Yasmine leaves in the morning again? I take my cover and take eight steps to her room. I knock on the door but she doesn't reply. I lay my cover outside her room and roll into it like a caterpillar. I imagine waking up and being able to fly outside to see what is going on. I would be purple and yellow circles; mama's favourite colours. I can't wait for school so I can walk down the streets and see if it looks any different. The streets look eerie at this time, but I still don't see a war. Nobody is dressed in army clothes and no tanks patrol the streets, but there was a gunshot.

★

The sun is starting to rise and I wake up to the light right away. Yasmine's door is still closed. She is usually awake by now. She must be very tired. I get up and go to my room. I look outside the window and don't see anybody. It's a school day, there's usually more life. I pick up my book on the bedside table and start to read, waiting for everyone to wake up. Today I am reading *Animal Farm* by George Orwell. I only have three chapters left. When I first started reading I couldn't understand why the animals were talking. I read the first chapter 17 times. So I understood after that. George Orwell has special powers of speaking to animals, like Prophet Suleiman who spoke to ants and birds. Now that I understand the idea, the story is still weird, but I can only guess what this man means. I sometimes have to read things over and over again before I can understand them, especially jokes or sarcasm. How do I know if someone is joking or being sarcastic? I think the author should give a warning in the footnote. That would make everything clearer.

I can't believe Yasmine is still asleep; she is usually the first to wake up. 'Yasmine… Yasmine… Yasmine.' I knock on her door three times. Mama said three is a blessed number. Yasmine still doesn't reply. I push the door a little and it opens. She usually locks it every night before she goes to sleep but this time she didn't. I stick my head in-between the gap and see Yasmine lying on the bed, on top of the covers. She looks grey, like the way mama looked when she was sick. She looks so much like mama. It makes my heart drop heavily like a rock, something surges through it and I hold my breath. Is this what an electric shock feels like? I walk slowly towards Yasmine and knock on her bedside table.

'Yasmine… Yasmine… Yasmine.'

She doesn't answer. I see the purple bruise in her face that I saw yesterday. She is bruised inside but I don't know how. I gently tap her legs to wake her up. She opens her eyes a little. They are red and she quickly rolls to her side and vomits violently on the floor. My eyes start spinning around the room; I notice boxes of pills on the floor. This can't be good. Mama had boxes of pills all around her room when she was sick. No, no, Yasmine can't be sick too. I don't know what to do. Yasmine stops vomiting and lies there, her head hanging over the bed. I run out of the room and knock on Baba's door.

'Baba… Baba… Baba!'

Baba comes out still wearing his pyjamas.

'Baba… ummmm…' I try to tell Baba to go and see Yasmine, but nothing comes out. My mind is filled with letters but I can't put them together to form a word. I hold my head and can faintly hear Baba talking to me.

'What's wrong Adam, are you okay Habibi?' I shake my head and point to Yasmine's room.

'Yasmine? What does she need?'

I walk towards her room and he follows me. He runs in and sees Yasmine still lying in the same position. His voice starts to fade out and the boys come running to the room. Suddenly everyone looks grey, not only Yasmine. I am really scared. I don't want Yasmine to go to mama. I need her. I don't want to miss her as well. Khalid runs out and slams the front door. Baba and Tariq come out of the room carrying Yasmine. She looks like snow, just like mama. No, no, no, no. The words now swim around in my mind and I start to feel dizzy, everything is spinning so fast and the room is running, taking me with it on a marathon. The walls try to speak to me, I can faintly hear their chanting but it doesn't make sense. The light is a line of rainbow across the sitting room. I can see Isa running to me in slow motion and his voice is like a robot. I feel like vomiting. The walls are crumbling down as I fall to the floor.

Chapter Four

BURGUNDY

I WAKE UP to white walls surrounding me. I don't know where I am or how I ended up here. A curtain separates me from the noise. I suddenly remember Yasmine and what happened to her. I don't know how long I have been here or why I am here instead of Yasmine. I can hear Baba's voice from afar and I feel safe again.

'Baba… Baba… Baba…'

Baba opens the curtain and smiles at me. His face looks like it is melting.

'Where is Yasmine?' I ask right away. Scenes from Yasmine's room replay in my mind in slow motion. I can't piece them together well. They are fragments of her in pain and suddenly silence enveloping me.

'She's in a room resting Habibi, she had a rough night.'

'How long have I been sleeping for?'

'All day, it is nine in the evening now.'

My eyes start twitching and my fingers tug at the elastic band on my wrist. I start tugging more and my wrist starts to get red. I keep shaking my head and whispering under my breath to stop myself from tugging but my body isn't listening to my brain.

'Adam stop that! Don't hurt yourself,' Baba says.

Baba comes towards me and taps me on my shoulder; he knows I don't like anybody touching me so he doesn't do it for long. I don't move away because I know it is his way of making himself feel better. I never understood human contact.

'Can we go to Yasmine please?' I ask Baba. He helps me out of bed and leads me to her room. We walk 17 steps straight then turn five to Yasmine's room. Baba doesn't knock before opening the door, which makes me uncomfortable. I knock three times on the wall as we enter. Suddenly I see mama on the bed, her eyes closed and rested. My heart starts beating fast and I whisper mama's name three times in a row quickly. Baba notices and comes towards me.

'Adam, Adam,' he raises his voice and holds my shoulder. I push him away and go to the corner of the room. Why would he bring me to mama? She is in heaven. What is happening? Am I in heaven? I know I am not going crazy because I know the shape of mama's eyes perfectly. I used to stare at her when she slept so I could memorise their shape. They look like round olives filled with black eyelashes that curl at the end. I even remember the way they feel. I can't hear what Baba is saying any more as I walk towards the bed to touch mama's eyelashes. My fingers start twitching like an insect's legs. I am scared to touch her and scare her. I can't keep my fingers straight. My nails are digging into my palm as my fidgeting becomes more violent. I close my eyes and imagine the colour ruby-red to calm myself down. I steady my breathing and think of Yasmine when she looks ruby. My heart suddenly calms down and my fingers straighten. Baba is still behind me when I open my eyes and look back. He is still walking towards me as I have the courage to lean down and touch mama's eyelashes.

'Baba! Baba!' I shout. 'It's not mama!'

Tears start falling down my face and I start to feel hot and sticky. I feel the exact same way I did at mama's funeral. My mind is filled with the number three jumping from one corner to the other like a Microsoft screen saver.

★

I calm down after the boys come in and try to speak to me. Yasmine is lying still on the bed and Baba is telling me what happened. He says she had her stomach pumped because she took too many pills. I wonder why Yasmine did that? Was she in pain? I don't want Yasmine to feel pain and leave me as well.

★

Yasmine got up a couple of hours later but she hasn't spoken since. She usually talks a lot and is ruby red, but now she is green. Tariq drove us home and made her food. The boiler in the house isn't working so it's really cold. I feel the air touch my bones, I can imagine my bones moving in on each other to keep warm. The more I imagine that, the warmer I get. The electricity and water keep on cutting out and there's nothing we can do. We can't shower as often or as long as we would like any more. I don't know who keeps cutting it. Don't they feel cold and dirty?

I put Yasmine's favourite romance movies on for her to watch and sit by her bed. I don't like these movies very much but I don't want to leave her alone. Sometimes the electricity comes back on, and the movies work. All the movies she likes have two people kissing each other in the end and tasting each other's spit. Why do people kiss and hug each other? It's uncomfortable and it gets hot. What is so special about exchanging saliva that makes people fall in love? It's a disturbing quality. I will never fall in love and do that. Yasmine says that if you loved someone you would want to kiss and hug him or her all the time. I don't believe that. I really dislike pressure on my skin.

Yasmine keeps going to sleep and waking up again. It's like she travels to another place when she sleeps. She wakes up with a completely different look. I wish I could see where she goes. I want to travel like she does. I have never travelled before but I always watch travel documentaries and feel like I have been to the place they show after the programme finishes. If I travelled I wouldn't go to tourist attractions. Why would anybody want to go to London and just stare at Big Ben? It's just a clock. You can see clocks everywhere. Travelling is not about staring at a brick wall or statue and pretending to be interested!

I can hear Isa reciting Nizar Qabbani's poetry from his room. He recites every night. I know all the poems by heart now. My favourite is 'A Damascene Moon'. When Isa reads my favourite line from it, 'a stream flows and poetry is a sparrow spreading its wings over Sham', I see sparrows flying around the room and rivers with orchids and Yasmine floating. It makes me feel like I am travelling on the river but today crows fly over the Damascene landscape and the sparkling water turns into a green gooey liquid.

I wake up to the sunrise as usual and straightaway get up and peek into Yasmine's bedroom to see if she is okay. She looks better today; she has spring in her cheeks. I decide to skip to the bathroom, which takes fewer steps than walking, so in four steps I reach the bathroom and go into the shower. The water is really cold today, the boiler light is on but it is not warming up. Why would the light be on if it isn't giving the right message?

'Adam! We all need to shower, quick,' Tariq shouts through the door. I quickly rush my shower in the cold. Goosebumps climb up my body and I shiver. It feels like insects are crawling all over me. I hate cold showers. I rush out and run to my room before anyone sees me. Thank God no one saw me or I would have to run to the bathroom from my room 17 times. I get dressed and brush my hair and put perfume on. I spray it on my right shoulder, then my left shoulder and then the centre of my chest. I can hear Yasmine's voice. I quickly put my school bag on my shoulder and run to the kitchen where I can hear her voice. Her face is a canvas of spring and winter. Each one is fighting to take over. I hope spring wins.

'Yasmine, are you going to work today?'

'Yes.'

'Why did you take a lot of tablets Yasmine?'

Yasmine suddenly looks up and it looks like concrete bricks are veiling her eyes. Her face sinks down. In this moment she looks like the dead rabbit I once saw at gran's farm.

'It was for my stomach Habibi, don't worry about what happened,' she quickly says and turns around to fry the omelette.

'Yasmine I don't want to eat, I am going to be late for school. I'm leaving now.'

'You have to eat Adam, you know the rules.'

'But I am going to be late for school.'

'At least take this labna sandwich to eat on the way with tea in a flask.'

'Thank you,' I say taking them and leaving in a hurry.

'Wait for me Adam, I'll walk you to school.'

'Why Yasmine? I always walk alone.'

'It's not safe out there any more darling, I want to come with you to make sure you get to school okay.'

'It is safe, I always walk to school.'

'Just wait for me please Adam, I'll just get my coat.'

I open the front door and see rain pouring down. I run back in for my umbrella and before I count to ten I run out again. The rain is pouring down very hard but there is still a bit of sun shining down on me, which makes me smile. I don't like the rain; it is so hard to walk in without my shoes getting wet or my umbrella slipping down and my body getting wet. I just like the sun. There aren't as many people on the streets today. The street lamps aren't working and it looks like a dark morning with nobody and no lights. Thank God the sun is shining, even if it is behind many layers of clouds. I start to imagine what it would be like with no sun on such a rainy day with no street lamps. It would be too dark to walk the streets and insects would crawl onto us without us seeing them, but I would still have to because I have school. The cry of a child upset about going to school disturbs my dark thoughts and I notice many banners on the ground ripped up with red paint on them. The streets still haven't been cleaned. There is usually somebody who cleans the streets every morning. Nothing is normal today, I can't wait to go to school and see everything normal. We take the turn onto the high street and it looks like we have entered a different city. The market stalls are on the ground with wooden splinters all around. It looks like Godzilla attacked it. Is this why there isn't anybody on the streets? There is a guy lying on the ground on his back and he looks like he has been sleeping for ages. His face looks like tree bark: aged, wrinkly and cold.

'Don't look at him Adam!' Yasmine takes my hand and starts running.

'Do you think we should wake him up? It's raining on him.'

'Just move Adam!' Yasmine shouts. I don't know why she has been so bad-tempered lately. I wanted to put my umbrella on the man but Yasmine pulled me too hard to start running.

We run to school and there isn't any assembly going on in

the courtyard. I look at the time, and it is usually the time for assembly. Maybe because of the rain we should just go to class. I go into school and up two flights of stairs and walk to my classroom, which is the third on the left. I look through the window and there are only five people and the teacher. Yasmine knocks on the door for me and tells me to go in while she talks to the teacher. Inside the classroom everybody is sitting apart and no one looks up when I enter the room. There isn't a single sound in here apart from the wind from outside hitting the windows. Someone is sitting in my seat today. I don't want to speak to them but I can't sit anywhere else. I have been sitting there all year. I stand by my desk and the girl looks up. She has skin that looks so fragile and thin it could fall off her face. The veins are painted in the shape of chicken's feet. Even though her cheeks look sick and unhealthy, her eyes are the darkest brown I have ever seen. You can see yourself through them without even meaning to. She gets up without saying a word to me and gives me my seat. Usually my classmates make fun of me before getting off my seat, but she didn't. I like her. Yasmine calls me from outside the classroom before I even get to sit down.

'Yes?'

'Your teacher says it will be better to go home, everybody is waiting for their parents to pick them up,' she whispers to me.

'But it's not home time yet.'

'Yes Habibi but there isn't school today.'

'Of course I have school.'

'Let's make a deal. If you come back with me and listen to what your teacher says, I'll take you to the market with me to choose the fruits you want to eat.'

'Really Yasmine?'

'Yes, come on, let's go.'

Yasmine says bye to the teacher and I look back at the girl in my class. She is still looking down reading. We walk out of the classroom and Yasmine looks at me in a funny way. Her eyes look huge and her smile feels like it is mocking me.

'What is it?'

'Who is that girl?' Yasmine smiles for the first time since the accident.

'I don't know her name.'

'Ooo, you like her,' she laughs.

'No Yasmine! I like her eyes.'

'Why her eyes?'

'They look like a tub of Nutella.' I start to think about her eyes. I looked right into them. It was like jumping into a chocolate factory.

'Snap out of it Adam.' Yasmine snaps her fingers in front of me and I'm dragged away from my chocolate factory heaven. We walk back on the empty streets we came on and nothing has changed, everything looks just as empty. We turn into the market road and at last I can hear some voices from afar. Yasmine suddenly pulls me towards her and tells me not to look to my right. I quickly look and see a man lying on the ground with his face towards the wall and his arms wide open. A bird is walking around his body and pecking at his fingers. It doesn't wake him up. I look again and notice blood in-between his legs.

'Yasmine! The man is hurt, he's not sleeping. He's bleeding!'

'Walk on quickly Adam, I told you not to look!'

'But Yasmine if we leave him he will die!'

'Adam!' Yasmine shouts at me and I look away and behind me at the guy who still doesn't move. The bird is pecking his eyes. This is the second man we have seen today lying on the ground.

We can hear more noises now and people shouting fruit prices out loud. As we take a right turn the market comes into sight and the busy atmosphere hits me after the lonely walk here. The fruits and vegetables on display paint the market-place with a vibrant look. I walk towards the brightest stand with dragon fruits, passion fruits, mangos, kiwis and starfruits on display in the shape of a huge smile. My mind plays around with the colours and I sketch an image in my head of the man on the side of the road made of fruit juices bursting out of him.

'Adam, I was looking all around for you, where did you wander off to?'

'Sorry, I was looking at these fruits.'

'Okay Habibi, just stay by me. I picked strawberries, a pine-apple and some grapes for you here.' She points at her basket filled with all my favourites.

'Thank you Yasmine!' I smile at her.

'Come on, let's look for some vegetables to cook for to-day.'

I walk behind Yasmine to the vegetable stand on the far corner of the market. Sitting on the corner of the pavement a father is recording a video of his daughter singing the national anthem in a loud voice. They both look orange. Before I get to look back at Yasmine I hear a deafening sound and in a second all the fruits jump at me and the stalls break to the ground. I turn frantically looking for Yasmine and see the video camera by my feet and the father and daughter nowhere in sight. I feel Yasmine grab me and we run. She drops the basket and the fruits tumble down to the ground and burst into a rainbow. Yasmine runs faster and I try to keep up with her. Another bomb goes off but it sounds further away. Screams surround us like a suffocating bubble and my mind zones out to one of my paintings on my wall with a family running away from a bomb. Something suddenly falls out from under Yasmine's shirt and she stops to quickly pick it up.

A loud siren goes off in my mind when I see the gun. Yasmine doesn't pause to look up at me. She picks up the gun and continues running. My heart sings the dreary national anthem of our country, and every beat gets heavier. There's a war, there's a war, there's a war. I didn't believe Yasmine, I didn't believe the news, now I am in the middle of the war and I want to run away.

'5-3-2-1, 5-3-2-1, 5-3-2-1, 5-3-2-1, 5-3-2-1, 5-3-2-1, 5-3-2-1, 5-3-2-1, 5-3-2-1, 5-3-2-1, 5-3-2-1.'

'Adam! Keep running!'

'5-3-2-1, 5-3-2-1, 5-3-2-1, 5-3-2-1, 5-3-2-1, 5-3-2-1.' Yasmine pulls me harder and every nerve in my body freezes. I stop in my spot and she tries pulling me harder but she can't.

'Adam? Adam look at me! What's wrong? We have to run, we could get hurt!'

Yasmine's voice soothes my nerves and I run really fast to show her that I can run as fast as a cheetah. I can hear Yasmine's breath behind me and I run even faster.

★

We run into the house and lock the door tight behind us. Yasmine turns around to me and looks me up and down to see if I am okay. She has a scratch from her lips up to her ear. I can't see myself so I don't know how I look.

'Yasmine, you're hurt.'

'As long as you're okay then I am.'

She walks into the sitting room and tries to put the light on but the electricity is out again. Everything is getting so bad. Nothing is working and the war has started. I start to fidget. I hate this, why is there a war? What did my country do to have a war?

I go to my room and look at the painting on my wall that I remembered when the bomb went off. The picture has a woman running while holding a young boy's hand. The colours are like a fruit cart has exploded all over it and blood has come out of the fruits. The painting resembles what happened in a strange way. I look at the other paintings on my wall and pray to God that none of those happen as well. My room is filled with war paintings that now scare me. I bring out my painting kit and start to sketch the girl and her father right away. I remember their faces clearly like I have known them my whole life. The father's eyes looked like they were about to close before the bomb went off, like he knew what was going to happen. The girl was happy singing our country's national anthem; the anthem that was supposed to protect us under its wings. But she fell to the ground in the middle of it all. Now our country is turning against us, we are not one any more. I finish sketching the father with a video camera in his hand and the girl facing him with her long hair flowing free. I then open up my paint palette and change the innocent scene into a painting with the premonition of death. Death was lurking above them, ready to pounce, to gulp their fresh flesh. Tears fall down from my eyes.

Yasmine comes into my room and I run to her.
'Yasmine I'm scared.'
'Adam, don't worry darling, I'm here for you.'
'But Yasmine, what if you leave me?'
'I won't leave you.'

'Why did you have a gun?'

'Mmm let's talk about it later.'

'Please tell me Yasmine, I don't want you to kill yourself with the gun.'

'No, no! Don't say that darling.' Yasmine leans down and holds my hand for a few seconds before she lets go.

'I found it at the demonstration and picked it up without thinking. I thought about it when I got home. It's not safe and if anything happens I might need a gun.'

'Don't kill anyone Yasmine.'

'I promise I won't.'

Chapter Five

WHITE

BABA WALKS UP TO ME and leans down and whispers in my ear, 'I'll show you a trick when the lights go out next. Go get me one orange and olive oil.'

I jump up and run to the kitchen. Yasmine is sitting at the table writing in her diary. She closes it as soon as she sees me.

'What are you writing Yasmine?'

Yasmine doesn't answer me. What is wrong with everyone today? Khalid walks in without saying 'hi' and goes into the fridge and takes three bananas out. He goes to the gym every day and eats bananas every time he gets back. He always tells me he'll take me to the gym but he never does. I look for the oranges in the fruit basket and find one at the very bottom.

'The oranges are finished Yasmine.'

'What do you want me to do about it?'

I don't like it when Yasmine shouts at me but I don't want to cry because I will look like a baby. I quickly take the olive oil from the cupboard and run out. I can hear Khalid speaking to Yasmine but it sounds like a code language that I can't understand. I give Baba what he asked for and he pats the seat next to him on the sofa for me to sit. I sit and wait for him to explain.

'When you're afraid of the dark, just remember that you're not alone. God is always with you and he will help you find eternal light. This trick will help you find temporary light.'

Baba starts cutting the orange in the centre and giving me

some slices to eat and then putting the rest in a bowl. He carves out all the juices and leaves the stem in the middle. It looks like a candle. He blows on the skin until the juices dry up completely. He then puts two spoons of olive oil in the centre and rolls it around the sides. He takes a lighter out of his pocket and lights the stem. The room starts to glow. It is the strongest candle I have ever seen.

'Do you like it Adam?'

'I love it Baba.'

Baba smiles and he looks better now.

'Do you want to play a game?'

Baba hasn't played a game with me for a long time so I grin in response. I am so excited.

'First show me the painting you have over there.'

I go and get the painting and hold it up for him. He doesn't say anything for a long time and my hands start aching. I can't see his face because the painting is covering it so I decide to put it down and look at him. Baba looks red like he has been crying. He smiles at me and I look into his eyes. I see my painting in them. I can't explain how weird this is but it's like my painting got imprinted into his eyes. Even his eye colour has changed.

'It's beautiful Adam I love it. I never knew you could do this.'

'Thank you Baba, what game are we going to play?'

'Let's play I spy with my little eye.'

'Can I start?'

'Of course.'

'I spy with my little eye something beginning with O.'

Baba keeps guessing all the Os in the room but missing the one O on my mind.

'I give up.'

'Are you sure Baba?'

'Yes Habibi.'

'Oxygen Baba!'

Baba starts laughing and messes my hair.

'You can't see oxygen Adam,' he says and he continues laughing.

'I can.'

'How can you?'

'If I look closely I can see oxygen in the air…'

Baba continues to laugh then picks a word with the letter L.

We continue playing and laughing and then Yasmine and all the boys join us and we have tea and start to play a card game. It's been a very long time since we all got together. I feel comfortable around them all. I feel happy and almost forget about the bombing. While everyone is sharing a shisha and I drink my favourite mango juice, Yasmine asks me about my friend Nabil.

'I haven't seen him since the last day I went to school Yasmine and he wasn't in the class this morning.'

'Do you want me to take you to visit him?'

'Yes I do, I like playing video games with him and talking about books.'

The rest of the night we laugh and Baba tells us stories from his childhood. My favourite story is when his two older brothers got into a fight and one of them was about to throw his slipper at the other one and Baba was walking past and the slipper hit him in the face instead. Yasmine always laughs a lot at that story and that makes me laugh. Baba tells us another story that makes me cry out of laughter. His younger brother was once desperate at night to go to the toilet and was too tired to run there so he peed in the flowerpot in the corridor and their mum was sitting on the sofa there and he didn't see her in the dark. Baba always has these funny stories that make me imagine him when he was young. Khalid then tells Isa to read us one of the latest poems he has written and we all sit closer to each other and listen to Isa recite his poem:

A river of cryptic ink flows through the city.
Little is heard but the whispers of the peasants
and their weeping.

The streets spell out the names of their late
companions with their remaining cement
and the trees howl for their favourite shepherds.
In silence we turn a deaf ear to nature.

On the right corner of the street the nostalgic
drink Aristotle's theories from a silver-plated cup
as others bathe in the remnants of Romanticism.
Their bodies rot in art's finest clothes.

Walking into the house I see my mother sitting
there, stitching me a sweater from the alphabets
of her heart, as father recites to himself Khalil Gibran's
poem 'The Lake of Fire'. He recites until dawn.

Where does literature end and love begin when
words dance ceremoniously to wed my country to
the title of 'the blessed' yet we are stripped of pen and paper?

When he finishes reciting his poem 'Anthem' Baba starts clapping so I do too. As Isa read I felt like I was being spun into a cocoon of literature. The silk strangled me but when Isa let out the last word I was able to breathe again. I have never had this feeling before so I don't know what it means.

Baba gets up and goes to bed and we all stay seated and talk. Eventually, I start fidgeting. Yasmine smiles at me and tells me to go to bed. I fall asleep the moment I put my head on my pillow. I didn't twist and turn this time and I didn't even think of mama.

★

I wake up to an unsettling sound in my mind: something like the sound of a dolphin's cry. I put my hand on my heart and feel its fast beating. As my heart settles down, my dream starts coming back to me. It's all a mess in my head but I remember sitting in the school playground with the girl with Nutella eyes and eating rose petals with her. I can still remember how soft they felt in my mouth and the way they melted as soon as I put one on my tongue. I didn't care about eating petals because I was in the girl's eyes eating chocolate too. Suddenly she screamed like a dolphin and that's when my dream ended. I wish she hadn't screamed. I feel relaxed after seeing the girl's eyes again. I don't know her name so I'm going to call her 'Chocolate'.

I skip to the bathroom and close my eyes to the smell of coffee. I then go the kitchen but Yasmine is not here. Her diary is on the table though. It's turquoise with a picture of a candle on the front cover. I sit down at the table and open her diary to the first page:

> I gave him my last letter today. I can't do this any more. I love him and the pain is unbearable but I have no choice but to ignore it. My family is more important. Everyone has been going through a hard time ever since mama left.

SUMIA SUKKAR

Even though it's been a few years I still have to pretend I'm okay in order to patch things up. I only feel happiness with him. At home I'm just a pillow for tears, but with him I'm a woman with feelings. If it wasn't for Adam I would run away with him, but Adam needs me. I just have to live like a shadow. I miss him.

I put the diary down and slowly slide onto the floor. I don't understand what is going on. Is Yasmine joking? Is she always feeling black oil in her heart? I don't want her to feel that way because I know the feeling from after mama left. I should run away so Yasmine doesn't have to feel that way. I love Yasmine and I don't want her taking pills any more or looking yellow. I want Yasmine the ruby. I run to my room and take my school bag and run out of the house. I want to go to Nabil's house. Yasmine said I should go and visit him. I feel a grey cloud on my shoulder, like it's going to rain on me. I walk to school without looking around in case I see something scary. It's too early to go to school and I have never been out at this time. The streets have shadows that look like crooked superheroes. I can see the one-legged Batman following me from the corner of my eye. I don't know if he is my enemy or friend. I keep a look out for him just in case. I stand outside school and try to trace the route Nabil takes to his house in my mind. I see a fork-like shape in my mind with three colours sprouting out: brown, purple and orange. I don't know which one to take. The orange has a more calming feeling to it so I take a right from the school gates and walk up the street. The roads don't look familiar. I am not sure this is the right route. I keep walking and my heart gradually starts to tighten. I am losing my breath. 7,7,7,7,7,7,7,7,7,7,7,7. I start twitching and repeating his seat number in class in my mind. The route will come to me if

40

I keep repeating his number. 7,7,7,7,7,7,7,7,7,7,7,7,7,7,7. My hands keep twitching and his seat number takes over my mind. I can't stop repeating it. There is a man coming towards me in the tight alley. I don't recognise the houses. I wonder how far away from home I am. I suddenly feel dizzy. The thought of being far from home makes me wheezy. The man is getting closer and my neck starts to twitch. The alley is so tight there isn't enough room for my pounding heart. I can smell home-made bread and I calm down at the familiar smell.

The man is now speaking to me but I can't concentrate on what he is saying. His words are scattered in my mind and it sounds like the heavy buzzing of a bee. His voice is giving me a headache and I close my eyes and put my hands on my ears. I feel his touch on my shoulder and I run away with my hands still on my ears. At the end of the alley I reach a wider road with cars and motorcycles. I have never seen this road before and I don't know where I am. I start coughing in pain. I am scared. I don't know what to do or where I am and I can't speak to strangers. I miss my house. I wish Yasmine was with me.

I turn around and see the man right behind me reaching out for my shoulders again. A weird sound escapes my mouth. He gives me a green look with his eyebrows drooping down at each side and I try to listen closely to what he says. I hear him say God's name so I follow him. Maybe he knows where to take me. I walk down two blocks with him and can see his mouth moving but I am too scared to listen. He points at a building and goes in. I don't know if I am meant to be going into a building with a stranger. Mama would shout at me if she knew this. I quickly turn around and start to run out so I don't upset Yasmine and don't get into trouble, but as I try to leave he holds me back by my arm. I turn around and look at

him and see a different person, this time in a police uniform.
Why is a policeman holding me? Did the man bring me to a
police station? I don't want to go to jail. I didn't do anything
wrong. I repeat the number seven to the policeman in case he
knows where my friend's house is but he just tells me to sit
down and gives me water. I don't want to drink water; I just
want to go to Nabil. The officer starts asking me questions and
other policemen walk in and look at me. I haven't said a word
since I sat down and now the officer asks to look through my
bag. I don't want him to see my drawings. I need to tell them
I want to go home but my words aren't coming out and I hold
my bag tighter so they don't search it. I look outside the glass
doors and see three men with green army uniforms on. I suddenly want to go home and tell Yasmine I don't want to die.
I write down my address for the police officer and hear him
speak to someone about collecting me. I hope Yasmine or Isa
come. The others will shout at me for going away. I don't even
know why I did it. I just know I don't want to see Yasmine upset. Maybe I can write her a letter before leaving next time.

I sit down looking away from the officer and right up at
the clock. My mind is ticking with the clock's hands. Does
the clock feel as grey as me with every tick? I look around at
the certificates on the wall to zone out the monotone sound.
There are so many frames around the walls; it looks like a university rather than a police station. There's a picture of the
president on top of the desk. I wonder if it fits with the rest
of the frames. His face is grey. I don't know if it should be, he
should be happy and proud to be ruling a country, but there is
something in this picture that I can have a conversation with.
Something about his forehead, he is trying to cover the frown
lines and it doesn't look like he has any. But I can still see them
and it doesn't look very nice. I forget what I was trying to

reach through these thoughts. I try to trace my thoughts back to the beginning with my fingers, drawing out a map of my mind in the air. I see shapes in my head and then a loud sound I cannot describe. It's like King Kong just put his foot down. The policemen start moving around and I look outside the window, all I can see is fog. I think it is smoke because it's moving past quickly. Grey smoke. Everything is grey today. I don't like it. I put my hands on my ears. Everyone is being so loud and someone's laugh is ringing on a higher frequency than everyone else's. Why is someone laughing when there is smoke outside?

I suddenly feel a flutter in my stomach and I see Yasmine rush in through the door. She has dust all over her but I am so happy I can't control myself. I start jumping up and down. It's when I'm the happiest because I can feel every part of my body jumping with me and I have this extreme energy coming out of me. I can touch the sky right now. Yasmine has a smile on her face but she doesn't look as happy as me. I stop jumping and walk closer to her. She pulls me into her arms and squashes me. I want her to stop, I feel uncomfortable. I start to squirm in her arms until she lets go. I move back and start twitching my neck from side to side trying to leak my discomfort out of my ears.

'Where did you go?' She has a tone I have never heard before. I don't know whether to be scared or happy.

I don't know what to say so I don't reply.

'What is the smoke outside Yasmine?'

'I don't know. Let's go home and see what the news says. Everyone is worried about you!'

'I wanted to visit my friend but I couldn't find his house. Now it's time for school.'

'Let's just go home, we'll talk about everything when you

get some rest, today must have been a shock to you.'

'It was scary Yasmine, I have been waiting for you for a very long time.'

'Don't go off alone next time, you got us all worried. Yalla.'

'But… But…'

'Khalas, Adam.'

Yasmine walks out of the station and takes a short cut to get away from the smoke. I follow behind and can see her turn slightly to make sure I am there from the corner of her eye. She is grey too.

Chapter Six

BLUE

WE PUT THE NEWS on as soon as we get home. Nobody else is home. All the lights are off. I put the sitting room light on. Yasmine just sits in front of the television and doesn't turn around. The woman on TV has a lot of pain on her face, which makes me want to paint her. She is talking about young boys being kidnapped in Syria and burnt. They were tortured and their nails were pulled out. Yasmine tells me to leave the sitting room so I don't hear this, but I don't want to leave. The woman shows a picture of the streets of Syria with drawings and words all over the walls that say 'Down with the regime!'. I don't know what that means and why the kids got tortured because of it. The thought of it makes me shake in anger and I start to pull my hair out. Yasmine runs up to me but I run away and lock my door. I can't be around anyone when I am angry, I feel like a volatile chemical reaction waiting to explode. I feel an unfamiliar emotion grow inside me, like spiders are crawling up my chest and to my throat to strangle me. I don't know why I suddenly feel this way but it's choking me. I have the urge to paint and I can already see the painting in my head. Two young boys lying in the water with their bodies spread open, free, but their faces disfigured, burnt. You can't even tell where their eyes and nose really are. It would be a black-and-white painting with the faces a spectrum of colours. It's going to be horrible and beautiful all at the same time.

As soon as I finish my painting it lets off a bitter scent, like vinegar. The power goes out. Yasmine knocks on my door and gives me a candle to put in my room for when it gets dark.

'Yasmine, I'm hungry.'

'If you're hungry I'll prepare your meal, nobody else wants to eat.'

We go to the kitchen and this time there is no fruit on the table and when Yasmine opens the fridge the first two rows are empty.

'Why is there no food in the fridge Yasmine?'

'Because everybody finished it Habibi, we'll buy some to-morrow. Don't worry and just eat.'

Yasmine puts out some bread for me to eat. I know we don't have food at home, but I don't know why. I wish I could have some rice with red soup now. Mama's rice and soup was the best.

I can hear the boys come in with Baba. I sit down on the chair and have my bread. Khalid comes in and picks Yasmine up and twirls her. Yasmine giggles and hits him to put her down. He pretends he is going to throw her in the bin and she screams. I don't like seeing anyone else make Yasmine happy, but it's been a long time since she was my favourite colour ruby so I laugh with her too.

'So what's to eat?' Khalid asks Yasmine as he puts her down. Yasmine doesn't answer, she just looks at me and then Khalid does too.

'Well I ate already so I was going to tell you there's no need to make a lot of food.'

Yasmine smiles and pats him on the shoulder. Isa and Tariq pop their heads into the kitchen too and then Baba joins us and asks why everyone is in the kitchen. I start laughing for no reason. I suddenly feel a surge of electricity run through me, and my laugh keeps getting louder. I have tears falling down my cheeks from my laughter and as I look around the kitchen everybody looks like they're drowning in my eyes. Tariq starts laughing too. It feels like I have party poppers going off in my heart and I have to release all my energy.

We all go and sit in the sitting room and Baba takes the Quran from the shelf and goes to his room to read. Mama said that when I was young I always used to sit next to Baba when he was reading the Quran and smile at him. He has a voice that flows like cool lemonade down my chest and makes me feel relaxed. The words of the Quran always comfort me and, even though it is so poetic and written in classic Arabic that I don't completely understand, there is something about it that speaks to me.

Tariq, Isa and Khalid start talking about what is happening around us. They don't say the word 'war' once but their voices sound like bullets. The droning sound of their heavy words hurts my head.

'Don't say their name,' Tariq whispers to Khalid.

'Whose name?'

They both look at me and tell me to go to my room but I don't want to.

'They can't keep controlling us! I am fed up with this, we need a revolution!'

'They have us in a corner, you know if you say anything they will kill all of us, be careful Khalid!'

'I can't live like this any more! I feel like a lab rat! Those kids that were burnt today for asking for freedom, why? How is that fair?'

'You will be too if you're not careful!'

'I'll die for freedom, I am not following any sects, I am just following my religion and they can't keep messing around with it or my freedom!'

'Assad,' I say.

They both look at me with a blank expression. I don't know why I said his name or why I am now repeating it but it keeps rolling down my tongue like it enjoys the ride. Tariq tries to explain to me in a low voice that I shouldn't say his name. But why shouldn't I? It's just a name, why should I be scared? I continue to say his name until all of a sudden Isa gets up and kicks the table and then storms off to his room. The sound freezes the name in my mouth and I have to swallow to get rid of the block in my throat. Isa's face looked like a jigsaw puzzle. I don't like what the war is doing to my family. I don't know who to listen to, they all have opinions and the news has a different one. I don't want to listen to any of them. I just don't want my family and me to get hurt and I don't want school to stop and I don't want blood on the streets with people dying. I just want my normal life. I hate the war. I am still hungry but I don't want to ask Yasmine for more food, she's been in a bad mood lately.

Baba is an orphan and he once took me shopping and told me that there were days when he would be treated badly by his foster-parents and they wouldn't feed him and he would hide bread under his pillow and soak it in water for it to soften up and then eat it before he went to sleep. He said sleep made him forget about his childhood because he remembers the dreams he had and he thought he was living them. Baba then bought me a dessert called sahlab and told me the story about him running away from school every week to eat this dessert and get away from the scary school he hated so much. He used to always get into trouble but he said it was worth it because that warm dessert made his insides happy.

A knock on the door and a loud voice calling Khalid's name disturbs my thoughts. He gets up and opens the door to one of our neighbours who's holding a platter of fried dessert. I can faintly hear their conversation but I know it's going to end up with Khalid going out. I wish he would stay at home for a bit longer. I like company.

Khalid walks back in and puts the platter on the table. The honey glazing on top is melting and my mouth is watering for it. Why do the neighbours have food and we don't?

'Want to walk down the streets with us?' Khalid asks me. He never asks me to go out with him and his friends. I jump up and clap my hands and stand in front of the door ready to go. His friend laughs and we walk out. It is starting to get dark now and we walk past the café's that used to be filled with men playing backgammon and drinking tea and are now half empty and some even closed. We pass by kids playing hopscotch and my heart feels heavy. I wish my neighbours would play with me. I feel sad when I hear kids playing outside and nobody rings on my door to call me out. That's why I like Nabil, because he likes to play with me.

The further down we walk, as they talk and I listen, the louder the sounds of people marching is getting. There is an echo of people chanting 'Down with the regime' and I can spot a flag being held up high. Is this the revolution that Yasmine has been telling me about, the one they went to? There is a strong smell of petrol coming out of Khalid's friend's mouth. I am not sure if I like him or not. I usually sense people's auras but his is difficult to pinpoint. I don't feel comfortable with that so I move away from him and stand by Khalid.

Five minutes later it's like we've entered a new world. There are buildings that are half-collapsed with rubble all around them. One of the buildings looks like a sleeping troll. The streets are packed with people chanting and holding flags. They look like a hungry army of ants going for attack. They also remind me of a scene from *Braveheart*. Many people are greeting Khalid and his friend. They seem to be well known here. Khalid is walking differently to how he does at home. His chest is pushed out and one of his eyebrows is raised. He looks serious. I didn't know people change in different places.

I jump on Khalid's shoulders to see things from above but I think I am too heavy because he is breathing loudly. There is a rectangular box with the Syrian flag and flowers on top of it. I think it is a dead body. I feel sick. I hit Khalid on his shoulders and shout to be put down. He puts me down quickly and asks me what's wrong but I just run to a pavement and vomit. I do it for two minutes and four seconds. All the violet in me is on the floor now. The pavement around me is violet. I look up and Khalid is violet too.

★

I wake up to Yasmine moving my hair out of my face. My hair has grown below my ears. I need a haircut. I don't remember going to bed. The last thing I remember is the overwhelming sensation I got at the revolution. I sit up and look around and find three bags on the floor with clothes in them.

'Yasmine, are you going somewhere?'

She smiles and continues to play with my hair.

'We are going away for a few days to the beach, would you like that?'

'Yes! Yes! Yes!… Yasmine I saw a house… a house that is half gone and there were two kids looking out of the window. The half of the house had bullets all around it with the shape of a UFO. I had a dream that a UFO came and destroyed everything.' I don't realise I am crying until Yasmine tells me to calm down and stop crying. She continues to play with my hair because that's the closest I will let her come to me.

'Did you see that yesterday Habibi?'

'Yes.'

'Don't go to the marches outside, you might get hurt.'

'Khalid took me out, I get lonely at home.'

'We are going to the beach to have fun, come on, get up!' Yasmine pulls me up and pushes me to the bathroom. We both start laughing and I have energy because I made Yasmine ruby again.

We all get ready in half an hour and I put my cap on for the sun, I love holidays. There is a taxi waiting outside for us and we all get in and start singing road songs all the way out of our city. The moment we leave, I can see the sun again and my heart feels like a blooming rose. I hope the sun lasts for the few days we are away. We stop at a petrol station on the way and I run around the car 17 times before I get dizzy and get back inside. I am already having so much fun. I wish things could always be this fun. The boys and Baba are smoking outside the window so I close it before the smell suffocates me and I am strangled to the ground. I put my hands around my neck and pretend their smoke is strangling me. I knock on the window with my elbow so they can turn around and see me. I love making people laugh.

We get to the seaside in two hours and 23 minutes, south-west all the way. It's warmer here.

'Yasmine put sunscreen on me.'

'Wait till we get to the house.'

'Whose house is it Yasmine?'

'Aunt Rana's house.'

'Is she going to be home?'

'No Habibi, she lent us the house for a few days.'

'Yayyy!' I run to the house where Khalid is standing outside smoking and the driver and the boys are taking the bags into the house.

The house looks very different to ours. The sun is shining on it and for a moment I forget there is a war back home. I run upstairs to look around the house. I decide to stay in the room that overlooks the beach. Then I change my mind. I don't want to imagine sea monsters at night when I look down. I settle for the small room next to it. I can still hear the waves from here. The smell is like a shell mama once bought me when she came here to visit her sister. This makes me think of mama but I run downstairs and shake my head before I get sad.

I tug at Yasmine's dress and ask her when we are going out to the beach. She says we have to eat first. I can't wait to go swimming. Baba used to take me to our neighbour's swimming pool every week when I was young. I love being in the water, I feel so free. It's the only time I can ever be myself and laugh till I can't any more. The water on my skin reminds me of a story I heard about a prince who thought that the sea was a magical place. He built a palace on top of the water and learnt to live underwater because the water against his skin understood him more than any other person ever had. The water is my best friend because it plays with me for as long as I want.

Baba goes to the shops around the place and brings us two roasted chickens ready to eat. After I have eaten I change into my swimsuit and run to the beach. The sand under my feet makes me shiver. It is hot but the sinking feeling makes a shiver run down my spine. I jump into the water and start clapping and singing a nursery rhyme mama used to always sing when we used to go swimming. The boys come running to me and all jump into the water at the same time. It's like a waterfall of their perfume and water. The three of them come up from underwater with their hair soaked and stand around me. I feel like I'm drowning in a rainbow of perfume. All of them have different perfumes on and I can smell them all so distinctly. But when I'm not paying too much attention the smell attacks me as one perfume monster tries to drown me, fighting to push me down underwater.

We start playing a game of ball and whoever drops the ball has to go underwater for ten seconds and the seconds keep rising the more the ball is dropped. I don't mind going underwater because I know if I don't have a house, I can live underwater like the prince. I don't know if the story the teacher told us is real or not, but I know I can live underwater and even try to pretend I'm a fish. I wonder how fish think though. Will they know I'm human pretending to be a fish or will they think I'm a fish? We have one Spanish girl in our class who has been brought up in Syria and she thinks she's Syrian but everybody else knows she isn't. Is that how I am going to be underwater?

After playing the game for long enough for all of us to get tired and our fingers wrinkly from the water, I sit on the sand and start to build a sandcastle.

'Yasmine look, do you like my sandcastle?'

Yasmine is sitting on a lounge chair with Baba under a parasol, she doesn't like getting red, I love it though.

'Keep going Adam.'

I get up quickly to drink some water and suddenly a pain that I have never experienced flies through my body and I scream and fall to the ground. I close my eyes and everything turns purple. Did I press a purple button in my body by accident? Yasmine says I twisted my ankle.

I spend the rest of the day sitting on the sand by Yasmine

with ice on my ankle. There are many people around that are speaking a different language to us and look very different. A woman wearing her underwear in the water has purple hair. I didn't know people could be born with purple hair. I guess she's from somewhere far like America. Isa comes and sits by us after swimming. He puts some music on his phone and we all sing along.

I see two kids speaking a fast weird language running up the beach and laughing and I get upset that I pressed a purple button in my body and now I can't run around.

Chapter Seven

YELLOW

WE HAVE SPENT three days away from home and the sun only went away today. The moment we get back into Aleppo a dark square rests on my heart, pushing it down. I don't know if it's because of the dark skies or because these three days have really changed our town, but everything looks like the shadow of a black angel. One of the buildings with a car parked outside resembles an angel with his head down. Maybe bad angels haunt our town, or maybe this is the bad angel's town.

I hold Yasmine's hand for the first time. I whisper the prayer that Baba taught me under my breath. I feel a spider weave his web around the linings of my heart. I repeat the prayer under my breath waiting for a release of good thoughts. Our taxi isn't far from our house. I can feel Yasmine's eyes on me for holding her hand, but I don't look at her. I am afraid I might notice something around me I don't like. My feelings are usually right; I am hoping this feeling is nothing close to a bad premonition this time. Baba opens the window and lights a cigarette. I look at his hand reaching for the window and I don't recognise the lines on it.

I start to feel a little better after repeating my prayers. We arrive outside our house and as soon as the car stops I run. My ankle feels better. I speed down the small alley leading to our door on the right and to my surprise the door is open a little. I shout out to Yasmine to ask if someone forgot to lock the door before we left. Isa comes running, swearing he locked the door and checked twice before we left. He pushes the door slowly and walks inside, I follow him and run back out. I see a black angel running towards me, I run to Yasmine and tell her to come in and see. Yasmine follows me as I run. She walks inside slowly and sees Isa picking up our furniture from the floor. Yasmine screams and falls to the floor. I try to pick Yasmine up and Isa comes and helps me. We lie her down on the floor inside because all the furniture is either broken or thrown across the room. Isa looks up and says a prayer, asking God for forgiveness and for God to help us. Baba and the other two boys come in with the bags and drop them in shock. They all have the same reaction; they go around the room and say the same prayer. Isa has brought Yasmine water and is blowing in her face. I walk over to the chairs and start picking them up.

Tariq sits beside me and asks me if I'm okay. I don't answer but look down at the floor. He moves me back slowly and puts his finger on his mouth telling me not to say anything. I stand back where he put me and wait for something to happen. I don't know if I'm expecting the worst or hoping for the best. Either way, I am frozen in place waiting to be told what to do with my body. As for my mind, it is pounding like a drum with the song in the background muffled by my fear. Why is everything upside down and the door open? What happened? There was a war outside, and now a war started inside our house.

Tariq tells me to go to the kitchen and get some fruit for Baba because his sugar level went down. I am watching my family fall one by one. I never thought this day would come. I thought that I would be the one who would always need help but now I am on the other side of the table and I don't know how to deal with things. If mama were here she would know what to do. Mama was our wings; now we are hopeless without wings.

I walk into the kitchen and to my surprise it looks like it hasn't been touched. Everything is in place and I open the fridge and take out an apple and cut it in four and put it on a plate. Baba is sitting with his hand on his forehead and Yasmine is lying down with sprinkles of water dripping down her face. I have a painting in my room that resembles this very moment. I hold the plate tighter in my hand and feel sick from this realisation. Tariq calls my name and I run with the plate to Baba and put it on his lap. His face looks as white as a ghost. I have never seen a ghost but I have heard this simile many times so I am going to assume that a ghost is white. I sit on the floor by Yasmine and Baba and think about how we got to this place. Our lives had a perfect routine that I was so comfortable living in, and now, I don't know who we are any more or what is happening. The war holds so much uncertainty above my head like a grey cloud waiting to pour and thunder down. I don't want it to thunder on me.

The doorbell rings and Khalid, who was fixing the furniture, goes to open it. If I don't think about it, I can erase the memory and it will be like there was just a light earthquake. I have always wished a board and rubber would appear in our minds when we close our eyes so we could rewrite our memories or simply erase them. When I grow up I want to study the brain so I can come up with an invention like this.

I hear an unfamiliar voice and then a girl walks in with her suitcase and stands by the door. She looks so much like Baba but I don't know who she is. Baba jumps up and hugs her as she cries on his shoulder. I don't think I have ever met her before so I get closer to see her better. Her perfume is strong and she has a lot of make-up on like she is not from around here. Baba sits her down on the floor while Khalid and Tariq put the furniture back in place. I listen to their conversation as Yasmine slowly gets up and greets the girl as well. She asks about what happened to the house but as Baba starts explaining, she tells Baba her husband died. Baba stops mid-sentence. So many things have been happening lately, I don't know what he is thinking now. I just hope he doesn't fall to the ground. She goes on to explain that her husband went out one night and was shot by the army.

'I have been out on that open road and I need a home after he left me.'

She introduces herself to me as Amira and her lips pout out like the opening of a rose. She is beautiful. Amira means princess in Arabic and even though I have never met a princess before, I don't believe she's far from being one. She takes her headscarf off and her hair flows down to her shoulders and falls perfectly in place. I stare at her intently until Yasmine gently ruffles my hair and laughs a little. She is still in shock. Amira laughs a little too but her tears are still falling. I want to paint her.

Amira is going to stay with us for a while and sleep in Yasmine's room.

★

Amira sits by the window with her make-up bag in front of her, fixing her face. She has an opaque look to her eyes, a cloudiness you can't erase. For the rest of the afternoon, we clean the house and Yasmine makes dinner. By the time the night falls Amira moves from the window and goes to the bathroom for far longer than normal. I wait 20 minutes in desperation to go to the toilet.

Now that Amira lives with us we have less food. I like her, but I am always hungry now so I feel tired most of the day. Ever since she moved in and school closed down I haven't been able to do much other than paint and read. Baba says I can play games on the computer to relax when the electricity works. I haven't showered in four days because there has been no water. I stink and I can smell myself but everything is changing so quickly and I can't catch up. I looked in the mirror yesterday and my face had a shabby look to it which I refuse to embrace, so I won't look into the mirror again until I shower. Everybody at home looks tired and seems to be dragging themselves around the house. We hear gunshots and shelling every other night now. It has become a normal part of our lives.

★

Tariq comes back home a few days later with a huge grin on his face. We haven't had any happiness for some time.

'I have a surprise for you Adam!'

'Surprise! Show meee.'

'Close your eyes and come outside.'

'But I can't see where I'm going…'

'Come, I'll cover your eyes with my hand and lead you.'

Tariq's hands are big and overlap when covering both my eyes. His fingers are cold and long, they feel unwelcoming. I put my hands in front of me as a precaution. We walk 11 steps and stand without saying a word. I touch his hands trying to find the knot between his fingers. He lets go and for a few seconds I can only see shooting stars coming towards me.

'Surprise!'

I can't focus on what Tariq is pointing at because my town is crumbling to pieces behind it. There are huge rocks and dust in front of a line of shops opposite our house and in the far distance there's grey smoke covering most of our sky. I look down and see the bike that Tariq is pointing to.

'For me Tariq?'

'You like it?'

'Yes… Yes… Yes!'

'Do you want to learn how to ride it now?'

'Yes!' I jump on the bike and fall on the other side. Tariq laughs at me and picks me up and puts me on the seat steadily. He arches his body over me and holds onto the handles telling me to peddle my feet. I do it and move slowly. I thought bikes were faster. We go around the block with Tariq still teaching me and I soon go a little faster and then faster still. I can fly if I go faster and peddle harder. I love this feeling like I can let go of everything and fly with my bike like in *E.T.* I never knew it could be this much fun.

'Where did you get this bike from Tariq?'

'I found it broken on the side of a road and fixed it.'

'Did you fix it at your university?'

'Yes I did.'

'I wish I was at university!'

'Haha it's a pain! Have fun being young and free.'

'But I feel old.'

'ADAMMMM!' Baba calls out for me and I look back at Tariq's face once more and run inside. I don't know why he answered me in a scary way. I just want to be older so I can do things myself too.

Baba pushes me inside as soon as I walk in and he calls out for Tariq to run. He closes the door after us and tells us to fol-low him. We go into his room and he opens up another door I always thought was a cupboard. We go down a few stairs into a room painted white, with the paintings I gave mama hung up.

'Those are my paintings Baba.'

'Boys, if anything happens and you have nowhere to go or if the army comes in to attack, sneak into this room and lock the door. It looks like a cupboard; they're never going to guess you're here.'

There is a record player in the corner of the room with a pile of vinyls stacked up.

'Are you going to come in with us Baba?'

'Whoever gets in here shouldn't worry about who is outside; everyone is their own man. You're a man now okay Adam? You have to stand on your own feet, we might not find each other in the end.'

'Does Yasmine know this?'

'I told everyone, you're the last to know.'

'Baba, I don't want us to be separated.'

'Adam you're a man. Men aren't afraid. You should only be afraid of the sound of your crying.'

Chapter Eight

RED

We haven't had electricity for the past week; we live in a different world now. Everyone is dark and depressed apart from Amira who still sits by the window with her colourful make-up. She still cries though. I haven't been able to sleep well lately. I can't stop thinking about mama and who is going to visit her first. I have been thinking of going back to the room Baba showed us so I can sit and play records but there's no electricity. I want to know what vinyls he has. I walk out of my room and look down both sides of the corridor before tiptoeing to Baba's room. I put my ear on the door to figure out whether Baba is in there or not. I don't hear anything and so I slowly open the door. Before I get to walk in Yasmine calls me from the kitchen. Why is everyone always calling me!

'Take some food to the neighbours Habibi.'

'Why Yasmine?'

'Don't be greedy Adam, we have to look out for our neighbours, it's good manners.'

'What are we having for lunch Yasmine?'

'Rice.'

'Rice with what?'

'Just rice.'

I want to shout and tell her to keep the food at home for us because we have no food but I just listen to her in case she gets upset. Yasmine used to always change colours depending on her mood but now she is a constant grey. I don't know if it's because I have no energy to pay attention or because she really is very dull now. I think it's because she can't see the man she loves. I wish I knew the truth rather than always trying to understand everything like it's a mystery. I love mystery but I am tired of being Sherlock Holmes.

I smell the plate Yasmine gives me. I am so tempted to move the foil and take some food. I look back and no one is looking so I open the foil but as soon as I see the rice I close it again and ask God for forgiveness. Maybe the neighbours need it more than me. I knock on the door three times and wait then knock another three times and call out for the mother.

'Auntie I'm here with food.'

There's no reply.

'Mohammed? Uncle Jamal?'

I push the door a little and find it open. The house smells like nails scratching on metal. The graphic image pierces my mind and I have to close my eyes and cover my ears from the impact. The thought is sickening. I walk into the sitting room with my plate of rice and out of pure silence I hear the movement of what sounds like a mouse. The sitting room has a bend that doesn't allow me to see the end of the room so I turn to the right, the smell gets stronger. I don't hear my heartbeat any more and I drop the plate of rice on the ground. I see the whole family curled towards the wall with dry blood on them and a pool around their bodies. They are all dressed well and the women have headscarves on their heads. That means that they were getting ready to go somewhere. The smell reaches deeper into my mind and I can almost smell their fear before all of this happened. I walk a little towards them to see their faces and they all have their eyes closed apart from the mother whose eyes are still open. I run out. Her eyes poured the colour pink. I pass by the spilled rice and for a split second see a

shadow come from the other room. I freeze. What if someone is waiting to kill me too? I don't want to die. I scream so
loud but my legs aren't carrying me away. I always wake up in
tears when I can't move in my dreams. But now this is reality
and tears won't do anything. I breathe in and out silently and
tiptoe out of the house. As soon as I see the daylight from the
door I run through it and without realising I look down to a
shirt full of vomit.

'Adam.' I hear a whisper behind me. I run to Yasmine in the
kitchen.

'What's wrong Adam, what's wrong?' Yasmine shakes me.
I can't catch my breath or find the words. I can't even move.

I vomit again.

★

I wake up to the neighbours' youngest son's face. Everything
comes back to me and I don't understand how he is here. Maybe I imagined everything. I really hope I did.

'You passed out again.'

I get up and look at Yasmine in the corner of the sofa, her
face so pale.

'Yasmine, what happened?'

Yasmine looks over at Ali, our neighbour.

'I'm sorry you had to see that,' she says. Yasmine used to
call me Habibi and always explain things to me simply, but
now she doesn't even look at me when she has something to
say.

'What happened to them?'

Ali starts telling me everything like it didn't even happen
to his family. Ali is two years older than me, which means he
is 16.

Apparently the army came into the house and started swearing at them and calling them names and they lined them all up and shot them. Ali was hiding under the bed. Even though he is 16, he looks ten and he can fit under anything. This happened yesterday and Ali did not move or run out till I went into the house. It was him that I heard move and whose shadow I saw. After I passed out, Tariq and Yasmine went to the neighbours' house and saw everything. They found him and brought him back here.

'Is he going to live with us as well Yasmine?'

'Adam! Don't be rude!'

'I'm asking, I'm not being rude.'

'Yes he is.'

Everyone is moving in with us. Our family is falling apart. I didn't know how disgusting a war could be till now.

'Are we going to bury them?' I ask Yasmine. I won't be able to sleep knowing there are dead bodies in the next house.

'We can't move them out, we don't have enough money for four coffins.'

'Are you going to leave them there?'

'Yes for now.'

I don't want to have dead people as neighbours.

'We want freedom, we want the regime down! We want freedom, we want the regime down!'

Yasmine gets up and slaps Khalid on the face as soon as he walks in and starts chanting.

'What the hell?'

I run behind Yasmine.

'If you want to chant you do that outside, don't bring your opinions into this house, understood? I don't want a revolution here as well. It's bad enough as it is. We are all losing our minds and people are dying for no reason and you're asking for more!'

I have never seen Yasmine speak that much or get that angry.

Khalid storms out and Yasmine swears after him.

'Calm down Yasmine, you can't control everything that happens in this house,' Baba tells her.

'WELL THEN LET ME LIVE MY OWN LIFE INSTEAD OF LIVING YOURS!' Yasmine shouts and runs to her room. Both of our guests look away as if they can't hear what's going on. I can't take my eyes off Yasmine's door.

★

'Let's go get some food Adam.' Baba gently shoves me to wake me up.

'We are buying food?'

'Yes, let's go, just you and I.' I jump up and before I count to 50 I am ready in front of Baba. I've been hungry for days. I've been craving stuffed vegetables and rice and apple pie. I think I even dreamed of it.

Baba and I walk out into a dead town. There isn't a single person around. There are spiderwebs on the neighbours' door. Baba tells me stories about the Prophet Muhammad as we walk down the street. These stories always inspire me to be the best I can be. When we get to the market we only find two stalls open in a whole street. There are two men sitting behind each stall praising God with their prayer beads. One of them is cleaning his teeth with a brown stick called the Miswak, which the Prophet PBUH used to use. Baba used to have one and I tried it but it has a funny smell that I can't get used to. It looks cool to watch people do it though. The stalls aren't as colourful as usual but everything looks tasty to me right now.

There are mostly dates on the side.

'Why are there so many dates Baba and nothing else?'

The man hears me asking Baba and pats me on the head.

'Young man, a house without dates is a starving house said the Prophet PBUH. Three dates every time you feel the pangs of hunger and you'll forget your hunger.'

I smile and look at Baba.

'That's true Adam, come on, let's pick the dates you want.'

I like my dates quite soft and shiny brown. They're the sweetest kind. Baba buys a huge bag of dates and a few bananas and gives me one.

'Thank you Baba.'

'Do you want to know something interesting?'

'Yes Baba…'

'I once read in a book that many fruits and vegetables resemble certain body parts and are in fact good for those body parts. Like walnuts, they look like a brain and are proven to be good for the brain. Grapes hang in a cluster that looks like the shape of the heart and are good for the heart. Isn't that strange?'

'Are you sure that's true Baba? It sounds like a story.'

Baba laughs and assures me it's true. I love hearing Baba tell me facts and stories. He knows everything. One day I want to know everything like him. But I don't want to be a teacher like him though because I'm not good with people. We walk home holding the two bags full of dates and bananas. I can see my school building from here. The lights are off and it looks like no one has entered it for a long time. I hear heavy footsteps behind me. I look back and see four men walking two by two behind each other. They walk fast and start walking in front of us. From here I notice the two at the back holding guns pointed at the front two.

'Baba, they have guns!'

Baba puts his hand on my mouth and pulls me back to the corner of a house.

'Adam, don't say anything, we could get killed.'

I freeze in my spot. How can everybody talk about death so easily now? We never used to talk about dying at all before. I hold onto Baba's shirt and stand behind him. He doesn't say anything. I can hear the voice of somebody shouting from afar.

'Have faith in God, never lose faith in God!'

'Shut up you…' I am guessing the guys with the guns replied to them. I can't repeat the word they said but it was very bad. Baba covered my ears. But I had already heard it. Baba says it's okay to walk out and we walk slowly behind them. They are 14 feet in front of us I count quickly. Baba puts a finger on his lips and I just follow him slowly. I don't take my eyes off the men. I can hear the men with the guns talking loudly but I can't understand what they're saying. It sounds like Arabic but it's a very weird dialect that doesn't belong to any Arab region. They sound like foreigners speaking Arabic. I didn't know foreigners could join the army. I need to ask Baba about that. Before I can finish the sentence in my head, the two men at the front duck down and run faster than I have ever seen. They chant 'God is the greatest' as they make an escape. One of them falls to the ground and the soldier behind him grabs him and shoots him. I have never heard a gun shot that close or seen anyone being shot. I can't describe it. The world stopped for a second when the bang came out. The man on the floor jumped up when the bullet hit him and I could see blood jumping out. Then he lay still. The second soldier catches up with the other guy and as I am expecting a bullet and cover my ears, he twists his neck and spits at him. I can still hear the bones cracking now. Baba pushes me behind another building and looks at me. He mimes the word 'sorry' and lets me hold his shirt till we can't hear footsteps any more. I cry because I don't like war. I feel my body shaking but I can't control it. Baba is blurry. His voice is clear though; he is reading a prayer over me. I close my eyes really tight and think of how upset mama would be if I wasn't strong enough. I open my eyes and tell Baba I am ready to go. We walk past the two bodies on the ground. The first guy shot looks like he is dreaming and is only asleep. I wish he was. But the second guy has dark blood on his neck, but it's internal. His face looks horrified. It reminds me of a horror movie I once watched with Khalid. I couldn't sleep all night. The other man doesn't have much hair but this one has long hair down to his shoulders. His hair is the only thing that looks alive about him. I follow Baba quickly into our house three doors down and keep in mind the idea I got for a painting.

As soon as we get in through the door Yasmine jumps up and asks us if we're okay. Baba doesn't say anything and walks on. Yasmine keeps asking me what happened. This is the most she has spoken to me in a long time.

'Two men got killed Yasmine.'

'Did you see them?'

'Yes, it was very scary!'

'My poor Adam, are you okay?'

'Yes Yasmine I'm okay, can I tell you a secret?'

'Of course.'

'I have a new painting idea.'

'What is it?'

'Every martyr I see, I will take some of his hair and make a portrait out of it.' Yasmine jumps back.

'Are you crazy Adam? Don't touch anyone!'

'I'm just touching their hair.'

'No! Understood?'

Yasmine is shouting at me for no reason. I don't like it when she turns purple on me but I just say okay and go to the kitchen. I still want to use my idea. The dates have already been put on a plate and the bananas in a bowl. I pour less than a quarter of a cup of milk and have three dates. Baba was right, I don't feel hungry any more. I open the tap for some water but orange liquid comes out. I don't know why it's orange but I wait for it to fade away but it doesn't. I can't drink this water.

'Yasmminneee!'

Yasmine comes into the kitchen and doesn't say a word. I lower my voice and tell her there's no water to drink.

'I'll show you the only thing we can do.' Yasmine fills a saucepan with tap water and puts it on the stove to boil. The electricity now comes every day for an hour. That's when we do everything.

'Are we going to drink hot water Yasmine?'

'We don't have a choice. Go and try to put the boiler on in the bathroom to see if it works. The rest of us need to shower today.'

'The rest of us?'

'Ali, Amira, Khalid and Tariq showered yesterday when the water came.'

I run to the bathroom in four steps, I am getting really fast. The boiler is on but the light isn't red and the water is still cold. I really need to shower. I can smell myself and feel the grease on my hair. It makes my head feel heavier.

'Yasmine there's no hot water!' I say out of breath.

'Okay I'll warm some water for you to drink and bathe with, but you have to wash quickly so the rest of us can.'

'But how can I wash my body with the same water I'm going to drink?'

'Just do as I say, we don't have much choice.'

I leave the kitchen and wait outside for the hot water to boil. I thought war brought families closer together, now everyone is on their own. I never thought Yasmine would let me be alone.

★

I feel free for the first time in ages. Being in water makes me forget about all the things that make me sad. I lie back in the bathtub and think about my idea for my painting. I could do a series of paintings that unite the frozen blood of our country. I got that sentence from the news. It sounded good. I will have a lot of fun trying to work with hair and paint for the first time. I can already envision the eyes I am going to draw then line with hair. I don't know what 'a raw piece' means but I was watching a show once and the TV presenter said an amazing painting was a 'raw piece'. I want my painting to be a 'raw piece' too.

I start to play a game in my mind thinking of movie names with the last letter of the first movie name that pops into my head. There's a knock on the door and Baba tells me to hurry up. I don't want to leave the water. I drink some of the water around me because I don't know when I will be able to drink this much water again.

After I get dressed I put the TV on to watch something that will cheer me up while the power lasts. I have been getting very bored at home lately. Ali comes and sits next to me. He has never been my friend. Nobody at school used to speak to me and now he is making a conversation with me about when

I think we will be able to go back. His face used to always have a full look to it. Like he was satisfied with everything he had. I once had a daydream he wanted to be my friend and for the rest of the day I kept on staring at him hoping he could read my mind. In the end, he and his friends laughed at me for being weird. Now his face looks empty. I don't really want to be his friend any more. We sit down quietly and watch *Punk'd* with Ashton Kutcher. I think he's really funny and he reminds me of Tariq's friend Omar. He looks a lot like him. I even think he speaks like him but Tariq says I'm exaggerating. Ali and I both laugh very loudly at the prank with Zac Efron. We are of course watching the episode with Arabic subtitles. I am the best at English in my class, writing not speaking. But I find it difficult understanding different accents. The hardest for me is the Irish. Ali likes Zac Efron. I remember at school he came in with a poster of him and stuck it on his table. The teacher had confiscated it by the end of the day but he got it back a week later. I don't really like Zac Efron though, I prefer Leonardo DiCaprio. Yasmine loves all his movies and if one of them is on TV no one is allowed to talk to her.

I wonder if Ali misses his family. He seems to be quiet about it and is laughing normally. I wasn't able to laugh at all for a few months after mama died. Even now whenever I laugh it's not the same.

Isa comes into the sitting room and ruffles my hair.

'What are you laughing at? Let me in!'

'*Punk'd* had an amazing prank on Zac Efron.'

'Can I sit next to you on the sofa?'

'Yes, come Isa.'

Isa smells nice, he has a very musky scent, no matter what. Sitting with him makes me happy.

'Isa are you going to show Ali your poetry later?'

'Only if he wants, do you want to hear it Ali?'

Ali nods and smiles. He has been living with us for days now but he still hardly says anything.

The second episode comes on and Ashton Kutcher starts speaking. Before we even know who is going to be pranked, I feel the ground shake. I say my prayer instantly and look at Isa.

'Calm down, I'll see what is going on.'

I follow him to the window. Yasmine comes running in and tells me to move so she can see. We can't see much but the sky suddenly becomes dark even though it's still morning. The town is filled with smoke, I can even smell it come into the house.

'Put the news on quickly!' Baba comes running into the room.

The screen has breaking news on it and the same woman who has been telling me what has been going on down my street before I even know about it comes on.

'Two missiles were sent to the city of Aleppo today and the aftermath has covered the city in smoke. 17 people have been injured. A citizen reports what happened: I was cleaning my car with my son when we felt the ground shake for about five seconds and saw missiles being shot above us. It sounded like the trumpet of the Day of Judgement. It's a wake up call if anything.' Baba switches the TV off and tries to breathe in and out.

'Maha, get me some water please.'

We all turn around the moment we hear mama's name. I feel my spine click in place and the hairs on my face tickle me. I haven't heard Baba say mama's name since she left us. Baba doesn't even open his eyes or correct himself.

'Baba, it's Yasmine,' I tell him.

'Someone just get me water!'

Yasmine comes in with a glass of water from the jar we filled earlier. Baba drinks it all without taking a break.

The sitting room has never looked so busy before; everyone is looking out of the window. I look around and notice how the room looks like a palette of colours. I can paint the war with the colours on their faces. Tariq puts the TV on again. The news is still talking about the bombing. I concentrate on what they're saying. They are doing live coverage. I can see my school in the distance. So many buildings are now on the ground and people are running around. I run to the window just in time to see a tall building three streets down collect dust and collapse like a Lego house. The screams are louder now and we can hear sirens. The electricity goes out and the TV turns blank. A woman is running with her kid down the street and a few men are also running behind. One of the men runs past our window and I can see a gun. I don't know who is good and who is bad.

This war is unfair, there are no uniforms or clues. A woman that looks about Yasmine's age runs past our window a few minutes later but seems to be struggling with her dress. She stops for a second and turns to see us looking out of the window. I can see the confusion in her eyes. None of us offers to help; the window is like a barrier. We are watching her like it is a movie. She pulls her dress up and runs away. I feel bad after she runs away. We could have helped, but we all stood and watched.

Things start to calm down four hours after the incident. Our street didn't get the full force but we felt the shake and one of our walls is a little tilted now. It could fall on us at any time. Isa puts on the Quran on the battery radio. We all sit around like we did at mama's funeral. This all seems too familiar; all our faces are just as long. Baba coughs really hard and I can almost hear the dryness in his throat. Nobody is saying anything. I try to think of something to say or pretend to talk about but not only is my mouth dry, my thoughts seem to be too. The elastic band on my hand starts to itch for my tug. My head is turning in a circle around my shoulders and I start blinking fast. This place is making me feel uncomfortable. As I rotate my head, I start to notice everybody's facial expressions and movements. All seven of them are rocking back and forth in different timings. They look like some religious groups that sit in a circle and rock to a tune of religious music. I start to get dizzy looking at them and concentrate on Baba. His eyes look blurry; milky describes them better. I've only seen grandma with eyes like that but mama said it was because she was so old. But Baba isn't old, he's… I can't figure out how old he is, but I know he's not old. He's probably only 50.

'Adam, are you okay?' Yasmine asks me and I lose my concentration and turn to her.

'Yes.'

I get up and start tugging at my hair from the back. It has grown a lot since the last time I noticed. It's now past my neck.

'Where are you going? Stay here, we should all stay together for now.'

'I don't want to Yasmine, I'm bored.'

'You're right, we are all safe and together, we should be happy, let's all play a board game, what do you think Baba?'

Yasmine looks over to Baba who doesn't even flinch. I don't even think he heard her. I tap Baba's hand but he doesn't even move. I tap him harder and he turns his head around so slowly like his head is too heavy to carry. He reminds me of an owl I saw at the zoo with mama that turned its head around its whole neck. I had nightmares for a week after that I think.

Yasmine repeats her question but Baba just tells her to get more water. I run to the kitchen instead to get it. I need to get away; I'm starting to feel my chest tighten and turn dark green. There is hardly any water left but I fill up a cup anyway and walk slowly to the sitting room so it doesn't spill.

'Yasmine there's no water left.'

I hand the water to Baba and he knocks it out of my hand. I look him right in the eye and I swear for a split second his pupils looked greyish-white.

I look down and my hand is bleeding. I don't feel any pain but I start to smell it. The smell is getting to my head and I feel my arms and legs go numb.

'Yas... mine!' My voice quivers as I call to Yasmine but she doesn't turn around. I feel a hand on my waist and I am slowly lowered down onto the sofa. I look up at Amira's face. She has glitter on her eyelids. I close my eyes and try to breathe in and out so I don't pass out. Amira plays with my hair and starts to sing. I open my eyes and look up at her. Her voice sounds like it belongs to the girl with the Nutella eyes. She has a voice that resembles the waves in the sea. She takes me away to the beach we went to and I concentrate on the waves coming to shore in my mind. I feel my head start to settle and I smile. I wonder how the Nutella-eyed girl is doing now.

Yasmine walks up to me and asks me if I'm okay while Amira is cleaning the cut on my finger. I feel weird being looked after by two women. It's like Yasmine and mama, only it's not. The boys get up and smoke outside the house and the room looks darker without them. I sit up and decide to go to my room to paint, I can feel a painting. I'm lucky the cut wasn't on the finger I paint with. I bring out my pencil set and start to sketch my brothers standing outside the way I saw them. Two of them stand by the wall with one of their legs up and then Isa stands facing them. Their smoke unites in the middle of the triangle. I start to sketch their eyes but I'm finding it difficult. I see fire in Tariq's eyes, the Syrian flag in Khalid's but I can't figure out what Isa has.

I think his eyes are just vacant, like they're looking for something to cling onto. I giggle and decide to draw a lion in Tariq's eyes instead of fire. I love sketching lions. I am very good at it as I have practised a lot. I finish sketching the outline and pick another pencil with thicker lead to make it look darker.

Chapter Nine

MAROON

YASMINE IS ON THE GROUND with her hand on her face and Baba is standing up shouting at her.

'How can you do this to me?'

Yasmine looks up without saying anything. What did Yasmine do? I loved Baba for being caring and teaching us new things every day but now he is different.

'I'm Yasmine.' Yasmine's voice sounds shaky, like a salt packet would sound after shaking.

'Who's Yasmine?' Baba asks.

I put my hand through my hair and count to ten while tugging at it. I don't know what's going on. Things are always happening lately, there is no peace. Amira puts her arms around me and tries to move me away but I feel strong and angry now so I move away before I hurt someone. I sometimes feel heavy with how strong I feel, like I can punch down a wall. I have never tried though. When I feel angry I sit down and if I'm seated I lie down and say a prayer. Baba once taught me that that's what the Prophet Muhammad PBUH said we should do. Anger is the darkest colour I have ever seen anyone wear. Amira moves away from me and walks to the window to look out of it. I'm now scratching my hands together and the pain is mixing with my confusion. I don't like this at all. None of the boys are around and Baba is still shouting at Yasmine but I have stopped listening and started backing away.

'Maha you betrayed me! How are you still in my house?'

Yasmine crawls away from Baba and turns around to me. I

help her up, her eyes are puffed and she has tears coming down her face. Her hands are shaking. She walks back and pulls me with her into her room. I lock the door behind us after looking back at Baba again. He is still standing and shouting. His face is blue.

Yasmine starts to cry really loudly now and sits on the floor with her legs up to her chest. She looks like a ball.

'AHHHHHHH!'

Yasmine is making me scared now. She is crying louder now. In-between her loud gasps, it sounds like she is losing her breath.

'Yasmine,' I whisper. I don't know what to do. I don't want to be shouted at.

'I hate this house!'

'Do you hate me Yasmine?'

She looks up at me and slowly stops crying so loudly. She is still crying though, but no tears are coming down her face any more.

'No Adam, come sit by me.'

It's been a long time since Yasmine and I sat down together.

'I'm hungry.'

Yasmine laughs a rusty laugh.

'I haven't sat with you in a while but you're just as I left you, hungry!'

We both laugh and stare at a frame on Yasmine's wall. It's the Dali 'Atomicus' picture.

'Why do you have this picture up Yasmine?'

'Because I love photography. I wanted to be a photographer but mama told me to be a nurse. It's more feminine.'

'Do you still want to take pictures?'

'Yes Habibi, I think about it all the time.'

'So why haven't you gone to work Yasmine? Don't the hospitals need you?'

'I work at a plastic surgery centre Habibi, we have no patients for now.'

'So we don't have money?'

'Don't worry silly boy, go play with Ali, you have a friend at last.'

'I don't know what to play with him. I like playing in my room but I don't want him to see my paintings.'

'Go play hopscotch outside the door. Don't go any further,' she says and then takes a chalk out of her bedside drawer.

'Thank you!'

I run to the sitting room and look for Ali, he is lying down on the sofa, Baba isn't here any more.

'Do you want to play hopscotch?'

'With you?'

'Yes, outside the door.'

He jumps up and takes the chalk out of my hand. I run after him and watch him draw the grid. We play hopscotch and sing the national anthem the way we did every day at school during assembly. We both laugh when Ali falls on his face on the last box. I run to the end of the lane and pick up some stones from the ground for us to play with. Ali follows me and says we should go and walk around.

'I've been at home for too long.'

'I… I can't.'

'Why not?'

'Yasmine said we shouldn't go far.'

'We won't, we'll just have a little walk around.'

'I can't.'

'Well then I'll go and I'll be back.'

I wait outside the door for Ali while playing with the stones. I don't know how long he's been gone for but during the whole time I've been thinking about the girl with the

Nutella eyes. I want to see her again to be able to paint her eyes. They're slowly fading from my memory but I try to think of them a lot so I don't forget. Ali comes running back laughing.

'Oh I miss going out! You should've come.'

'Where did you go?'

'I ran all the way to school and found a cat sleeping outside so I scared it and came running back.'

'Why did you scare it?'

'Because it's fun.'

I am starting to dislike Ali. I love animals and I hate it when people mistreat them. It's not fun hurting people or animals.

'Come on let's play again.' Ali is circling around me and it's making me dizzy. I can hear a few gunshots in the distance but I'm not sure if I'm imagining things.

'Did you hear that?'

'Yes, but it sounded far away.'

'We should go in.'

'Let's just play one more game, it's probably no big deal!'

I look around and try to listen out for any more sounds but there's nothing. Ali starts to count to ten before we start playing hopscotch and I jump on the grid first and he tries to push me away laughing. We play till the sun starts to set. The sky is pink on one side and grey on the other. It looks beautiful but scary. It starts to get chilly so we decide to go in. I had fun today, it's nice having friends. I wonder if Ali knows where Nabil lives.

'Yes I do, do you want to go?'

'Yes!' I'm excited to see Nabil and tell him how Ali is now my friend.

I can smell food for the first time in ages. I feel so happy, I have a friend and we have food.

There's suddenly a loud bang on the door like someone is in a rush. I am scared to open it. Yasmine shouts from the kitchen for me to open it. A man out of breath is standing outside the door. I have never seen him before.

'Tell your family to come to the hospital down the road, Isa is injured!' He speaks really fast and then runs out and calls some guys and they all rush towards the hospital. I don't believe what he said. I run to the kitchen and tell Yasmine and she puts her hands on her head and slaps her face. Wasn't Isa just outside smoking?

'No, this isn't happening! Adam run and get me my scarf.' We run out of the house and down the road quickly. The hospital isn't far, it's only a seven-minute walk but we get there in five minutes. Yasmine asks around as soon as we walk in. There are people lying on the ground bleeding and some of them are on beds with doctors tending to them. This is the most blood I have ever seen. Even more than I saw at the neighbours' house. The smell is just the same though. Everybody is different but they all smell the same when they're bleeding. I try not to think of the smell because I don't want to embarrass Yasmine. There are so many sounds and voices. There are people talking and people shouting and people screaming and some moaning. I find Isa's friend who came to the door and I tell Yasmine it's him. She picks up her skirt and runs over to him.

'Where's Isa? Tell me where he is now!'

The guy just looks to his right and there Isa is. His chest has six bullet holes in it and his legs are bleeding. I can see this upside down. Yasmine runs to him and starts to kiss him. I follow behind her slowly. I still haven't seen his face. The closer I get the better I feel. I can smell Isa. His hand is on his chest with a bullet shot in it as well. He smiles when he sees me. His eyes are bruised and his lips swollen. I see crows flying around in my head. I don't want Isa to leave me. I can hear people screaming from two beds down. A doctor comes rushing in and pushes me out of his way quickly.

'Everybody move please, stand away from here.' Two nurses follow him in and the doctor takes a metal stick from one of the nurses and starts to put it into Isa's bullet holes. Isa moans loudly, it sounds like the cry of a donkey. It sounds black.

'What is he doing Yasmine? What is he doing to Isa?' I tug at Yasmine's skirt and she covers my eyes into her chest.

'They're helping Isa, just wait Habibi.' Her voice has completely changed. I can feel the echo of the words in her chest but the voice sounds like the way a sloth would speak. Isa screams louder and one of the nurses pushes us out and closes the door on us.

'Please save him God, please save him God!' Yasmine cries.

I hold really tight onto her skirt.

The doctor opens the door and Yasmine jumps up from the floor, I follow her. She peeks her head into the room but I'm not sure if she is able to see anything.

'May he rest in peace,' the doctor says. Yasmine starts shaking and screaming so loudly. I don't know why she is doing this; the doctor said he hopes he rests in peace. Isa should be fine after he rests. Yasmine runs into the room and the door closes on me. I can hear her screaming. I go in and see Isa's body covered in a white cloth, even his face. I hate it when my face is covered with something; it makes me feel uncomfortable and weak. Yasmine is on her knees by the bed crying and praying. I walk over and move the cloth from Isa's face so he doesn't feel uncomfortable as well. Yasmine jumps up and starts shouting at me not to touch him and moves me away. Why is she acting like this? I caught the look on Isa's face before Yasmine pushed me away; he looked happy to be resting. I can't wait for him to wake up and read me some of his poetry.

I can feel a cold breeze touch me. Yasmine is on the floor reading some Quran. I guess she is waiting for Isa to wake up.

'Isa is going to feel uncomfortable with the cloth on his face Yasmine.'

She looks up at me and then continues to read her Quran. I don't like being in the hospital. People keep coming in covered in blood and crying. There's a girl in the last bed with her leg cut off and the doctor is putting a huge bandage on it. I've been looking at her. She didn't cry once. Her eyes are closed.

'Let's go home now.' Yasmine gets up and closes the Quran. She kisses the cover and taps it on her forehead.

'What about Isa?' Yasmine looks over at Isa and she starts crying again. This time she doesn't make a sound. She leans and kisses him over the cover. Yasmine takes my hand and we walk out leaving Isa on the bed covered in white. I miss him already.

★

When we get home we see everyone sitting around.

'What happened? Where is he?' Khalid jumps up first. Baba looks good again. His eyes seem clear.

'NO! NO! NO! Don't give me that look!' Khalid starts shaking Yasmine for an answer.

'He's resting in peace,' I say.

Khalid falls to the ground and reacts just like Yasmine did. Tariq goes to his room and slams the door behind him. What is happening?

'Yasmine, what is happening?'

'Let's go and sit in my room.'

Baba doesn't say a single word but I see him cry for the first time. I freeze in place and stare at him.

'Why is Baba crying Yasmine?'

Yasmine looks back and walks over to Baba. She kisses him on the forehead and hugs him. I can hear her whisper some things to him but I can't figure out what she is saying.

I feel lonely standing here waiting for Yasmine. I miss Isa already. I want him to come back and watch TV with me. Baba calls me over and tells me to sit on his lap. I sit on the edge of his knees.

'Are you okay?'

'Yes Baba I'm okay. Are you okay?'

'Everything is in God's hands. I'm glad God has given me a vision to see with and not just eyes.'

'What does that mean Baba?'

'That means that you don't need eyes to see, you need a vision.'

It sounds like Baba is speaking French. French is the hardest language for me to learn so I don't understand anything.

'But Baba we see with our eyes.'

'You're right Adam, you're a clever boy aren't you!'

'I am!'

'Isa isn't coming back Adam,' Baba says. Yasmine is still crying. She is sitting on the sofa with her shoulders slouched down.

'Why Baba?'

'Because he has gone to mama.'

'What? No Baba! The doctor said he just needs to rest in peace.'

'Adam Habibi, Isa isn't coming back. We are going to say

goodbye to him like we did to mama,' Yasmine says.

'Why Yasmine? Why did he leave? We were having fun!' I start crying.

'I'm sorry Adam. Stay home and be a good boy today, I have to arrange his funeral.'

I can't believe what Yasmine said. I didn't say goodbye to Isa. My heart starts to pound really fast and I can feel the green dragon whisper in my ear like he always does after I hear bad news.

'Adam relax, breathe in and out,' Baba says as he rubs my chest. But I can't breathe properly. His hand is making it harder for me to breathe in and out. I jump onto the floor and start to feel my eyes swell up and my lips quiver. Khalid gets up from the floor and sits beside me.

'It's okay Adam, he's going to be happy with mama.'

'He didn't say bye! I liked playing with him!' I run to my room and cover myself under the duvet. It's dark here and my spot starts to feel damp with my tears but I don't want to go out. I want Isa to come back. Mama said 'bye' before she left so I knew she was leaving and got ready for a change. But Isa didn't say anything before he left. He can't just go.

Chapter Ten

BLACK

My heart is in my stomach. I think it fell because of how sad I am. It's like hot tar has spilt over it and drowned it. I'm really hungry. We didn't eat all day yesterday and my stomach is making angry sounds. It's trying to eat my fat. I leave my room and run into the kitchen. I spot my reflection in the oven. My hair is scruffy and under my ears and I can see my cheekbones clearly. I don't recognise myself. Yasmine comes in wearing a black dress and scarf and for the first time since she stopped working, she has red lipstick on.

'I like your lipstick.'

'Isa did too.'

'Where are you going Yasmine?'

'We are all going to Isa's funeral, get dressed.'

'I'm hungry.'

'Here, have a date, we have nothing to eat.'

'Didn't you cook yesterday?'

'Yes but it burnt when we left running.'

I eat the date and get ready. My eyes and lips feel heavy. I put my trousers on but they slide down. They're too big. I call out for Yasmine loudly and she comes into my room. Her eyes are black.

'My trousers are too big.'

'Wear a belt Adam.'

I didn't think of that. I wear a belt and a jumper that looks like it doesn't belong to me and leave my room.

Everyone in the sitting room is dressed in black but me.

Did they discuss what to wear?

'You have to wear black,' Ali comes and whispers in my ear.

'Why?' No one told me I have to wear black.

'Because that's what people wear to funerals.'

'I don't have anything black.'

Yasmine huffs and tells me to just walk on. I forgot something in my room so I run in and bring the painting I'm going to put with Isa. It was his favourite.

We all leave and find four men standing outside with a body wrapped in the Syrian flag on two wooden sticks. They pick the wooden sticks up and start walking.

'Who is that Yasmine?'

'It's Isa Adam. Stop asking me stupid questions.'

'Isa was in the hospital, how did he get here?'

Yasmine doesn't answer my question, she just starts walking on behind the four guys and crying. Everybody starts to chant 'There is no God but Allah and the Prophet Muhammad PBUH is his messenger'. The men carrying Isa started chanting and then the whole family joined in. We walk past the hospital and down the main road to where we said goodbye to mama. People on the streets start joining in and chanting with us. I don't even think they know Isa. I hear a guy saying 'see you in heaven dear martyr' to Isa. I start chanting along with them and holding on to Yasmine's dress. She's still crying. By the time we get to the cemetery we have a huge crowd behind us. The four men put Isa down and turn around to face the crowd.

'Everyone now please read Surat Al-Fatiha on the martyr's soul.' Everyone goes quiet and raises their hands up and starts whispering to themselves. I can't count how many people there are. I started counting them but couldn't see far enough.

I need to step on something to be able to see. They finish reading and wipe their hands on their faces. The four men carry Isa again and walk through the cemetery to an empty box of soil where they put him. Mama is on his right. My tears hurt as they come down my face. I miss Isa and want him to come back. I tighten my grip on the painting I brought with me. They cover him with soil and Yasmine falls to the ground. She digs her hands into the soil and starts screaming and crying loudly. Khalid leans down and whispers something to her. I tap Tariq's shoulder and tell him I want to put my painting on Isa. He asks me what's in it and I show him a picture of a tank with three people squashed under it and the prayer verse I wrote over it.

'You can't do that Adam.'

'Why? It was Isa's favourite painting.'

'Did you draw it?'

'Yes I did.'

'Okay then, let's go together.'

Tariq holds my hand and takes me closer. I look back and people start to leave. I put the painting down and in my heart I tell Isa to say 'hi' to mama. Yasmine gets up and puts the side of her scarf over her face and wipes her tears. Everyone is crying, even Ali. I wonder if his family are still in their house. He never mentions them. Yasmine puts her hand on my shoulder and squeezes it hard. We start to walk away and Baba's walking stick sinks into the soil and he nearly falls down. Everyone is purple today. We walk away slowly because Baba can't walk fast. People put their hands out and Tariq shakes them and thanks them for praying for Isa. I hear a group of people shouting and running really loudly coming closer to us. I look at Yasmine and before I am able to look back I hear a string of gunshots being shot and see bullets in the air hitting people.

Five people fall in front of us screaming. Yasmine pushes me down quickly and pushes my head onto the ground. I get soil in my nose and I can't breathe. I wriggle my head but Yasmine pushes me down harder. I can just hear gunshots but I don't know how close they are or if I am going to get shot. I can hear men shouting 'Assad is our master!' If they're with the president, why are they killing people from his country?

After 70 times of me repeating a prayer for God to help us, the shooting stops and the angry men's voices disappear. Yasmine lets go of my head and I jump up and breathe. I have soil up my nose and in my mouth. If it wasn't for the prayer I would have felt claustrophobic. We came for a funeral and ended up in bloodshed in the cemetery. Faces I recognise from the march up here are now on the ground with blood all around them. One of Isa's friends that held up his body has his mouth wide open and blood is still flowing out of it. It's bright red and fresh. I look away quickly before I imagine things and have nightmares. Yasmine tiptoes around the cemetery and I follow her steps.

'Khalid you're bleeding!' Tariq shouts from behind us and comes running down. Khalid and his yellow shirt now looks brown from the side where his kidney is. I think that's where his kidney is. He looks down and touches it and I can see blood on his fingers. I don't know if it hurts him because he is walking normally and isn't screaming. I'm never going to cry again from a scratch or if I hit my toe on the coffee table.

'I'm fine, I'll put coffee on it when we get home.'

Why would he put coffee on it? I don't think he heard clearly that he's bleeding.

'Khalid you're bleeding because you got shot, so you need to go to the hospital!'

'Don't worry Adam, coffee works, I'm not grieving over a

bullet when Isa took eight.'

I don't know what to say so I walk on and think of Isa's face. I put him beside mama in my mind. I have folders in my mind and now mama and Isa are in the closed ones. I lock them so that I don't think of them a lot and feel black spread over my heart. I'll unlock them only when I think of good things.

The call to prayer goes on as I put Isa in his new folder. It's the only thing that doesn't change so I smile when I hear it.

Yasmine pinches me on my shoulder.

'Why Yasmine?'

'You're not meant to smile after a funeral.'

'But the Adhan came on Yasmine, that means the sheikh is still alive and it didn't change'. I skip away so she doesn't have to say anything about me smiling. I like smiling. Mama once told me that a smile is charity and God said that charity puts out the fire of his anger. I don't know how God gets angry because mama said he's different from everything and anybody and that I shouldn't think much about it but I know that he's angry now because there's a war. I hope I didn't do anything to make him angry.

I used to like it when Baba took me with him to the mosque and I watched all the men pray and everybody used to go up and down at exactly the same time like it was rehearsed. I try to pray sometimes but Baba said I don't have to because I'm still young. When I pray I lose track quickly so I think that's why. I start reading a surah from the Quran and then I stop and think of washing my face because it feels itchy. I like just following everyone when they pray instead of praying alone.

'I want to pray in the mosque,' Baba says. His voice is really quiet now. After he shouted at Yasmine and he thought she was mama, he has been using his support stick more often and his voice is lower.

'Are you sure you can stand Baba?' Khalid asks.

'I'm still young, young man, I can stand more than you!'

Khalid laughs and tells Yasmine they are going to pray.

'Okay, I'll go and get candles for the house, meet you at home. Adam you go with the boys.'

'I want to go with you Yasmine…'

'I'm just going to get candles, go pray.'

'Please Yasmine, I'm scared.'

Yasmine's eyeballs go around in a circle. I don't know how she does that, I tried many times.

'Okay, I don't want to hear a word on the way then.'

Yasmine is being mean to me but I don't want to leave her so I walk behind her and count the houses that have balconies on them.

'Wait outside the shop, I won't be long.'

'Why can't I come in Yasmine?'

'I told you I don't want to hear any questions.'

'Can I buy some food?'

'What would you like?'

'Can you buy me a packet of crisps?'

'It won't fill you up Adam.'

'But they're yummy and you used to always put them in my lunch box.'

'Okay just wait here.'

Yasmine goes in and I turn around in circles and then stop and laugh at how everything looks funny upside down. It's so fun doing this. I keep turning around and stopping. I see three guys walking down the street carrying big guns on their shoulders. I see them upside down now because I feel dizzy. It looks like they're walking on their hands. I close my eyes really tightly so I stop feeling dizzy.

Yasmine comes out and I hide behind her quickly because the men are getting closer and their laughter sounds like a pig moaning. It's scary and I don't like how they look. They're all bald and big and they are stomping their feet like they want to kill all the ants on the ground.

'Come here young boy!' they shout. Yasmine holds my hand behind her. I think they are talking to me. No one else is around. The shopkeeper comes out and they shout at him to go in and threaten to kill him. I'm so scared. My heart is beating so fast I might vomit it out.

'Did you not hear me Ya Kalb? Come here!'

I don't like people swearing but they do and continue to laugh. I can feel Yasmine's colour change and she is slowly moving me back trying to get away. I just want to get out of this and go home.

One of the guys takes his long gun down from his shoulder and leans his hand on it.

Yasmine pulls a gun out and points it at the men. Her hands are shaking and the gun jumps up and down. She looks scared. Her whole arm is shaking but her face looks like she is ready to punch someone. She yells for them to back away and the men start laughing at her.

'I'll shoot. I will.' Even her voice is shaking.

The man with the rifle makes fun of Yasmine before pushing the gun away and hitting her in the stomach with the back of the rifle. She crouches in pain.

'I see we have a stubborn one here guys, eh?'

The other two laugh and come closer and stand one on either side of us.

'Master, do you want us to take action?'

'Bring the girl.'

The two big guys lift Yasmine up and she tries to fight her

way out. I hold onto her skirt tighter and cry. She is shouting and screaming for help. One of the guys pushes me hard onto the ground and spits at me. I can smell his green breath on my face.

'Yasmine, don't go!'

'Adam go home!'

'Yasmine where are they going to take you?'

'We're taking her to her new home!'

The biggest guy turns around and laughs at me.

'What can you do little boy?'

I don't know what to say, I keep running after them and trying to pull Yasmine down from their arms but she doesn't even move. They have strong arms. Yasmine is crying and screaming. I don't know what to do.

'Yasmine, please don't go!'

'Adam, go home, I'll come back.' She has brown tears coming down her face. It looks like she has patches of dirt and dry skin. She doesn't look like my Yasmine. Before I get to say anything else one of the guys picks his gun up and pushes the end of it into my forehead. I feel my head vibrate. I want to say something but my throat isn't letting me. I put my hands on my head to stop the spinning. I feel a wet liquid on my temple. I pull my hand down and see blood. I can see the word blood scattered around in my mind and it keeps on multiplying. It keeps getting darker and darker the more it multiplies. I don't think I can hold on any longer.

★

My head is pounding like I have a radio in my skull. It's silent music though because I can't hear anything. I open my eyes for a split second and close them again because it burnt the moment I opened them. There is a bright light shining right into my eyes. I can remember what happened last but I don't know where I am now. They took Yasmine away, why Yasmine? I start crying but I still don't open my eyes.

'Open your eyes, you're safe.'

The voice doesn't sound familiar but I can feel a soothing smell coming out of his mouth so I open my eyes. I don't recognise the man looking down at me. I lift my head up and feel every muscle in my body react. I look around and notice I'm in a shop. I'm really hungry but I have no money. The shop looks half empty. The shelves are dusty from what I can see from here and there aren't as many things as there used to be. I spot the crisps that I told Yasmine to get me. I wonder where she is. I don't want to imagine anything bad happening to her so I hope she will come back. I want to go home. I want to be in my room. Yasmine said she'd come back so I know she will. She can't just go and not come back.

'Do you know where you live?'

'Yes.'

I get up and touch my head where it was bleeding. I feel a cotton cushion on it.

'Go home young boy. God be with your family.'

I walk out and look both ways in case I see any men. I don't see anyone and I run home and count how many steps I'm taking. I can feel the blood on my forehead coming down my face but I run 52 steps until I get to the door and bang really hard.

Khalid opens the door really quickly.

'Oh thank God! There you are, what happened to your head? Where's Yasmine?'

I start crying and trying to explain what happened but whenever I start I feel too scared.

Chapter Eleven

INDIGO YASMINE

'ADAM RUN, RUN! Don't let them take you!' I try to shout but the words get stuck in my throat. I jump away from their grip but they hold me tighter. My arms are burning. 'Curse you people…curse you…you killed my brother and ruined our lives…. CURSE YOU!' I have a war going on in my mind, feelings of fear, hatred and sorrow thrown into conflict with one another. What did we do for this to be our fate? Adam can you read my eyes? Adam look at me! Don't give up now, stay strong! I know I'm talking to myself as he falls to the ground but I still try to reach out for him. The man raises his rifle and slams it against my head too…my sight is suddenly a blur… Adam…

I finally come to, dazed from the rifle blow. I look around only to find myself in a dark building. There is no light or entrance, only an overwhelming stench of urine. They look disgusting so of course they live in a disgusting place. They open the apartment door and throw me inside against the wall. I hold my tears in and pretend I'm not hurt. My back is aching and begging me to scratch it but I close my eyes and pray to God to help me. 'I need to get out of here… I don't want to be here… what do I do? Stay strong Yasmine, stay strong…' I tear up as I whisper these words to myself, hoping to find refuge in the hopes of escaping and being with my family again. The three men approach me and I learn that the master has no name but master. Those other two dogs must be slaves to a bastard. None of these men have dignity, they're just trash. I wonder how they've been brought up. They're disgusting. If only I can show them how much I despise them. The master kneels down and comes close to my face.

'What's your name beautiful?' His eyes are the clearest green I have ever seen on his dark skin colour. How can such beauty be enveloped in evil? I want to spit on his face and show him what I am made of. I wish Wisam was here to help me, he would protect me from these bastards.

'I see you like to play tough!' He yanks my scarf off with the force of a shameless man and starts to caress my hair. I shiver from disgust. If only he was a little closer. I struggle to kick him but find myself unable to do anything to resist. He laughs in my face and I can smell his rank breath. He must have had eggs for breakfast. I wish I could find eggs to buy for Adam. I hope he copes without me. God be with him please. I have to look after him till my dying breath, I promised mama.

'You like me caressing your hair do you? Did you see that boys? She shivered from my touch. I think we have a gem here.'

The other two men laugh and come closer and blow me kisses.

'Do we get a turn?'

'When I'm done with her, make yourself useful and go get me my tea.'

One of them goes running to make him tea like a spineless coward and the other stands in place until he is given an order. I want to cry so badly, my tears are welling up but I'm closing my eyes really tight and thinking of Wisam to cheer me up and give me strength.

'Open your eyes pretty girl, don't be scared.'

I keep my eyes shut.

'I said open your eyes!'

He shouts and his saliva lands on my face. I wish I had the strength I need right now. I open my eyes and look down.

'Go fetch a cold bucket of water!'

I am so scared God, I don't want to die. God please be with me. Please God protect me. A tear falls down my face as I plead with everything in me.

The two men come back and stand side by side waiting for more orders. The master gets up and sits on a chair and drinks his tea. I start to shiver in fear. Now that he has moved away from me all my feelings come tumbling down like a waterfall. I swear at myself in my head to stop the shivering and tears but I can't control anything. I have lost control. I am scared and feel bile rising in my throat. Control yourself Yasmine! They're nothing but animals!

I look up to see the men staring down at me, not saying a word. Now they know I'm scared. I gave them the best of me. If only all the poetry and stories I have read could help me now. My favourite line 'Let us leave this place where the smoke blows black and the dark street winds and bends' fills my mind. I am filled with both guilt and fear at the mercy of three men. I want to leave this place where black smoke blows into my heart. God, I can only turn to you for help. God please, if you save me now, I will be a loyal worshipper of yours and never turn a deaf ear to your words.

The only thing I'm glad about is that they took me and not Adam. I hope Adam is okay. As I start to think of his face I start to feel sick. I can't control myself any more and I break down and show my kidnapper's my life's fears and guilts.

'She's not so tough after all, eh? Bring the handcuffs and cuff her.'

My head is spinning and I can hardly see in front of me but

I can hear clearly. I hope I did not really hear what I thought. I hope I'm going crazy.

I close my eyes in the hope of stopping the spinning in my head but it gets worse and I can see a tunnel with an elephant blocking the light. I don't know what happened next.

★

I wake up to the splash of the coldest water on my bare body. I open my eyes and look around but my vision is covered in black dots. I try to concentrate ahead of me till I am able to see beyond the black dots. As my vision starts to get a little clearer I am surprised by another splash of freezing water and this time I choke on some. I try to cough it out but some water goes down the wrong pipe and I start saying my final prayers. I thought this was the end of my torture but I was able to cough all the water out painfully. My arms are tied up from the ceiling. I can't reach the ground. I am hanging on a wall naked and crying. I never thought this could ever happen. I haven't ever had time to look at my own body and now these three men see more than I have ever seen in my lifetime. I can clearly see the smirks on their faces as I choke and cry from pain. As soon as I lift my head up and look the master in the eye the A/C is blasted on full and I feel my skin shrivel up trying to find warmth. My whole body tries to reject this brutality and I try to imagine the warmth of my bed in order to block out what is happening. I don't know how long I have been out of it or how long I have been here. It feels like forever. I have always been around my family, always looking out for them, now I'm estranged from the only people I have ever known my whole life.

'Are you enjoying this?' one of the men whispers. He walks

closer and in his hand is a long fishing rod. I have always wanted to go fishing and be able to figure out how to use a fishing rod. I just never thought this might be the only way I can. He twists the top, clutches the fish hook and licks it.

'You're going to like this one Rose, yes, that's your new name.'

I close my eyes from the fear. I don't know what he can possibly do to me with the fishing rod but make me scream from pain. Please God save me.

He comes closer and licks my belly button. I am on display. I start to repeat my prayers in my mind hoping I won't feel any pain. Only I do. I have never screamed this loud. I have never even thought my voice box could reach this high. He hooks the fish hook into my belly button and I look down to a river of blood pouring down to my knees. I scream and shout for the help of God with all my strength.

'Shut up! No one is going to save you!'

I continue to shout for God's help and I can feel the hook push and pierce its way through my flesh.

'Shut up!' The master gets up and stands on a chair to slap me to silence.

I shout out God's name louder. I know he will save me. Curse these animals! As the hatred in me rises and my faith in God takes over my heart I stop screaming for a split second, sure that I couldn't feel any pain. But the other man hits me and all the pain comes flooding back. I have never known there was such pain.

'Stop!'

The master puts his hand up and both men freeze in their place.

'Prepare my bed!'

The master places his hand on my thigh. It seems like my

tears are going to be my only companion. Forgive me God. I can't fight back any more. I hang limp looking up and blocking out all that I can. I thought I had mastered the art of blocking out the present but I look down and see that I am alone in the room. I start crying loudly thinking that it's over. I look around and remember that I am still hanging and can feel the muscles in my arms stretching. I have a feeling that this is just the beginning. I'm sorry I left you alone Adam, I'll be back soon I promise. I know you're a big boy and can cope alone, I trust in you.

I see a shadow and then one of the followers walks in with a dog bowl. He puts it down and unties me without a word. He pulls me up from the ground as I slam down. He drags me into a tiny room and slides the dog bowl in and locks me in. I see a curled up lump in the corner. I stare but it doesn't move. I move back into a corner quickly. The other person is naked too and I can see their ribcage on their back. I don't know if it's a man or a woman. I look down at the bowl and see a small piece of bread with mould all over it and a bit of water. I thank God for the food. My stomach starts rumbling loudly. I try to push in my stomach for the noise to go away. I don't want to wake the other person up. I can feel the cold coming in from the cracks on the wall. It's freezing. I soak the hard bread in the water and eat. My tears add some flavour to the water. I curl into a corner and slowly bite on the last bit of bread and try not to cry loudly. I miss my family. I'm sorry Adam, I'm sorry I was horrible to you. I just wanted you to learn to be independent. I guess I used the wrong method. I'm sorry Habibi. I don't know what time it is but I hope you're eating and sleeping well. I love you. I close my eyes and pray for Isa and hope he is with mama.

It feels like I just closed my eyes for five minutes when

a huge bucket of cold water is poured on me. I gasp for air through the never-ending flow of liquid. I feel one of the men's nails dig into my shoulder pulling me up. I haven't opened my eyes enough to see who it is but nothing matters at this point. I can't imagine what is going to happen today. In the main room, the master is lying down on a few cushions and smoking his shisha like all this is normal. He points a finger at me and gestures at me to walk to him. I don't move. I can't move. I am pushed roughly to him and fall to my knees in front of him. I try to stumble up but he holds my arm down.

'Where do you think you're going?'

He blows his smoke in my face. 'Sit here beautiful,' he says. I look him in the eye and hope he can feel the disgust and hatred I have towards him. I sit down afraid of yet another vicious handling by his men.

'That's a good girl,' he says as he tilts his head up at the two men gesturing for them to leave. I have no fondness towards their abuse but I pray they don't leave me alone with him. They walk out and lock the door behind them with a key. My heart sinks to my feet. I can't move from how heavy my heart feels.

He hands the shisha to me and asks me to smoke it. I reluctantly take it in my hand and smoke it. He laughs as I choke my lungs out. He tells me to continue smoking as he gets up. I don't know what is going to happen. His face speaks of past monstrosities. I wouldn't put it past this guy to kill me. I can't afford to think of death, I need to concentrate on surviving and escaping. I wonder how long the person with me in the cell has been there for. Have they given up hope? I still haven't seen their face.

He comes back with a rope tied around his arm. I gulp the smoke as soon as he comes in and choke again. My eyes water but I can still see the smirk on his face.

'Please let me go!' I didn't expect myself to beg him or even say a word to him but my mouth uttered those words. As soon as I said them I could see his face glow. I need to keep my mouth shut. He yanks the shisha pipe from my hand and hands me the rope.

'Show me what you can do with it.'

I don't know what he means by that but I take the rope and extend it on the ground hoping that he'll let me go.

'You idiot!' He crawls to me and ties the rope around my hands and feet and ties them both together. I lie down on my belly, my arms and legs tied back. I am trying to hold my pain and tears in. I can't afford to show him another moment of weakness. He unbuckles his belt and I close my eyes and pray to God to help me. Please God help me. I have no one but you.

'Don't touch me you bastard!'

He laughs and pulls his trousers down. Forgive me God, forgive me Baba, forgive me Adam, I couldn't fight back. My crying gets heavier but that doesn't stop a cheap bastard like him.

Midway through his torture he calls in his men to come and have a go, and they all laugh. They won't get away with this. God delays but never forgets.

★

I remember closing my eyes really tight to a dizzying extent then feeling the weight of blacking out and thanking God the pain would stop. I look down and find cuts on my body I didn't notice before. I'm glad I didn't feel anything, I don't want to know what happened. I am back in the cell. I turn and stare at the other person still curled up. I am starting to doubt their existence. Am I imagining someone or are they dead? I move towards them slowly trying not to trigger pain in my body. As I get closer I can smell a strange smell, almost like urine but stronger and more concentrated. I poke their shoulder hoping to get a response. They lift their head up and turn around. I jump back and put my hand on my mouth before a scream comes out. I have never seen so many scars on someone's face. I notice it's a woman because of her chest but nothing on her face tells me of her gender. Her eyebrows have been shaved off and her upper lip is split. I ask God for forgiveness for being scared. I wonder how much worse she must have suffered. She smiles slightly and puts my heart at ease. I tell her my name and she whispers her name back. I don't know if I hear right but I continue the conversation.

'How long have you been here for?'

'Too long.'

I can't believe this. She has been locked in here for so long and nobody has found out about these bastards.

'Have you tried to escape?'

'Twice, that's why I look like this.'

I cringe and sit beside her. We don't say anything but I'm glad I have someone with me. I think about Adam and Baba and hope they're doing okay. Baba has been losing himself lately and he needed me by him too. I need to go back to look after my family. I can't sit here for months on end. I don't know how long I've been here but I'm hoping it hasn't been that long and that they're out there still looking for me.

I wake up in desperate need of a pee and run to the door and bang and shout. No one is coming or responding. It sounds like a dead place. I would have thought they would be guarding the cell. Maybe escaping isn't that hard after all. I don't know why the other woman kept on getting caught. I can't hold myself anymore and feel the warmth spread down my legs. It's the warmest I have felt for a while. The smell rises and I feel the embarrassment of what I have done sink in. It's disgusting but I have no choice. I wish I had some clothes to put on. I have been bare for too long. I look back at where I fell asleep by the woman and notice she went back to her former position. I think she sleeps all day. I look around the cell and try to find some way to escape. I can see a ray of light squeezing through a brick in the wall in front of me. I walk and try to see if I can reach it. I can't. I am sure the brick is loose and I can pull it out. Maybe we can get some help. I put my ear against the wall and strain my hearing for a hint of life.

I hear the door open and jump up. It's not my door though. I can hear more than three men. I can faintly hear a woman but I can't really tell. As they get closer I hear the whimpers of a woman trying to fight them. I think they covered her mouth because a few minutes later she starts to swear at them and make a scene. I guess this is a regular thing for them to do. I wonder if they have other cells with other women or if she's going to end up with us. We can all try to escape.

I wonder what's going on. Do they have the same routine with every woman?

I shake the other woman to wake up quickly. She mumbles and weakly shoves my hand away.

'Shh, wake up.'

'What?'

'How long did they torture you for before they left you?'

'I can't remember, leave me alone.'

'Try to remember, please!'

'I don't know how long it lasted, but when they got another woman they left me.'

For a moment I feel a happiness I didn't know it was possible in my current position. Will they really let me be? I can plan an escape quicker.

'How did you try escaping?'

'Keep me out of this, I've had my fair share and paid the price!'

'Just tell me, did you notice that loose brick up there?' I point and search her face for a reaction. Not even her eyes widen to the idea, she just shakes her head and curls up to go back to sleep.

I have a good feeling about this escape. I need to get out of here soon and go back home.

Just when I thought my time was over the door opens and I am pulled out by my hair. I scream and fight but nothing changes. I am thrown in front of the master watching TV as I look around for signs of the girl. Nothing.

'Bring it!'

I look back at what the master gestured at and see a shaver. I shiver and fall to the ground in fear.

'Please just leave me alone.'

He laughs and plugs the shaver in. I don't know what is going to happen but I am not ready to face any more pain. I jump up and try to run past the two guys standing behind me. I didn't know they were so close to me. I try to bite one of them and scream for help but instead I am pushed to the ground.

The master grabs my hair and starts to shave me. I wriggle and try to shout but the taste of blood in my mouth stops me. I can't stand the taste or smell.

'That's a good girl,' the master says and slaps my bare head. I can hear the impact of the slap but I don't feel anything. I now have no warmth in my body. My only warmth at night is now gone.

'From now on this is your house, you're going to live in that cell and I'm going to watch you starve and die! I am going to get rid of all of you slowly and painfully!'

Please God save me. My tears hot and powerful come flooding down and I let myself go and crumple to the floor. Please God take me back to my family.

I am grabbed by my leg and for the first time I look around me and notice pictures of beaten up men on the wall and drawings linking them together. There are scribbles on the wall that I can't read because they're too small. I notice the face of one of the men who used to work at the butcher's there. There's a normal picture of him next to the one I first noticed with his eyes closed and a slit on his throat. He has bruises all over his face. That's where he went. When I went to buy meat I asked for him because he used to always serve me and they said he was travelling. Everything is starting to make sense now in this country. No one ever travels; we are all stuck here but eventually 'travelling' because of the war. If only there was an escape. I wonder sometimes, if the leaders thought the way us normal people did, would all this be happening? Or do minds change the moment they lead?

The two men have their way with me again in their room and I lie there limp trying to block everything out. Please God save me. After they are all bored of me they throw me in the cell and I lie my head on the rock and imagine it's my mother's lap and start to tell her everything in my heart. She's the only one who understands. Don't you mama? I lie in mama's arms and sleep while speaking to her.

I wake up to the sound of a woman's scream from outside the door. I run to the door and try to look through the crack at the bottom. I can see bare feet moving on the ground. There goes another woman. When are we going to get saved?

Are we really going to die here? No, No! We can't! I know God will save us.

The girl's scream pierces my ears. I hope she is loud enough for others to hear and come for us. Keep screaming. We can do it. In front of them I want the floor to open up and swallow me from fear but now I am filled with anger and hatred, enough to fill a country with. If only I had taken the karate lessons Wisam said I would need one day. I hope he is okay. Is he alive? It's funny how things change from I hope he is doing well to hoping he is alive. Even though I couldn't see myself with him any time before Adam grows up I still prayed he would wait for me and not find another woman. I hope it wasn't selfish of me. I hope that's not why I am being punished now. I simply love him and want him to myself. Circumstances don't help though. I thought I was done crying over him because nothing can be changed, but I keep crying for everything happening.

Chapter Twelve

BROWN

'YASMINE! YASMINE!' I wake up in a hurry and run around looking for Yasmine. I can't remember when I last spoke to her. I had a dream she wasn't home when I called her name. I run around the house but I can't smell her. I knock on her door three times and then walk in. Her bed is neat and done. Her aura isn't in the room. Where's Yasmine? I walk out and see Khalid walking into the house. I run to him and grab onto his shirt. My mind is spinning with questions about Yasmine but nothing is coming out.

'What's wrong?'

'Where's... where's...'

'Yasmine?'

'Yes!...Yes!'

'She'll be back soon, just don't think about it.'

'Khalid I miss Yasmine.'

'I do too.' He leans down onto his knees and smiles at me.

'I have a feeling she'll come back soon.'

'Where did she go?'

'Do you not remember?'

'I remember men took her, but I don't know where.'

'Do you remember how those men looked?'

'Khalid they were big.'

'Do you remember anything else?'

'They didn't have hair and they had a green smell coming out of them.'

'If only I can find and kill those bastards,' Khalid whispers but I can hear him clearly.

We are not allowed to use bad words at home. I don't know what the word he said means but I know it's bad because he had black ink coming out of his mouth when he said it.

'Khalid I'm cold.'

'Come, we'll figure something out.'

I follow Khalid to the kitchen and we check for water but there isn't any. He opens the fridge and finds a bowl of water. I think Yasmine put it there before she left.

'Go get me coal Adam from that drawer and get me the lighter from on top of the stove and follow me to the sitting room.'

I quickly get the things he needs and walk slowly after him. I think he's trying not to spill the water. We go to the fireplace and I watch Khalid use matches and lighters to light up the wood. After many attempts and the strong smell of burned out flames, he manages to light up the fireplace. Isa used to be able to do so quickly. I hope he told mama how much I miss her and they're having fun together. I want to have fun with them. I miss them. The house is empty without Yasmine and Isa. I don't know what to do. They've been gone for so long.

Khalid spills the water into the pot Isa left by the fireplace before he left us. The fire is keeping me warm and we can at last have some water to drink.

'I know a trick.'

'What is it Khalid?'

'We can boil books with leather covers, it has good nutrients.'

'Yes, but I love all my books.'

'Shall we get Isa's?'

I don't know what to say; even though Isa is not coming

back I don't want to ruin his books. He loved them so much and I loved listening to him reading his poetry.

'Come on, what do you think?'

'Okay, but can I pick the books?'

I run to Isa's room and enter it for the first time. Isa never liked anyone entering his room. It's like a different world. There are books on the wall, on the bed, on the floor, on the desk, in the cupboard, on the windowsill. It's like a book wonderland. It's the most beautiful thing I have ever seen. I don't know where to begin so I start picking the books from the floor. I open one of them and find a poem that Isa once read to me and I loved but never knew which one it was. Now I know it is by Mahmoud Darwish, it starts 'O Homeland! O eagle.'

'Why are you crying?' Khalid asks and I look up and realise my face is wet. I didn't know I was crying. I was concentrating on how the poem made me feel. I wish Isa was here to explain things to me.

'Did you find books we can boil?'

'Not this one!' I shout at Khalid.

'No need to shout Adam, come on pick a few books.'

I don't know why I suddenly feel different and I don't want to burn any of Isa's books but I have to because I told Khalid I would choose some. I pick three from the floor that I've heard Isa read out of before and smell like real leather and give them to Khalid. We put them in the pot and I watch the ink spread into the water. We are going to eat Isa's favourite books.

'What if we hiccup poetry Khalid?'

Khalid laughs and looks at me without answering.

'Oh you're serious?'

'Yes Khalid.' I don't understand why he would ask me that. Why would I ask him if I wasn't serious?

'That won't happen Adam, don't worry.'

'How do you know?'

'It's just one of those things you know.'

'What does that mean?' Khalid is confusing me; I don't understand what he is trying to say.

'Sorry Adam I can't explain what I mean'. I like Khalid but I'm not used to talking to him and I don't understand him. I wish Yasmine would come back soon. I haven't been counting the days because my brain hurts whenever I try to think about it but I know it's been long because her smell isn't in the house and I miss her. Maybe if I close my eyes and try to send her a message through the air she will get it.

'I'm pregnant!' Amira comes running into the sitting room laughing.

'How did that happen?' Khalid jumps up.

'What do you mean?'

'Your husband died.'

'No he didn't! I was just with him!'

I don't know why Amira is lying, she keeps her hand on her stomach and repeats her last sentence.

'Come sit down Amira.' Khalid walks up to her and pushes her to the sofa.

'Do you think I'm pretty?'

'Yes I do.'

She smiles and her yellow smile becomes pink.

'I'm going to call my baby Khalid.'

'Why don't you call him Adam?' I ask. Mama said she was going to call me Haitham but she felt Adam fitted me better. I think so too. I can never imagine my name being anything else.

'Khalid looks like my baby.'

I don't know why Amira keeps on saying weird things that don't make sense. She hasn't even seen her baby, how does she know it looks like Khalid? I look back at the boiling pot and now it looks like ink. Are we really going to drink ink?

Khalid goes to the kitchen and comes back with three bowls and pours the ink in it. I haven't seen Baba and Ali for a few days and the moment I think about them I see Baba come into the sitting room. I don't think it's been that long since Baba has come out of his room but he looks very different. His jaw is long and looks like he has a sad face on it. He has more wrinkles than I last counted. I used to look at Baba and count his wrinkles because they looked weird on faces. How do wrinkles grow? It's like people grow extra skin on their faces. I hope I don't get wrinkles when I grow up. Baba's wrinkles are too many for me to count now. He has some on his cheeks, eyes, forehead, chin and neck. It's too much for me to count.

'Maha!'

We all look back at Baba and I can feel spiders crawling in my heart. My heart has been getting darker every day because I'm never happy any more.

'Where's Maha?'

'Baba are you hungry?' Khalid asks.

'I asked you where's Maha?'

None of us answer. I don't know what to say. I look around and Amira is still whispering to her stomach and Khalid's eyes are looking down. I think he is scared.

'Get me food then.'

Khalid jumps up and gives Baba his bowl.

'I asked for food not a blue drink, do I look like a kid to you?'

'We don't have food Baba.'

'Why? Do I not work hard enough to feed you?'

'None of us have any more money and there are no jobs.'

'What are you talking about? Where do you think you are?

I have always provided for you!'

Baba and Khalid continue their conversation and I start thinking of mama's food. Her roasted chicken with garlic was my favourite. My mouth is now watering and my stomach makes a funny noise again so I drink the ink and hope that I don't hiccup poetry. I don't want Isa to be upset that I am reading his books. Baba hasn't asked about Yasmine, only about mama. I don't know how he forgot that mama is gone.

'Just shut up and call Maha, I am fed up of arguing with you.'

'Baba mama is dead,' I say. I don't want Baba to get angry but my head is like a washing machine; twisting and turning and it hurts more when he says mama's name.

'What are you talking about? How dare you say that about your mother.'

Khalid sits Baba down on the sofa and starts reading the Quran in his ears. Baba doesn't say anything and his eyes start to close. I remember the room he showed me and I sneak out while Khalid is looking after Baba. I tiptoe into Baba's room and as soon as I walk in I smell a weird smell that reminds me of the smell of medicine. I look around and find bottles of medicine spilled on the floor. The smell reaches my throat and I nearly vomit.

I run to the small room to get away from the smell. I walk in and find Tariq sitting in the corner. He jumps up when I open the door.

'Tari!' His name gets stuck in my throat. I don't know why.

'Come sit with me?'

I sit down and look over at the number of records on the floor. They look like a column of rainbows.

'How have you been Adam?'

'I have been hungry Mr Tariq.'

Tariq laughs and tries to explain that he is asking how I am doing.

'Baba is a different colour and I'm scared of him.'

'What do you mean a different colour?'

I don't know how to explain to Tariq that I see in different colours.

'I'm sick of the protests every day, they're giving me a headache. Life was so much better before people tried to act clever and rise against everything. Now Isa's dead and Yasmine's gone,' Tariq says.

'Yasmine is going to come back Tariq.'

'How do you know? We don't even know where she is.'

'Because she told me.'

'Adam, we don't know where she is, we don't even know if she's alive.'

My heart becomes hot. Why would Tariq say that? Of course Yasmine is alive. She's just gone for a while and will come back. I know that.

'Are you okay?' Tariq puts his hand on my shoulder. I move away from him. I feel black smoke rising inside me. I want to be alone.

I turn away from Tariq and rock myself to get rid of the smoke. If I don't do this I'll get angry and hurt something. I bang my head on the wall to shake away the bad thoughts. Why did Tariq say that? Now I have black and violet smoke fighting inside my heart.

'Adam, are you okay?' Tariq's voice is now louder and he is starting to scare me.

The voices in my head start to get louder and I start to rock harder. I hear the record player go on and play a song that sounds familiar and soothes me.

The smoke in my heart starts to disappear and melt away

like ice. It's all gone now but Isa's face is now on my mind. I start crying heavily and my body begins to shake and shiver. I can feel every tear shake me.

I can hear Tariq's voice mixed with the song but they both sound like they're in slow motion coming out of a robot's mouth.

Tariq carries me and runs out. I try to fight out of his arms but he is too strong. He has big muscles. I wish I had big muscles. I start to calm down as I think about how I can fight him and run out of his hands. He smells like old rain. He doesn't smell nice. I wonder how I smell.

Khalid comes up to Tariq and I and asks us what's going on. His voice doesn't sound happy.

'Go get one of the pills I told you about from the kitchen' Tariq says and sits me down on the sofa. Something bad is happening. I can see snakes.

'What… What… Pill?' I ask. My voice sounds like it's cold, it's shivering.

'Just relax, you're going through a lot.'

Tariq holds both my hands down and leans over me. What am I going through that I don't know about?

Khalid comes back in with a box of pills and hands them over to Tariq who opens the box and takes out a pill and breaks it in half. Some of the powder from the pill falls onto me. I have seen these pills before. When mama died and I wasn't feeling well and Baba took me to the doctor. He said I was going through a hard time and in my condition I needed something to calm me down. I kept asking Baba what the doctor meant when he said that but Baba didn't answer. I know I'm different because I speak differently. I just don't know what condition I have. Those pills used to make me sleepy. I once slept for three days Yasmine told me. When I woke up I remember it felt like I just slept for a few hours.

'Tariq I don't want the pill, I'm being good.'

'Shh Adam, just relax.'

'No, no, no!'

It looks like Khalid and Tariq are speaking to each other but they're not opening their mouths and I can't hear them. None of them are listening to me. Tariq holds my head back and I start to move away and try to fight them off. Both of them hold me down and I can't move away. They open my mouth and put the pill inside. I don't want to swallow it. I don't know what this pill does. I try to spit it out but Khalid covers my mouth and tilts my head backwards so I swallow it straightaway.

I feel the pill go down my throat and Khalid and Tariq both let go of me at once. I really think they're secretly speaking to each other. I don't know what is happening. Were we playing a game? Both of them are smiling. I get up and run to my room. I don't like feeling confused. It's like a train track in my head is disconnecting.

I go to my room and stare at the painting I haven't finished painting because I was so hungry my hand started to shake. I have a pile of drawings on my desk but I have no space to hang them on the wall. The top one is of Isa smiling the way he did when he saw my paintings. The more I concentrate on his face the more blurry it gets. I try to speak to him but he isn't answering me. Why aren't you answering me Isa? Are you coming back? Do you know where Yasmine is? My voice sounds far away in my head and Isa still isn't answering me. He looks so happy in the picture but his face is frozen. Frozen. Frozen. I can't remember what I was saying. I'm still staring at the painting and now Isa is speaking to me but I can't answer. My eyelids and breath are getting heavy. I can imagine a night monster trying to close them for me. I wasn't tired before. Please monster, don't make me go to sleep. I try to say something but my throat is closing up. Come help me Isa. Come back Isa.

Chapter Thirteen

LIME

A GROUP OF MEN dressed in army clothes are outside my window with guns on their shoulders. Why are they here? I hide back under my covers before they see me. I don't want them to take me. I lie flat on my stomach and make a little hole I can peak through. There are now more men and they're not wearing uniforms. They have their eyes covered in a white cloth. What are they going to do to them? They make them sit down on the pavement and I can see a man's mouth moving but I don't know what he's saying. I keep staring and then notice someone who looks like Khalid walk up. I squint my eyes so I can see better but I can't tell if it's Khalid or not. I look at his clothes and he's wearing the same shirt Khalid has been wearing for a week. What is Khalid doing there? He is speaking to one of the men in the uniform. I don't know who the bad guys are. Is Khalid with the bad guys? I don't like politics or war. Everybody says different things about them, even when you see something, people say different things.

The man hits Khalid on the shoulder and my heart sinks down to my feet. Please don't take Khalid too. Khalid starts laughing and walks into the house. What's going on? Is this a dream? I rub my eyes hard and open them again. I see grey and yellow spots covering my eyesight. I don't know what pill the boys gave me yesterday, maybe I'm imagining all this. I once read about waking dreams where you are awake in your mind and can see and do things but your body can't move. Is this a waking dream? Am I really moving? My sight starts to clear up and I see the exact same faces outside but Khalid isn't there. I try to slither down my bed like the snake I saw on the National Geographic channel and reach for the curtains so I can close them. I start to close them slowly then suddenly I hear a bang on the window and I try to run back. There is another bang and before I can get up and run my window cracks and a gun comes through. What is going on? Why is my room being attacked? I pick myself up to run away and step on a big piece of glass. I feel it go through my foot like electricity and I look down and see the glass through my foot and blood around it. I scream so loud I feel my lungs shake. I never knew I was able to scream this loud. I hear footsteps from the sitting room and repeat God's name in my mind so I take my mind off the pain. Khalid bashes the door and comes in.

'What the hell happened!'

He looks at the window and starts swearing under his breath. He leans down over me and tells me to close my eyes. I don't want to close my eyes but I do because my brain hurts and everything is slowly turning blue. I can hear cracking sounds in my mind and see blue glass crash over and over again in my mind. The glass starts spinning and I try to follow it.

'Stop shaking Adam!'

I can't feel myself shaking but I can hear Khalid's voice clearly so I open my eyes and nothing is blue any more. Everything has it's own colour. Khalid pulls out the shard of glass from my foot quickly and I don't feel it until the end when it leaves my skin. I look down and see a slit as big as one of my fingers.

'It's fine Adam, it's fine.'

'Kh…'

'Speak Adam, don't worry, it's just a scratch. Let's go put

something on it.'

'The window…'

'Don't worry, it was an accident, they're outside, just come with me.'

'What are they doing Khalid? Why are they outside my window?'

'Let's just go Adam, it's not safe here.' Khalid helps me to the bathroom and is speaking to me but I'm not concentrating. I want the people outside my window to leave. I don't want the war to be outside my window. I can hear Baba call mama's name.

'Not again!' Khalid whispers. His mouth spits yellow words. He covers my foot with a bandage. I don't think it's going to make a difference. The more he squeezes the bandage on my foot the more it hurts.

'It hurts.'

'I know, just bear with it.'

'It hurts more with the bandage.'

'Adam, just listen to me, you need the bandage,' he says. I don't say another word. Only Yasmine understood me.

'Khalid why did you speak with the baddies?'

'You mean the army?'

'Yes.'

'I was tricking them into not attacking our house.'

'How?'

'When you grow up you'll learn that manipulation is a man's best friend.'

'What does manipulation mean?'

'It means tricking people into believing what you want them to.'

'You mean lying to someone?'

'Kind of.'

'Lying is bad Khalid.'

'Sometimes you have to do it to protect yourself.'

'But God said to never lie!'

'That's right Adam but I had no choice.'

I look into Khalid's eyes and don't see the same aura he usually has. Everyone is turning the same colour. Everyone is turning dark.

We hear swear words coming from outside. They sound like they're in the house. It sounds scary. Khalid tells me to tiptoe. It's not safe now. We peak quietly outside the sitting room window. Amira is sitting in her usual spot, she hasn't even moved. Nothing scares her. She doesn't even ask us what we are doing sneaking around. If I was her I would be curious and ask so many questions. That's what Yasmine said she hates before she left. When she comes back I won't ask her many questions. I just want her to be happy. I like sneaking around with Khalid, it feels like we are playing a game. I would ask Ali to play but he has been sleeping for days. I copy Khalid and stick my head out the way he is. I can see the same men with uniforms swearing and the other men sitting on the ground with their mouths open and the pavement in-between. They even have their eyes covered. I wonder how they feel not being able to see and sitting in the middle of the street? When my eyes are covered I feel suffocated and I keep fidgeting. I can't stop thinking of bad things and it feels like my whole body is shrinking into my brain because I'm scared. They must be very scared. The soldier hits one of the men on the head with his foot. Why is he kicking him? I close my eyes but I can still hear the same sound of his shoe hitting the man's face and the man shouting 'God is the greatest'. I open my eyes and see a puddle under the man which wasn't there before. I look over to Khalid who is whispering things to himself and I wonder if he too hates violence.

'What's that puddle Khalid?' I whisper. I know if I talk loud they might see us.

'The man peed on himself...' Khalid didn't whisper back. He spoke normally. Maybe he forgot we are hiding. I have never heard of a man peeing himself. I look back outside and squint at the floor. I think I can see a hint of yellow in the puddle. I thought only kids peed on themselves. Mama used to tell me that if I peed my bed once more she would lock me in my room for an hour to learn my lesson. I don't like being locked in so I never peed myself after that. Maybe his mother never taught him that.

'Why did he pee himself?' Khalid doesn't look at me or answer. He continues to whisper to himself. I start thinking about how embarrassed he is. I remember a girl in our class once peed herself and everyone made fun of her. I didn't though; I didn't even speak to her. Thinking about school I remember the Nutella-eyed girl and before I smile because of her eyes I hear shouts and screams and gunshots all at once. They all strike at the same time. I push my head up to see better and the seven men that had their eyes covered and were leaning with their mouths open on the pavement now have blood all over them and broken faces. There is one man left and the soldier steps on his head and in my mind I can see the way his mouth cracks open in slow motion. Blood flies everywhere. I always read in books about violent scenes with blood everywhere but I was never able to imagine how blood can fly everywhere. Now all those scenes come flooding back. Blood does fly everywhere. Khalid pushes me down and tries to cover my eyes but I have seen everything and now I am shaking. How could this happen? Why did they do that to them? I want to see what will happen to the soldiers. I move out of Khalid's arms and look back up.

'Don't look!'

I don't answer Khalid and watch the soldiers walk away from the men on the ground. There is pee mixed with blood and skin on the ground. It looks like papier mâché, but it's not. I can feel vomit rising from my stomach but I look away and try to breathe in and out the way Yasmine taught me so I don't vomit.

I run to my room and lock the door. My room feels empty and open. I never knew a window was that important. I sit by it and look outside at the men on the side of the pavement. The more I look at it the more it looks like a painting. Something Dali would draw like his painting 'The Face of War', but with more faces. I feel like I have seen this scene before but I know I haven't. It's this weird feeling I can't explain. It's like I know them. It's like I have been here before. But I know I haven't. I know I haven't.

I climb out of my window and am careful not to step on any glass. The window is low and I don't even have to jump to get out. Now that I am right by the men everything seems more real. I didn't know it could get any more real. It's like a painting that you don't feel until you sketch out every detail of it and piece it together. That's what I do when I like a painting. I once had a dream that George Orwell was speaking to me. It didn't look like him but he said it was him. Mama said it means that I really like the author. I do really like his books. He told me that blood is the substitute for paint. How can blood replace paint? But now with blood in front of me, I have a part of me that is pushing me to take some blood and paint. So I do. I look around carefully and make sure no one is around. I reach through my window and on my windowsill I have a pen holder. I empty the pens and collect blood into it. The blood is really thick but there is so much of it that it looks like water. Some blood touches my hand by accident even though I tried to be careful. It has a weird feeling. It's not like anything else. It feels warm and cold at the same time. It's almost like your feelings disconnect when touching blood. My senses are confused. I pull my hand back right away.

One of the men has long hair that has fallen on his shoulders. I lean down and pick a few hairs and run back inside through the window. I feel like I'm losing my mind. I heard Yasmine say that expression so many times I think she has passed it on to me along with the feeling. The war is making me feel dizzy. I can't even understand myself now.

I sit down and keep on thinking about Yasmine. Is she eating well? Is she far from here? How long will it take her to come back? She's my favourite person in the world. As I think of her I start to think of mama then of her funeral then of Baba and then everything comes crashing down on me like a plane crash and my shoulders feel heavy.

I look down at the pen holder with the blood in it and decide to start painting. I set everything up and pick up my favourite pencil. I start sketching a mouth wide open like the men outside but then it turns out like an eye so I start drawing one eye in the middle of the page with a pupil that has a story inside. I start sketching tall buildings then at the bottom a fire and a collapsed building. I never know what I am drawing or why I am drawing it until I finish my painting. I usually just let my brain do everything. That's why I love painting, it's the only time I don't have to think, I just have to move my hand and see what comes out.

I move back and look at the sketch. I don't know why but I see Yasmine in the picture. Is this her eye? Is this what she is seeing now? My stomach starts rumbling and making noises all of a sudden. I didn't realise how hungry I was. I forget when I ate last. I usually have a very good memory and keep track of everything, but I have been losing track easily nowadays. I don't like it.

I finish sketching and start painting, my stomach is still rumbling. I am scared to go outside, everyone is different. I start with the colour black for the outline. The smell of paint is my favourite. When I smell it I see triangles. I dip the paintbrush in the water. I haven't changed it in ages because we don't have any. I wonder if I can drink this water? But if I do I won't be able to paint. I keep painting and thinking about what I can eat. I can eat paint! I love the smell and the colours so why won't I love the taste? I have stacks and stacks of paint that I sometimes use but mostly use the three on the table that are my favourite. I lean down to the drawer with all my paints and pick one from the back because those are the ones I hardly use. These colours are all mixed up because I used to use them when I was younger and mama was teaching me how to paint. Mama used to paint when she was younger too, she had a gallery at her university before she got married and then got too busy. I won't ever leave painting though. I squeeze the green colour out of its tube and start to eat it. The moment I put it in my mouth my body shivers in reaction. I get the same reaction from honey. I am so hungry I continue to eat some more. I can taste the green colour. It's a weird feeling but it tastes green. I wonder how the other colours taste. I keep squeezing the tube into my mouth. The more I do, the gooier it tastes. I am starting to get sick. I put the paint down and try to swallow the remains in my mouth. I rub my tongue with my fingers to get rid of the paint. My tongue and lips are green in the mirror. I need to rub it before anyone sees. I pull my shirt up and rub the paint out of my mouth and tongue. There is still some left but it doesn't look like I ate paint. My stomach stopped making that funny sound. Maybe eating paint is actually a good idea. I have a lot of it. I won't run out any time soon.

I hear the phone ring in the sitting room. I haven't heard that sound for a long time. I run to the sitting room and answer.

'Allo!' I am so happy to even say 'hello' again.

'Allo! Can you hear me? It's me', says the voice. I don't know why people say that on the phone. Who is 'me'? Why don't they just say their name? It would be so much easier. I recognise the voice but I don't know who it is exactly.

'Yes I can hear you. Who is it?'

'It must be Adam! You're the only one who speaks politely. It's me, your aunt!' She laughs. I have many aunts, so this doesn't make it any easier.

'Which aunt is it?'

'Haha! You haven't changed one bit. It's me, Aunt Suha,' she says. I like Aunt Suha, she's mama's sister. She used to always come over and invite us to her house in Damascus. She has a big swimming pool I used to always swim in. I wish I was there.

'How are you? How's your family? Are you safe?' I don't know which question to answer first. She asked too many. I can hear her whispering to someone next to her but I can't hear what they are saying.

'Do you still have a swimming pool in your house Auntie Suha?'

'Yes! come over!' She laughs.

'How do I get to you?'

'Ask Yasmine, where is she?'

'Three men took her away. I think she will come back soon.'

'What do you mean three men took her? What happened? Speak quickly.' Whenever I am told to speak quickly I don't know what to say. It's like my brain shuts down. Why can't people just listen to what I say instead of telling me to speak quickly.

'Are you still there Adam? Is there anyone else I can speak to?'

I look around and see Khalid coming into the room.

'Who is on the phone?' He runs to me and smiles for the first time since Yasmine left.

'Auntie Suha.'

He grabs the phone out of my hand and starts speaking fast explaining everything. Why can't I do that? Why am I so different?

I walk to the light and put it on. Light really makes a difference. The power is back.

I tug on Khalid's shirt but he doesn't move.

'Khalid!'

'Shhh!'

'Khalid how do I go to Damascus?' Khalid doesn't answer me and continues to tell Auntie Suha the whole story. Why does he have to explain everything? I can hear her loud voice from across the phone.

Khalid puts the phone down and sits down on the chair. He doesn't look at me, he looks down at his hands then puts them through his hair. He breathes in and out heavily like a boy in my class who has asthma. Khalid doesn't have asthma though.

'Khalid how do I get to Damascus? I want to go to the swimming pool.'

'I don't have time for you now Adam.'

How does he not have time for me? There are 24 hours a

day and 1,440 minutes. He doesn't use them all. He is just sitting down not doing anything now.

'Why Khalid? What are you doing?'

He looks up at me and his eyes are red. It looks like veins exploded in his eyes.

'Adam please, just leave.'

'Where shall I go?'

'Wherever you want.'

I walk out to the door and open it to get some fresh air. I can't see the dead men outside because they are around the corner but I know they're there so I can feel them looking at me. There's a cat lying by the neighbours' house. I wonder if the bodies are still there? Does anybody else live there? I get up and walk over. The cat starts hissing the moment I get near the door. I lean down and start caressing its fur. It's a black cat with white eyes. I think it's blind. I can feel the ribs when I touch it. I wonder if it eats anything. Mama used to throw food out to the cats but I don't know if Yasmine ever did. Is it hungry? I pick it up and put it against my chest. Maybe I can hide it in my room and look after it. I can have a new pet. I'll name it Liquorice because it reminds me of my favourite sweet. I open the neighbours' door and the cat starts hissing again. I caress its fur so it can relax. Maybe it just wants food. It doesn't stop hissing though. The house is dark inside and the smell is so strong. I don't know what it smells of but it gives me a headache straightaway. Liquorice is trying to get out of my hands, I hold it tighter but it runs out.

'Come here Liquorice!'

I have never told anyone to do things, I am always the one being told because I'm the youngest. It feels good.

'No Liquorice, come here!'

I run after it but the smell gets stronger and I can't go any further.

'Come…'

I'm too scared. I don't want to go in any more. It's like the smell is ganging up on me ready to punch me in the stomach. I stop and open the door where the cat snuck in. I open it slowly, something doesn't feel right. The only thing I can see is Liquorice's tail moving from side to side. What is she doing? I open the door a little more and hear the cat sniffing around. There's no light but I can see everything clearly. This is where the smell is coming from. There are so many dead people lying on the ground. I can't count how many people there are. They are all lying face up next to each other covered in white cloth. I don't know if Ali's family are there. I can't recognise any faces. Why are they all here? Who put them here? It smells of feet, blood and mould. I can't describe how horrible it is. I can feel my thoughts becoming more distant the more I stare. Liquorice is going around sniffing them. She's hungry. I know the feeling of me losing track. It means I'm going to faint. I start to feel nauseous. I gag but don't vomit. I run out of the house as quickly as possible before anything happens. I don't want to faint in-between dead people. No one can help me. I reach the entrance and breathe in and out like I haven't had fresh air in years. My lungs feel tight. I didn't realise I was holding my breath inside.

Why did I go in there? I sometimes get too curious and end up feeling sick. I wait outside for Liquorice to come out while saying my prayers. Who is dumping the bodies at the neighbours' house? I feel like I am in a detective movie. Maybe I should take this case on and find out who dumps the bodies next door. I can be the Syrian Sherlock Holmes.

Liquorice comes out at last and we run into the house. I look out to see if there is anyone in the sitting room before running into my room. I put Liquorice onto my bed and sit down and breathe in and out. I don't know why I am out of breath. I didn't run much.

I lie down on the bed and the cat climbs on my stomach and curls up. I think it likes me. I like the feeling of having a warm stomach. I feel sleepy. I don't do much all day but I am always tired. I don't want to end up like Ali. I don't even know if he got up. He never comes out of the guest room.

★

I wake up to Liquorice still on my stomach. I don't think I slept for that long. It's still just getting dark. I had a bad dream. I wish Yasmine were here. I always go to her after I have a bad dream. She usually warms up milk for me and lets me sit in her room. I was dreaming of the girl with the Nutella eyes. She was running to me and I felt happy. I was thinking that I at last have a friend that I really like. She reached me and fell to the ground and started kissing my feet. I jumped back and then she stood up and her eyes turned into mama's eyes and she was telling me to run back with her. I was trying to escape but I couldn't run. That's when I woke up. I don't know why Nutella-girl's eyes would turn into mama's? They look wrong but right at the same time. They look familiar I guess.

Liquorice purrs at me.

'Did you sleep well Liquorice?'

Liquorice looks up at me but doesn't answer. I need to train her to understand me. This is going to be fun. I don't need any more friends. I think it is a she. Liquorice sounds like a she.

I suddenly hear gunshots outside and I look out to see a tank coming down our street. My heart sinks to my feet. I have never seen a tank in reality. I run out to look for every-one and tell them.

'Amira! There's a tank outside!'

'No, there isn't,' she replies without looking back. I need to look for Tariq and Khalid. I knock on Khalid's room three times and wait for him to tell me to come in.

'Khalid come out, there's a tank outside!'

'What? Those bastards! Do you know about the secret room?'

'Yes.'

'Go there till I tell you to come out.'

'Can I take Liquorice with me?'

'What are you talking about? We don't have liquorice.'

'Liquorice is my new cat.'

'Adam! Just go to the room!'

I can hear people screaming outside. I pick Liquorice up and run into the room. This time it's empty. I sit back and whisper a song to Liquorice that mama used to sing to me. Come back Yasmine. I don't know how to do anything without you.

I hear Ali's voice and jump up. I have been waiting for him to get up. I put my ear against the door and then open it a little so I can listen. Baba's room's door is wide open but I can't see anyone in that line. I hear a door break down and Amira shout. What is going on? I can hear deep voices coming closer. How many men are coming into our house? I see the shadow of a man but I don't know who it is.

I hear Baba's voice, but I am scared to go out. Khalid said I should stay here. I am scared. What do they want from us? God please don't let them hurt any of us. I can hear plates being crushed along with shouting and screaming. I push myself back to the corner and cover my eyes in Liquorice's fur.

'You want freedom huh? I'll show you freedom you sons of dogs!'

'I beg you let us go, please. I'll kiss your feet' I can hear
Amira's voice.

What are they doing to them? I suddenly hear the sound of
Amira screaming. I don't hear anybody else's voice. What are
they doing? I sneak a look through the crack again but I still
can't see anything.

I don't know how long I wait in the corner singing quietly
to myself but after some time I hear nothing and see no shadows. The house is silent. It makes me shiver. I step out of the
room quietly and pass through Baba's room. Liquorice doesn't
squirm in my arms. She stays still. I enter the sitting room and
find the sofa's ripped up and upside down, plates on the floor
smashed and our TV in pieces on top of the table in the middle of the room. Baba is in the middle lying on the ground.
His eyes are open. I can see them, but he doesn't blink. I run to
him without looking for anybody else.

'Baba! Baba! Can you hear me?'

'Khalid…'

'Baba, I'm Adam!'

'Khalid…'

I look to see if I can see Khalid but I don't see him around.
Ali is holding onto Amira's waist while she gets up to start
cleaning up.

I stroke Baba's face and try to get him to get up. Amira goes
on cleaning without moving Ali off. She sings quietly to herself. I can just hear a low humming sound. Everything is dark
and messy. Even her humming sounds dark.

'Baba, get up.'

Baba doesn't answer, he holds my hand and I try to pull
him up slowly. Where's Khalid? I'm scared to ask.

'What happened Baba?'

'Khanjar,' Ali answers. I don't know what he means.

'What do you mean?'

'He's a mercenary. I have been hearing his name.'

'What was he doing here?'

'Ruining our lives.'

'Where's Khalid?'

'They took him.'

'What?'

'Yes, there goes another one of us.'

I run to the door and scream Khalid's name. They can't take him as well. They already took everybody else! I scream till I feel my voice become grainy. I stop before I lose my voice completely. My mind is still screaming Khalid's name though. If Yasmine was here she would know what to do. Come back Yasmine, come back Khalid. I don't want to miss anyone any more. I want them to be with me. Why are they taking my brothers and sisters? What did we do to them? I have never taken any of their family. I wipe my tears away and feel my fingers scratch my face. I look down at my hands. They look like Baba's. My skin is hard and rough and it looks like I have been scraping it on wood. I spit on my hands and rub them together so I can moisturise them but I can't spit a lot. My mouth is too dry. Are my hands like this because I paint? I go back in and ask Ali to look at his hands. His are like mine.

I sit next to Baba and try not to cry. Baba is crying. His body is shaking.

'Will Khalid come back Baba?'

'I don't know Adam. I hope you never feel the pain of your child being taken away from you.'

'Khalid is not a child Baba.'

'He is my child!'

Baba doesn't explain what he means as he usually does, he just gives me the same answer. I wish I understood. I rock myself and try to sing in my brain. Music makes me calm down. I get up and start praying. I don't have my Wudhu but I have the sudden urge to just get up and pray to God. I know God will help me.

'I spoke to Yasmine in my dream yesterday,' Baba said.

'How Baba? What did she say?'

'She didn't say anything, she stayed quiet, I was speaking.'

'What did you tell her? Did you tell her to come back Baba?'

'Yes I did. I think she is okay. If you dream of speaking to someone apparently it's a sign.'

'Yes! Yes! Yasmine is coming back!'

'Shh Adam, it's just a saying I don't know if it's true. Let's just say God willing.' Baba wipes his tears.

'I know she is coming back Baba.'

Chapter Fourteen

GREEN

IT HAS BEEN 32 DAYS and four hours since Yasmine left. I started counting her missing days ever since my head stopped hurting me. I wait for her every day by the grocery store she last left me at but she hasn't shown up yet. I go there every day at 3:30 p.m and hope that the men will let her go. I know she'll be back, I just don't know how long she'll take. I really miss her. The house has been quiet without her. Baba is always in his room and the boys are out protesting and come back late at night tired and go to sleep. I have been starving and no one is eating. We have no food at home but Amira is helping me boil water every day on the fireplace. The electricity hasn't come in eight days. We have been living in the dark. Every day the sound of the prayer is mixed with gunshots or bombs. Ali has been sleeping most of the days. He wakes up for two hours and goes back to sleep. I don't know why. Amira's face now looks like a slab of wood. It's thin and long. She still puts her make-up on every day.

'Come, I'll show you something.'

I follow Amira to the bathroom where she tells me to come in. I have never been in the bathroom with somebody so I just wait outside.

'Come in, I have something.'

I tiptoe inside. I can't think properly when I'm this hungry so I just do as I am told.

Amira reaches behind the toilet and takes one of the tiles

off. I squeak as I try to say something but no words come out. Why is she breaking the floor? She pulls out a jar of honey. My eyes widen and I think of how bees widen their eyes when they see people coming for their hive. I just want to eat.

'Where did you get it from?'

'I brought it with me when I came, I knew one day we would need it.'

'Can I have some?'

'Come, sit down.'

I sit down and hear my knees crack. My arms look long and yellow and so do my legs. I never look in the mirror any more. I don't have a choice anyway because Amira broke it one day. I was painting in my room when I heard a scream coming from the bathroom. I ran and saw Amira on the floor with glass all around her and one piece in her cheek. I have seen a lot of blood lately but my reaction never changes. I hate the smell.

'Open your mouth,' Amira says. I stop thinking and come to reality. Amira has her two fingers dipped in honey. I don't want to take honey from her hand. I don't like people touching my food.

'Can I put my finger in?'

Amira closes her eyes and smiles.

'All you men are the same.'

I don't know what she means but she gives me the honey jar so I put my finger in on the side where she hasn't touched. No one is the same so how are all men the same? I hardly speak to Amira. So I have conversations with my paintings. They never confuse me, they always say the right things. I put the honey in my mouth and I shiver straightaway. The sweetness of honey always makes me shiver. It feels good to have something that isn't water.

I want to have more honey but Amira is closing the jar and

putting it back.

'Why are you closing it Amira?'

'We need to keep it for other days, if we finish it we'll starve to death.'

I am not sure how people starve to death. I haven't eaten in days. I have only drunk hot water whenever we can light the logs with fire. I am starving and feel tired all the time, sometimes I daydream of dying because of the pain but I never die. I wonder how long somebody has to starve before they die.

Amira gets up and leaves the bathroom. I am now alone with the jar of honey and I am really hungry but I can't steal. If I steal I become a bad person and I want to be good so I can go to heaven. I have to pray to God so he can give us some food. I crawl out of the bathroom because I am too tired to get up. We are not allowed to pray in the bathroom because the jinns live there. It's not a good place to stay for long. I put my hands up in the air and ask God for food and to bring Yasmine back. I know God won't leave me alone without helping me. I close my eyes and hope my prayer flies right up to God.

It's 11:47 p.m now. I'm really tired. I am lying in bed and thinking of how I can dream about Yasmine. I try to think of her without getting distracted so I can sleep and dream of her. Maybe she will speak to me in my dream. Why did she visit Baba but didn't visit me? Does she not miss me? My heart feels like a rock in my chest when I think of that. I get up and decide to go to Yasmine's room to sleep there. Maybe I will feel like she is there too. I walk into her room and feel a cold breeze. The window isn't open. I look around. I remember when we sat down after Baba slapped her and we spoke for a bit. I liked it. I replay Yasmine's voice in my head then I try to replay her laugh. Her laugh isn't clear in my mind though. How can I forget Yasmine's laugh? It's my favourite sound. I keep trying to replay the sound in my heart but every time it sounds different. I settle at the sound I think she makes. I think it is close enough. Her eyes squeeze together and her mouth opens really wide when she laughs. She has nice teeth, I notice them whenever she laughs. The dentist used to say I have very good teeth. I am really scared of dentists because of the tools they use but my dentist is nice. I like him, he doesn't put metal in my mouth because I told him I don't like it. It makes me shiver whenever metal touches my teeth. I don't know how my teeth are now. I roll my tongue over them, they don't feel as straight. I can feel the dirt on them, that is what is making them bumpy. I never realised how important water is and how much we use it until we didn't have it any more. Yasmine's room used to always smell like her, of rose water. Now it smells like cold air. I pull her duvet up and curl into her bed. It's cold and lonely. It doesn't feel like Yasmine's room. I sit up and put my hands together and pray to God for Yasmine and Khalid to come back and for this war to end. I look around the room and see mama looking at me from Yasmine's table. It was when mama was young. She's wearing a red dress with white flowers on it and she is smiling. She has the same smile as Yasmine. I wish she could come out of the picture and sleep in the bed with me. It's cold. I close my eyes and start to hear shooting outside. It happens every night at the same time. I cover my ears with the pillow and think of things that make me happy. Baba's room is next to Yasmine's and I can hear him breathe heavily through the door. Baba has changed so much. He is very thin now and has to hold onto things while walking. He looked good before. Liquorice sneaks into the room and jumps on the bed. I think she traced my smell, I'm glad she came, now I can warm up and sleep knowing she is in the room.

★

Ali comes running into the room without knocking and wakes me up. How did he know I was here?

'Wake up quick Adam! Quick!'

I squint my eyes and look around. The sun is so bright, I don't usually sleep in this late. I jump up and trip over the cover, I can't see properly.

'I can't see properly!'

'Just rub your eyes, it's the dust from outside. All our eyes hurt.'

'What dust?'

'Come.'

Liquorice follows us.

'Where did you get the cat from?'

'Her name is Liquorice.'

'That's a funny name.'

'I like it.'

Baba, Tariq and Amira are crammed at the door. What are they looking at? I look over Amira's shoulder, she is shorter than me, and see the street is nothing but rubble. Did all this really happen when I was sleeping? I didn't feel or hear anything. I see a face and a leg next to each other through some of the rubble and clothes in-between. Our house and Ali's old house are standing. Blood is mixed with water on the ground and now it doesn't even make me sick any more. A man is sweeping the ground with a broom.

Baba walks out and Tariq follows him.

'Where are you going Baba?'

Tariq looks back and gestures for me to follow him. Amira holds my hand and walks on. Where are we all going? I let go of her hand and walk alone after Baba. We get on the main street and I see my town in a completely different way. It's like I am in a war story. What would I say if I was one of the characters? I guess I would be describing everything but it's beyond words. They need to see it with their own eyes. There's a river under the bridge we are walking towards, the water is brown. I don't know if it is dust or blood or both. We walk on and I keep staring at the river. I want to jump into it. The water looks so free. I lick my lips and feel my dry skin peeling off. I'm thirsty. When we start going down the other side of the bridge the water looks clear. Even though the water is connected, one side is different from the other.

'Why is the colour of the water different on the other side Tariq?'

'This part belongs to the government, the other side is the part where the free army lives.'

'It looks like two different cities.'

'It is now.'

A group of men are joining hands and forming a human chain that links into the water. I can't see what they're doing from here so I walk faster to the front. There are three men at the front pulling out a body from the river. The body is covered in a black bag with a rope wrapped around it. They pull it up and lie it on the floor and go down and pull another body out. This one looks like a young child, maybe seven years old. Where are they getting these bodies from? Everyone seems calm like they have always been doing this. They all link hands and hold on tight. The third body they pull up is naked and one of his legs is missing. I turn away. I have already seen it though, I can't erase the image from my head. The image is stuck in my head.

Now I try not to look back but I do. I see another body being pulled up. I look for the body I saw earlier, I don't know why. I just need to see it again, there's something in my mind that's forcing me to. I look around but can't see it. I spot the first body with the plastic bag on it, but I can't see the other one.

Walking into the government part of the town, the buildings are still up even though they have bullet marks in them, but at least they're not on the ground with people under them. I wonder if the people living on this side hear and see what we go through every day. Something seems wrong. Nothing comes easy mama used to say, but maybe this did. There are exceptions to every rule I once read. I remember everything I ever read and hear.

There are rats running around the streets like they have taken over the town. On my right, the pavement is filled with rubbish bags that a young kid is going through. That's a clever idea to find food. I'm starving. Everyone walks on without stopping; I stop and look to see what she is going to find in the rubbish. She takes out a box of what looks like microwave food and starts licking the insides. The whole place smells really bad, I don't want to know how bad that box smells. There are kids running around and playing. In our area no one plays around. I wish I lived on this side. There are four kids carrying their friend and playing 'a funeral'. I don't see how that's a game. I don't understand. I stare at them and one of them sticks his tongue out at me. I catch up to Tariq and look back at them as they walk away and chant a prayer in their little voices.

'Tariq why are we walking here?'

'I don't know, we are following Baba.'

'Doesn't Uncle Shady live on this side?'

'Oh yes, I forgot about that. Maybe we are going there. You're a clever boy.' Tariq winks at me. I know I am clever. Mama told me that sometimes I can be cleverer than other people and at times I need to be patient with myself. I get frustrated when words don't come out and I have so much to say. During those moments I want to pull my hair or punch something. It's like a waking dream you're trying to escape but you can't. The only difference is that people don't know what is going on in my mind and they start to make fun of me. I don't like it when people laugh at me, so I prefer not to talk to people.

'Yasmine! Yalla!' I feel my heart stop beating when I hear Yasmine's name. I knew she'd show up! I turn around following the sound of the voice and see a young girl running to her father. I feel cold but I am sweating. Yasmine's name took all the energy out of me. I feel like I ran a mile. I didn't move a centimetre though. I don't like being disappointed. I see the colour purple when I close my eyes when I get disappointed.

Baba is knocking on Uncle Shady's door just like I guessed. He knocks twice and waits. I walk up to the door and knock one more time. We always have to knock three times: it's a rule. Nobody uses it though, because I made it up.

'Move back Adam,' Baba hisses like a snake.

We wait for 73 seconds before Baba knocks again. We are all standing behind each other like we are scared of one another.

Uncle Shady at last answers the door, but not the way we expected. He is now sitting in a wheelchair with his legs cut off. Baba gasps for a split second before going in and kissing Uncle Shady. I stand on the side trying to avoid the kisses and notice them look at each other in a familiar way. Uncle Shady cries silently still staring at Baba and then wipes his tears and welcomes Baba in.

'I missed you big brother,' Uncle Shady says.

'I trust you've been doing well?'

'As you can see, I'm great.'

This conversation doesn't make sense. Baba didn't reply to Uncle Shady saying he missed him. Uncle Shady says that he is doing great even though he is in a wheelchair with his legs cut off.

'What happened to you Uncle Shady?' I ask.

Baba looks at me and hisses again. I can't make out what he is saying but apparently Uncle Shady can because he tells Baba not to be harsh on me. Was I meant to pretend I don't see?

'It's a long story, let's sit down then speak,' he says. They go to the sitting room and sit on the sofa. I haven't been to Uncle Shady's house in ages. We used to always come before mama died but when she left we never came here again. I don't think Baba and his brother spoke for a long time. I can see yellow circles coming out of both their mouths when they speak, it means that they are both shy. How can you be shy in front of your brother?

'Adam do you still paint?' my uncle asks me. I feel my cheeks go red because I don't like talking about my paintings.

I look down and play with my elastic band. Baba comes closer to me and ruffles my hair.

'Answer Adam. Don't be shy in front of your uncle, you remember him right?' I wasn't being shy. I want to tell Baba I know he is shy himself but I don't.

'Yes I still paint. Yes I remember Uncle Shady,' I say.

They both laugh and my uncle tells Baba that I haven't changed. Of course I haven't. Why would I change? If I changed I wouldn't be me.

'So who did you come with?'

'That's Amira and that's Ali. It's a long story but they are both a part of our family now,' Baba says and smiles. He is actually happy.

'Where's Yasmine, Khalid and Isa? Are they doing their

own thing as usual?'

Baba looks down. I want to tell Uncle Shady that I don't like him for bringing them up but I don't know how to say it without him laughing at me. I mean it, it's not funny.

'God be with us,' Baba says and tries to get up.

'It's time for us to go.'

Tariq helps Baba up and stands by him. He looks like his bodyguard. Tariq has huge shoulders and chest. His shirt looks bumpy because he is really big and strong. He is the most muscly out of all of them, but I have never seen him use his strength and I don't want to! It would be like a scene out of the movie with Arnold Schwarzenegger and his little twin brother. The movie made me laugh a lot. That's how Tariq and I look together. I laugh to myself and Tariq looks at me without anything in his facial expression. I stop laughing in case Tariq really punches me like in the movie. I don't want to go flying back. The twin brother seemed fine after that, but I am sure I won't be.

'You just got here, stay for a bit more. Hanan is coming back soon, she just went to her mother's house down the road.'

'Just tell her we send our regards, we have to go. Adam doesn't like staying out for too long.' Does Baba read minds? I hate being out of the house for too long. Is that really why he is going home? I can't say anything because I can't wait to walk back home. This house looks familiar but unfamiliar at the same time. I don't like the feeling. It's better to just go home.

'I don't know if I'll ever see you again big brother, people keep on disappearing nowadays. Look after yourself.' I don't know why Uncle Shady calls Baba big brother instead of his real name. Am I meant to call Tariq big brother?

Baba walks on and I stick to Tariq's side and whisper to him 'Are we going home big brother?' Tariq laughs a little and shakes his head. I like being funny and making people laugh. I like making Yasmine laugh the most. I feel good today. I know mama is looking down at me today. I wish she would look down more often. We all say bye to Uncle Shady and I look back at him, his eyes are black.

'Adam, how are you feeling?' Baba stops and looks back at me. I forget about Uncle Shady right away and tell Baba I'm okay. I am happy Baba looked back at me. I missed looking at his face. I walk beside Baba with our shoulders brushing against each other. I remember when mama and Baba used to walk in front of us and I used to count how many times their shoulders would brush against each other.

A man wearing the Islamic dress for men stands on the opposite pavement from us and starts calling for prayer. He puts his hands around his ears and shouts. His voice echoes through my body. I feel his voice shiver my insides. Why isn't he in the mosque calling for prayer? I ask Baba and he tells me the mosque was bombed. So why is he doing it on the streets?

'When it's time for prayer, nothing will stop us, not even a war,' Baba says.

I don't reply and start thinking how important prayer is. If not even the war will stop it, what will? I used to like watching people pray in Makkah all together. It was exciting when the whole crowd went up and down at the same time as if it was rehearsed. It's the only thing that brings all the Muslims together Baba once told me. Mama used to say it was beautiful, so I think it is too.

We pass by the river and get home without me even realising. I was thinking about prayer and I didn't even know where I was any more. I love it when that happens, when for a few minutes I leave. If only I knew how to get away for good.

There's a carton box outside our door. It looks like a parcel.

I love parcels, you never know what's in them.

'Baba! Look we have a parcel!'

'Don't touch it Adam!' Baba grabs my hand.

'Why Baba? It's a parcel!'

'I don't have a good feeling!'

I don't have any feeling about it, I just want to open it. I love parcels. Baba carries it and takes it in. I follow him to the living room to see what is inside. Everybody else goes to a room and closes the door behind them. It's like we don't even live together.

'Baba, are you going to open it?'

'Get me scissors.'

I run to the kitchen and get Baba the scissors. I hold them down the way Yasmine taught me. Maybe the parcel is from Yasmine! Maybe she is coming back soon. My heart is beating fast. I am so excited. When Yasmine comes back I am going to tell her I love her and to never leave again.

Baba starts opening the package and my heart beats faster. Is it a card picture from Yasmine? Is it her address so we can pick her up? It is none of those. Baba opens the package and I can feel the air being sucked out of the room. Baba gasps and throws the package out of his hands. I can't breathe. I can't say anything. All the air in my body has been punched out. I am moving my mouth but I feel suffocated. My face starts getting hot. The package is Khalid's hands. His chopped hands in his blood. Khalid doesn't have hands any more. I know his hands by heart. Their size and colour and the hair on his fingers and... and... the tattoo on his finger that mama kicked him out of the house for. I regain some breath and start panting.

'No, no! Not Khalid! He's alive! I know he's alive!'

Baba is rocking himself forwards and backwards and slapping his hands on his lap.

'Khalid! My son! Khalid!' Baba is crying and shouting. He starts pulling his hair and crying harder. He repeats those four words until everybody comes out of their room and runs to him. I want to explain what happened but I start imagining Khalid without hands and I can't look straight any more. Does Yasmine still have hands?

I fall to the ground and close my eyes. I don't want to see anything else ever again. Tariq kicks the table in the middle and starts swearing.

'Why are you swearing! You should be praying to God!' Baba shouts at Tariq. I open my eyes and see his face get so red. I don't know whether I want to block my ears or eyes. If only I could block both.

'Those bastards! They have no shame! No life! What the fuck is happening to this country?! What is happening to the people?! Where did all these animals come from?!' Tariq punches the wall and runs out of the front door. 'I'll show those bastards what it means to touch my brother!'

'Come back Tariq! We can't do anything!' Baba shouts after Tariq. He doesn't look back though. Amira holds Ali and is covering his eyes.

I bang my head on the edge of the sofa over and over and over again. Over and over again. Khalid... I remember when blood made me vomit and made my head spin, now blood is like water and body parts are parcels. I don't even know why there's a war. Why is there a revolution? Why are they taking my family? What happened while I was painting and going to school? Why is everyone suddenly talking about politics when they used to talk about art, fashion, religion and travelling?

'What happened!' I shout and scream. 'What happened!' I don't know who I am screaming at. Nobody looks at me. Baba is still crying and repeating the same words. Amira is still rocking Ali in her lap and covering his eyes while he covers his ears. I don't know who we are any more.

I run to Isa's room and start ripping books and kicking his bed. I've never felt the colour black take over my body. I see black and white now. Everything is a target with a focus point. Everything is different. I hear a car stop outside our door and stop everything for a split second of hope. I run outside the room and don't see Baba any more. Amira and Ali haven't moved. They look frozen.

I hear the car drive away and run to the door. Why did they stop outside our house? I open the door and see the lights slowly disappear. It was a black car. I look around and don't see anyone. Did they pick someone up from here? I notice a log on the floor a little down our street. It looks as long and thick as a log but why would they drop a log there? I couldn't see their faces. I leave the door open and walk up a little. It's not a log. It's a person. Did the car dump a person here? I am scared to walk over but I do. I am filled with curiosity.

The person's feet are tied back. Their body is rising up and down. They are alive! Oh my God they dumped a living person! I run towards them and lean down. They need help. I start praying under my breath and take a look at their face. It's Khalid! It's Khalid! Oh my God! Khalid is alive! I shout as loud as I can for someone to come out and help me. Ali and Amira come out quickly and ask me what I am doing out here in the dark. I don't reply and start untying the rope around Khalid's feet and they come and help me without saying another word. We carry him inside and lie him down on the big sofa. We all stand back and stare at him. We all know what to do nowadays. Khalid's eyes are bruised and one of his cheeks is puffed up and purple. His neck has scars that look like they go deep down but I can't see because he is wearing a shirt. There is blood on it and it is ripped on his shoulder. I lean down and whisper 'hello' to him. I see his eyeballs move under his eyelids but he does not open his eyes. Amira tells me to move back from him at the same time as her stomach makes the loudest hungry noise. Her face goes red and she pretends nothing happened. Her facial expression is fighting to say something but she keeps the same face.

We don't have any clean water for Khalid to drink. I try to think of somewhere we might have hidden some water. I remember the honey Amira hid and run to the bathroom. Honey is better than nothing. I come back to the sitting room and see Khalid's eyes open. I don't know if he can see us though, his eyes are really puffed. Amira sees me holding her honey jar and jumps up.

'Who told you to touch it?'

'It's for Khalid, Amira.'

I have never seen her this angry.

'It's for me and my baby! He will die if I don't feed him.'

I don't know what to say. Amira looks skinnier not pregnant.

'Can I give some to Khalid please?'

'Okay, some!' Her eyes look down then she makes a stern face and takes the honey jar out of my hand.

'I'll give him some, you go call Baba,' she says.

'Where did Baba go?'

'Look for him in his room.'

I run to his room and knock on the door three times. I don't get an answer but I open it slowly. I can see Baba's legs then I open it fully and walk in. I see Baba sitting on his knees like he is praying but he is holding a box in his hands. I can't see what he is doing with it from here so I walk closer. I can't believe what I am seeing. I cover my eyes and open them again. Baba doesn't look up at me, I don't know if he heard me come into the room.

'Baba...'

Baba jumps up, he has hands held against his face with blood dripping down to his knees.

'What are you doing Baba?'

Baba doesn't reply. His pupils widen.

'I'm feeling Khalid's agony.'

I don't know if I should go near him. I'm scared. He doesn't look like Baba any more. His face looks completely different.

Why would he touch Khalid's hands? Why would he touch the blood? Is this what people do when they lose someone? I have never heard of it. I think Baba is really upset. I once watched a movie with a woman acting crazy and she didn't know what she was doing or who she was. Is Baba like her?

'Baba... Khalid is here.'

Baba's eyes open up. He replies when I call him Baba.

'Khalid? Did they send his dead body?'

'No Baba, he is in the sitting room on the sofa.' Baba jumps up, drops the hands and runs out. He doesn't even wipe the blood. I look down at the box and a shiver runs through me. The box looks messy with blood and Khalid's hands. How can Baba touch that?

Khalid is slowly sipping honey from the spoon.

I sit down on the sofa and just stare at him. Baba is sitting next to him holding onto his arm but Khalid keeps moving it away. What happened? I always have to connect the dots myself. Khalid closes his mouth tight so Amira doesn't feed him. He tries to move away but his face scrunches up in pain. Why isn't he speaking? Can he not speak any more?

'Talk to me Khalid, are you ok?' Baba asks.

I want to ask so many questions but I fight the voices in my head. I don't want to upset anyone. Everything is always happening to people around me. What about me? Is it my turn next?

I am happy Khalid is back home, but where is Yasmine? Is she coming back home soon? Is she going to be hurt as well?

My eyes start to feel heavy. When I think about Yasmine when I'm tired I get really depressed. I try to stop thinking about her and get up and go to my room. I'll pray tonight that Yasmine comes back home tomorrow. She's been gone for too long.

★

I wake up all of a sudden and look around. It's still dark outside and my heart is racing loudly. I had a nightmare, which I was stuck in. I was trying to get out but I couldn't. I don't want to think about it. I don't know what time it is, it feels like I slept for a whole night but it's still dark. I couldn't have slept more than a few hours.

I get up and rub my eyes. I have crust in the corners. I try to take as much off as I can but it needs to be washed away by water. I go into the sitting room and look at the time. It's only 2:30 a.m. I slept for three hours. There is nobody in the sitting room. I go back into my room and take my books from the bedside table. I haven't had time to read lately. Nobody has time to read when there are bombs and blood everywhere. I wish I had more time though. I start to read and feel good. I love reading, it feels like I am travelling. I miss this feeling, like you're invincible. But I can't feel invincible during a war. I learnt that word at school when a boy was pretending to be Superman and stood on the table to jump off and shouted 'I'm invincible!' He's a clever boy, he always gets good marks.

I went home and searched for what it means in the dictionary. That's why I am using it now. Whenever I learn a new word I try to use it as much as possible in any sentence. Yasmine used to always laugh at me whenever I'd say a new word in every sentence.

I hear the sound of a car engine outside. The street is pitch black because we don't have any more street lamps. But I can see the car headlights coming towards me. There is no other sound on the streets but the car driving up. Are they going to throw Yasmine outside? I go a little under my covers so they don't see me. I don't want them to know I'm here. The car stops on our street on the neighbours' side. I can still see it very clearly. A man comes out of the front. His face is covered with a cloth. He looks around him and then closes the car door after him. He walks to the back of the car and opens the trunk. He looks around again. What is he doing? Are they going to kill us? I should sneak out of bed and wake Tariq up. I remember that he left the house earlier, but I think he has come back home now. He never stays out at night any more like he used to. It's not safe outside.

I shuffle down my bed a little trying to get to the edge slowly without making any sound. The guy buries his head into the trunk for what seems like a long time then comes out again grabbing two legs. They are wrapped up in a white cloth, but I can now recognise a dead body from miles away. Another man comes out from the front and opens the back door and three men follow. Two men take the body from the first guy and carry it together and the other two take the next body and follow the first two. They are walking towards Ali's door. Are they the people who dump the bodies inside? Should I call the police? I don't even know if the police station is working any more. I don't know if anything is any more.

Everything is different. I don't move and just watch the first two men come out of the house and take another body from the trunk. How many bodies are in there? How did they fit them in? The last man carries a body alone and walks towards the house as well. I can't tell if he is holding a small child or half a body. It just looks like a small body without a beginning or an ending. Who are they? Are they good or bad? No one ever knows who's good or bad these days. I just know that I want this to all end.

It starts raining really hard out of the blue. It hasn't rained in ages. I want to go out and drink the water. I can feel the cold breeze come into my room and I pull the covers tightly on me. I want to go out in the rain but I'm scared of the men. They all come out at the same time and run into the car and drive away quickly like they are being chased. Is there someone in the neighbours' house who is alive? The thought of it scares me. I don't know who to tell about what I saw. Maybe I'll tell Tariq if he is in a better mood. I jump out of bed and run to everybody's doors. I knock three times and run to the next door. I shout 'It's raining!' I shout once and hear all the doors open. I don't even think they were sleeping. We all run outside and gather the water in the palms of our hands and drink it. I rub my body with the fresh water and imagine it's a shower. I open my mouth and face the sky and let the water fall.

'I'll get a few buckets to fill up,' Amira shouts. Her voice sounds happy. I go in and help her, she looks really tired. We let the buckets fill up and play around in the rain. I can hear other people coming out of their houses and laughing. This is the happiest moment of my life. I can see butterflies playing around with us. It feels like we are living a normal life again.

I see Khalid walk slowly outside. I run to him and smile.

He doesn't have his shirt on and he has bullet marks on his skin and scratches. He has a hole next to his belly button. It looks like it was cut out. I look up at him and try not to look down again. His body looks scary.

'How are you Adam?' Khalid speaks at last! My voice gets stuck in my throat. I am really happy.

'I am good Mr. Khalid.' Khalid smiles and walks to Baba. Baba looks at Khalid and Khalid falls to his knees and starts begging Baba for forgiveness and crying. I don't know why he is doing that. Baba holds Khalid's head against him and rubs his hair. Baba starts crying too and everyone else stops playing with the rain and watches them.

'What is happening Amira?'

'I don't even know.'

Khalid stands up and kisses Baba's forehead and starts laughing. Baba put his hand on Khalid's face and doesn't say anything. He is still crying. Even when we are happy, we still have tears because the war is just above our heads. I want to paint this scene.

We all go in with our three buckets of water.

'Go put a shirt on Adam, you'll get sick,' Baba tells me.

Tariq goes to the fireplace and lights it up. Everyone sits around and dries off. I can't wait to go to my room and start painting. I can't sleep any more.

'I can't sleep any more Ali, can you?'

'I can sleep forever!'

Amira laughs and rubs her belly.

We all get up and I go to my room and get my painting kit out straightaway and start painting the scene under the rain. We look like a happy family, but behind us there are collapsed buildings and the sky looks darker than it ever did, even at night. I don't know how to explain how black the sky is.

There is no sign of the moon in the navy-blue sky; just black smoke covering it. One day, when the war finishes, I'll have my paintings to show people what was really going on. My paintings don't lie.

Chapter Fifteen

GREY

I SIT IN THE ROOM Baba showed us and listen to music; the power is back on. I forget about everything until Tariq opens the door and comes in. Whenever I come here he is here too. Does he come every day? I want to tell him about the neighbours' house but I'm scared he'll shout at me for going in. Liquorice squirms in my lap while I think about what to tell him.

'Can I tell you something Tariq?'

'Where's the cat from?'

'This is Liquorice. Liquorice this is Tariq my brother.'

'Nice to meet you Liquorice.' Tariq pulls out his hand to greet her. Tariq is funny. We laugh together.

'Sure, tell me.'

'You won't be upset?'

'Just tell me Adam.'

I don't know if I want to tell him any more. I don't like people ignoring my questions.

I tell him everything anyway and how I found Liquorice and try to feed her whenever I have something to eat. His facial expression keeps on changing the whole time.

'Wow. You're really brave Adam!'

'Really?'

'Yes! If I were you I'd be having nightmares.'

'I have been having nightmares.'

'Well I'm glad you told me.'

'So you're not upset?'

'No Adam, things like this happen. A war isn't a pretty thing.'

'So you'll let me keep Liquorice? I don't have to hide her any more?'

'Of course. There's an Islamic saying that a prostitute once fed a thirsty dog and all her sins got wiped away and she went to heaven.'

'What is a prostitute?'

'Mmm, a bad woman.'

'So what does that mean?'

'That means that looking after a needy animal is a very good thing and God likes it.'

I smile because it makes me happy to hear that I am doing something good. We sit in silence and listen to Abdel Halim Hafiz.

I go to the kitchen and drink a lot of water from the bucket. My mouth is dry. It's weird, my mouth usually gets dry when I speak a lot, but now it gets dry when I don't speak. But I don't really need to think much about that now because everything is getting better. We have water, Khalid came back and it rained. Khalid's arms look scary though. I don't like looking at them. His arms end at his wrist and a piece of thin skin grows over them. We have to help him do everything. I don't think he likes it. He used to like doing everything alone.

I take Liquorice out because she keeps on squirming and hissing. I think she wants some fresh air. I don't think she likes staying at home. She runs away the moment I put her down on the ground outside.

'No Liquorice! Come back!'

I run after her until she stops next to a bin. She jumps in and goes down into the rubbish. The bins smell very strong and disgusting. I never take the bin out, I hate it. How does everything we eat stink when put together in a plastic bag? I can hear Liquorice scratching around inside the bin. She comes out with a bone in her mouth and keeps licking it. The bone looks yummy. This is the closest I might get to the taste of meat again.

'Can I have some please?' I try to pull it a little from her but she holds on tight. Then she lets go and jumps inside again. I take the bone and start sucking it. I can taste the faint taste of meat. Liquorice is so clever! This is how she feeds herself!

I tip up the whole bin and Liquorice comes jumping out and screeching. I laugh and apologise to her. She jumps back in as if nothing happened and we look for food together. Everything together smells horrible but when Liquorice finds something it smells nice alone. She continues to find bones and even some rotten cheese. Who would throw away food? Or maybe nobody has looked through this bin in a long time. Maybe we are lucky. I love Liquorice for finding this food. I kept her to feed her, but now she is feeding me.

Liquorice and I walk home now, full for the first time in a long time. I have a bag in my hand with some things for everybody at home. I look up at the sky and try to look beyond the grey smoke and think about the blue sky and sun. It's a cosy feeling, it makes my heart feel warm, like I am home again and everything is good. Some buildings that we pass are now half dust. A huge white mess remains behind them. Ali told me that all these people move far away and live in tents. How do people do that? How can a family fit in a tent? I just want to stay at home until the war finishes and be able to go back to school and see the girl with the Nutella eyes. I wonder if she knows that her eyes look like a tub of Nutella? She didn't seem like she spoke a lot. I think she is shy, maybe she is like me. Maybe there are people out there like me.

We walk home and I run straightaway to Khalid's room because he is the most sick. When I walk in I see him sitting down facing his cupboard. Maybe he didn't hear my knocking.

'Khalid?'

'Mmm…'

'I got you some food,' I whisper. I am scared of him turning around, what if his scars got uglier?

'I don't want it.'

'But you're sick.'

'Where did you get food from?'

'From the bin, Liquorice helped me.'

Khalid turns around quickly and I can sense an explosion. His eyes turn maroon. I hope he doesn't shout at me.

'What?' he shouts.

I close my eyes and pretend I'm with Yasmine. I don't know what to say. Why does he have to shout? Did I do something wrong? I brought him food.

'Are you a scavenger? Why are you eating food from bins?'

Even though I am pretending I can't hear, I did hear what he said.

'I'm hungry,' I whisper.

Liquorice rubs herself on my leg. I think she feels that I'm upset and feeling gloomy.

'We are all hungry Adam!'

I don't know what to say. The food was yummy and I haven't eaten in a long time. I miss food. I drop the bag on the floor and run out of his room. Liquorice follows me, I can hear her steps. I run to Baba's room to go to the small room so no one can find me. I don't think they will even notice

I'm gone. I want to live with the vinyl records until Yasmine comes back.

I pick Liquorice up and knock on Baba's door and walk in. I don't know where he is. I wonder if he is hungry and wants the food I brought or if he would shout at me too? Baba is lying on the bed, still. His eyes are closed and his chest is still. No, no! Why isn't he breathing? He couldn't have died. I drop Liquorice and run to Baba's bed and start pushing my hands down on his chest like I saw on TV. I don't even know if this is what I should do but this is the only thing I know. Baba opens his eyes and looks confused.

'What are you doing Adam?'

'Baba, you're alive!'

'Of course I'm alive, are you trying to kill me?'

'No, I was trying to bring you back to life.'

'I was just sleeping!'

'Thank God! Are you okay Baba?'

'Yes, where's Maha?'

Baba is doing it again. It makes me feel uncomfortable to think about mama during the war because I am already always sad.

'I don't know Baba,' I say. I try to pretend I know what he is talking about. Baba is acting like a child. What happened to him? Is he sick or are all old people like this? But Baba didn't use to be old before the war.

'Baba I'm going into the other room.'

'What room?'

I am confused. Does he not remember the room he showed us?

'The room you showed us Baba.'

'I don't know what you're saying. Are you speaking Arabic?'

I don't know why Baba is acting this way. It's like he doesn't know who I am or what he is doing.

'Get me my lunch.'

'We have no food.'

'I said get me my lunch!' Baba shouts, suddenly his facial expression completely changes. What is he doing? He whispers 'Ahh' after he is done and I look down at him and his bed is wet. Baba just peed himself! What is happening?

'Baba!' He doesn't look up and closes his eyes to sleep again. I think Baba is dying… I don't know how it is for people to die slowly but I think this is it. I run out to the sitting room and find Amira cleaning. I don't know why she cleans every day. There is nothing to clean.

'Amira! Can you please help me?'

'Yes Adam,' she says as she smiles and rubs her stomach. She is always doing that.

'Can you come into Baba's room? He peed himself.'

'What?'

Amira runs into Baba's room and slaps one of her cheeks in shock.

'Oh my Lord! What has come upon us?'

'Is Baba dying Amira?'

'Don't say that Adam. He's just having a hard time.'

'He asked for mama again and didn't know what room he showed us.'

'Don't worry, I'll deal with it Adam. You go and do what you were doing.'

'Are you sure?'

'Yes.'

I run into the room and keep the door slightly open and

keep my eye on Amira. She kisses Baba on the forehead the way Yasmine used to and starts to wake him up. She looks like Yasmine from the back. But she is not. She's not Yasmine.

Chapter Sixteen

BYZANTINE YASMINE

I'VE BEEN EATING my hard bread with a mouse that comes to visit me every day whenever my food comes. The girl in the corner hardly ever speaks. Sometimes I speak to her but she doesn't reply and in the end I'm speaking to myself. How long have I been here? I don't know how to count the days in this cell. We have no light and no hope. I think I should sit in the corner like the other girl and forget about time and the world, but I can never stop thinking about Adam. I am always imagining what he is doing or not doing without me. Is he being looked after? Is everyone still alive? Every day I have been monitoring the screams and how many women they have brought in so far. I can't see if they're torturing everyone in the same way but the screams are the same. My heart always shrivels up when I hear the sound of torture with a whip or when I hear their moans. It makes me cringe and want to die inside. If only I could chop my ears off. I wouldn't be the first one to do it. I sometimes try to count as long as I can to waste time and figure out how much time has passed. I once counted to 8,457 before I got tired and fell asleep. I try to sleep as much as possible because there's nothing else to do.

'What? Where is he! Bring him to me now or you're going to die!'

'Master, they took him.'

'And what were you doing you idiot? Were you just smiling and giving him to them?'

'Master, I had to run away.'

'If he gives away our secrets and hideout we are all dead! You know that you bastard!'

'Master! I will do my best!'

'Go! Go! I don't want to see your face until you bring him back.'

The shouting is so loud it feels like I am sitting in the middle of them. Maybe this is a good thing for us. I hope they kill them. I hope we are able to run away. I just want to go home. I'm cold and lonely. I wonder why they have been giving us bread and keeping us alive. Don't they want to kill us? Or is this their way of prolonging our pain? I wouldn't put it past these bastards. I am not eating anything from now on. I'd rather die sooner than later. I want to die and let go of all my worries and pain.

I hear the main door slam and the master speak to someone. I guess he is speaking on the phone.

'They took Wael hostage!... I know, I sent him back to get him, but let's be realistic, he's not coming back. We need a change of plan!'

He doesn't say anything for a while and keeps punching walls. I can almost feel his punch.

'Stop the attack for now. We need to make sure they don't make him snitch. Well what can I do? If I go out there they'll kill me for sure. I don't even know if Haitham is coming back after I just sent him... Khalas, I'll deal with it. Don't worry.'

They're planning an attack? I pray that he says more so I know where it is. I just hope it's not by our house. I can't do anything anyway but please God don't let it be by our house. He doesn't say anything else so I'm guessing he's put the phone down. Damn!

I know a huge thing but I have no power to make change.

I don't know how many people they intend to kill with this bomb but maybe I can make a change. I keep thinking about how to escape then look over at the woman in the corner and shiver from fear. Am I that brave? I don't know. I am already scarred with pain.

I pray all day and cry to God to listen to my prayers and save us. I know he is listening. Please God, save us, please keep my family safe. I look down at my naked body and cry even more. I don't even have the guts to look at myself any more. They made me hate being a woman.

I hate the state I am in: weak and needy. I have never relied on anyone before. I have always looked after my family from day one and have never had a day for me. I don't even have a family of my own. No child to name or laugh with, my only child is Adam, and he isn't even mine.

I lie down on the cold concrete and close my eyes really tight and enjoy the stars I see forming behind my eyelids. This is the best entertainment I can provide for myself. Different shapes form and merge into animals then houses and then people then I cannot stop thinking about Wisam and his face is formed inside my eyes and pieces of him fall down my face with every tear.

I open my eyes to the sound of a loud hammering and chainsaw. That's what it sounds like. A chainsaw has a peculiar sound: it cannot be mistaken for anything else. What are they doing out there? I feel guilty about feeling relieved at not being out there. Soon I hear a girl screaming and my guilt increases. I don't know if I have the right to feel relieved. I should pray for the girl and not be selfish. My prayers are my only company. I know my prayers will save me. I have faith, I know this isn't the end of me. The screaming stops a few minutes later and another woman starts to scream the exact same way. I hope it's not what I think it is. I hope I am not next. I crawl to the girl in the corner and tap her shoulder. Her eyes pop open. They are so big, and her jaw is pointy and thin. I almost forgot what I wanted to say after seeing her. She stares at me in an intimidating manner, it feels like I am being scolded. Her silence is so strong. It seeps into me and plants fear inside my tears. I swallow the saliva building up in my mouth and muster up the courage to ask her if she knows what's happening outside.

'I don't know and I don't care as long as I'm in here!'

I don't feel so bad any more because I'm not the only one who feels this way. Everyone is selfish I guess.

'What if we are next?'

'I want to die anyway.'

'Don't say that!' I jump at her but then think about how I have the same thoughts. Is everybody stranded in this place experiencing the same waves of hopelessness? Is there actually any hope for us?

I sit next to the woman and try to touch her shoulder slightly. I want to feel the comfort of another human being. I want to feel alive. She doesn't move and I close my eyes and stay bundled up in my own limbs close to her. I start thinking of what I would do if I came out of here safely. I would write a book and go to protest against these bastards. I would get revenge for Isa's blood, I would find Wisam and tell him I want him no matter what. Or would I? Do I really have the guts? If I go back, will I just go back to living the same mundane lifestyle?

My mind spirals around these ideas for what seems like an eternity. It feels like my thoughts are slipping from my brain down to my neck and are about to strangle me.

★

It's been days I think since I have been given some bread or water. My throat feels like it's closing up, it's giving up on me. I haven't heard any screams or any of the men's voices since the last screams with the chainsaw. What is happening? I have no way of looking out to see what is going on. I can only guess that days have passed because I have thought about my whole life and prayed for hours and hours for God's help. I have no sense of time. Who would have thought that time was this important? You lose track of life itself without time.

I get up and walk around the cell and stretch my legs. My limbs keep getting numb because my blood circulation is wrong. I keep moving around trying to find the warmest position possible with no clothes and no warmth. I think it rained a few days ago because I can smell the humidity through the walls. That's how thin they are. What if I keep banging, would someone hear me? I have nothing to lose any more; I am going to lose my mind if I stay in here another day. I start punching the wall and kicking it. I can hear the echo in the room. Would the people outside be able to hear me? Or is there no hope? I can't remember if we are on the ground floor or if we are on the upper floors. Maybe nobody can hear because my wall isn't on the ground floor. I have never felt this disoriented. Is this how Adam always feels when he says he is lost? I know I haven't been the best support. I know he needed a special school because of his condition but we couldn't afford it so I turned a blind eye to his needs. How horrible was I to do so? Why didn't I think it was wrong back then? Was I too blinded by mama's death?

I hear the slamming of a door and people shouting. It sounds like a huge group. They start shouting God's name and praising him. I run to the door and stick my ear on it. I try to hear as much as possible. I hear gunshots being fired but I don't know who they're shouting at. I hear no screams. Are all the other women trapped here as lost as me? Or am I the only one who is noticing these things? I look back at the girl in the corner and she hasn't even flinched.

I hear the bunch getting closer, they aren't chanting any more and there are no gunshots. Are they coming to get us? Are they the people the master spoke to on the phone? Is there worse yet to come? Question after question races through my mind and I just sit back and wait for fate to take its course. I don't know why I can't sit still even though I can't do anything. Is there something wrong with me?

I can hear doors opening and men calling out to people.

'By the name of God, come out!'

Is this a dirty trick they're using on us, calling us in the name of God so we trust them? I can hear them getting closer so I run to the woman in the corner and act like her. Maybe they'll think we're dead and leave us alone? I wait and wait but nothing happens. I start counting to comfort myself and the moment I count to 15 our door slams open. I feel a breeze sweep over us and try not to shiver. You are dead Yasmine, you are dead. I squeeze my eyes shut and repeat to myself that I am dead.

'By the name of God, come out, we have come to free you.' What filthy bastards they are, they think we will fall for this trick? I don't move and can hear footsteps approaching me. Please God save me, please God. I try to hold my breath but I am running out of willpower. Someone taps me on the shoulder but I do not move. You're doing a good job Yasmine, keep going.

'Sister, get up, I know you're awake. We are here to save you.'

He puts a blanket on my shoulders and my heart relaxes. Maybe we really are being saved at last. I open my eyes and look up. I see the man smiling down at me, his face glows with confidence. Maybe we really are being saved.

'Where do you live sister?'

I don't know whether I should tell him or not, what if he captures my family?

'Around…'

'I promise I'm the good guy,' he says as he laughs.

'How do I know?'

'Because I haven't done anything to harm you so far…'

He's right but I can't act like a fool and end up in something worse so I still don't answer.

'Well, we've got everybody some clothes outside, so grab something and leave, you are free.'

I jump up and run before he changes his mind. I run like I have never run before. I look up and try not to look down. God forgive me. I grab the nearest piece of clothing and run out of the door. My forehead is sweating and I feel dizzy. The intensity of my heart beating has got to me. I put the dress over my body and wrap myself in the cloth and walk down the stairs and out of the building. There is no sun or blue sky but the natural light outside makes my eyes hurt. How long have I been inside? I pick my dress up a little and run for my life. It's not an expression: I am running for my life.

Chapter Seventeen

RUBY

I AM PAINTING THE SCENE outside today. It looks scary. There
is blood and in the distance there's a collapsed building. I'm
painting the blood on the floor with real blood. I'm happy that
I am painting even though I am painting a sad scene. I think
the sun is out a little more today. I finish the painting and then
wait for it to dry off before taking a pencil and sketching Baba
holding Khalid's hands with blood dripping. I fill him in with
different colours especially navy blue and black. Because that's
the way he made me feel when I saw him. If anyone sees this, I
wonder if they will know what is happening? I don't want to
paint Baba like a bad guy, but I want to paint the truth.

I decide to combine a little of the rain that fell with the sun
that is coming out today. I am not lying, I am just mixing the
days. Our days are mixed up anyway because we are always on
the edge of our seats. In English class we had a sheet handed
out that described the reaction to a horror movie as someone
sitting on the edge of their seat. This isn't a movie though
and I am literally sitting on the edge of my seat. Miss Basma
said that it's a metaphor for fear when I asked her why someone would sit on the edge of his or her seat. I have never understood what a metaphor is. How can you say something is
something else when it isn't? She gave me an example: 'Time
is money'. But time isn't money so why are they teaching us
lies? I really like school, but sometimes it doesn't make sense.

I look out of the window and see a man running fast down

our street. It looks like he is running to me because my window is broken and I get confused between being inside and outside. I stare at him running, he is breathing heavily. I can't hear him because he is far away but I can see his chest go in and out really fast. The closer I look the more it looks like a woman. The body looks like a woman's but they're bald. I keep staring till I can get a better view. They're getting closer and now I am sure that it's a woman but it's the first time I have seen a bald woman in real life. I see them in movies when they are cancer patients, but it's weird seeing it in real life. Her face looks familiar but I am not sure how. I don't know how to describe her familiar features. She has eyes that look like rubies. I only know one person like that: Yasmine. But Yasmine has hair and she wears a headscarf. Could there really be someone else who has eyes like Yasmine's?

The girl stops in the middle of the street and bends down. I think she is catching her breath. She looks up and it feels like she is looking right into my eyes. I know I've seen those eyes before! I can see tears coming down her face now and she comes walking towards my window slowly.

'Adam!' she says.

My mind freezes. Yasmine? That's Yasmine's voice? Those are Yasmine's eyes! But that's not Yasmine's hair! Yasmine? Yasmine doesn't have a scar on her face.

'Adam!' she shouts this time and comes running towards our door.

I run to the door and open it and before I am able to take a good look at her she hugs me so tight and my hands stay at my sides, frozen. She smells weird. She smells dirty. That's not how Yasmine smells, but her skin is like Yasmine's and she feels like Yasmine. My heart starts beating really fast and I want her to let go of me so I can see her face.

'Yasmine?'

I can hear her sniffing from crying.

'Yasmine, is that you?'

She moves back and her face is covered in tears. Some parts of her face look white and clean from the tears and the other areas look dusty and dirty.

Oh my God it's Yasmine! It's Yasmine! I want to cry and I want to laugh at the same time. I end up making a sound like a duck. Yasmine is back! God accepted my prayers. I reach out to her scar. She smiles and hugs me again. I really don't like being hugged, even by Yasmine after all this time. I wriggle to be let go. She smiles.

'You haven't changed a bit...'

'Where were you Yasmine? You've been gone for so long.'

'I'm back now Habibi, I'm back now.'

'You look different.'

'Where's everyone?'

'Khalid! Tariq! Baba! Amira! Ali!' I shout.

Yasmine laughs and wipes her tears. I don't know if she is happy or sad. She cries and laughs, they are both different emotions.

Khalid and Tariq come out at the same time and they both have the same facial expression. Their eyes open up wide and they come running towards Yasmine. Tariq picks her up and twists her around. Yasmine laughs and hits him on his shoulders to put her down. She goes to Khalid and hugs him then looks down at his arms. They both start crying and she hugs him again. Baba comes out and rushes to Yasmine. This is the fastest I've seen him move in a long time.

'Maha! Maha!'

Only he doesn't know who she is. Yasmine hugs him and doesn't say anything. He touches her bald head and starts swearing and then thanking God that she is home safe. We are one family again. Only without Isa.

'What happened to you Khalid?'

'Don't worry about me, are you okay?'

'I'm okay now…'

We all sit in the sitting room and Tariq lights up the fireplace. We have water from the rain that Tariq warms up.

'How have you been Adam?' Yasmine turns to me. I am happy she asked about me first. I am still in shock that she is home. I have never been this happy in my life. Her face looks pale and thin and her body doesn't look red any more, she looks purple. Dark purple but her eyes are still red.

'I'm okay thank you Yasmine.'

'You haven't changed one bit,' she says as she ruffles my hair. She smiles so wide I can nearly see all of her teeth.

I don't know why she keeps on saying that, am I meant to change?

'The family is all together again at last,' Tariq says as he comes and sits next to me.

'Are you happy as well Tariq?'

'Happy? I am flying from happiness!'

I get up and start jumping up and down. I can't hold back my happiness and everyone starts laughing at me. The sound of laughter sounds like honey melting in my ears. If I had wings, I would fly around now.

'Yasmine will your hair grow back?'

'Ahh I missed your questions! Of course it will, don't worry Habibi, I'll be back to normal in no time.'

'Were you sad when you were away? Where did you go?'

Yasmine's eyes change but she doesn't pause to think about an answer.

'Very, but I am happy now.'

'I have a cat Yasmine. Her name is Liquorice.'

'Really? Where did you get her from?'

'I found her outside our door.'

'How do you know she's not anybody else's?

I didn't think about that, but I didn't see anyone looking for a missing cat.

'I don't know Yasmine, but she was really thin so I wanted to feed her.'

'Good boy. Where's Amira and Ali?'

'Ali is always sleeping in the room. He is hardly ever awake, and Amira is always cleaning and putting on make-up.'

'Go call them to come Habibi. I want to see them.'

'But I don't want to leave you Yasmine.'

'I promise I'll still be here when you come back.'

I start to walk then look back at Yasmine.

'I promise. I promised to come back and I did.'

'I waited every day for you at the shop where you left until we couldn't go out any more because it wasn't safe.'

'I'm here now Habibi, go call them…'

I keep looking back making sure she doesn't disappear.

I quickly knock on the room Amira and Ali sleep in and open the door. They are sleeping, just like I said. I don't want to go in and lose sight of Yasmine but she wants me to wake them up and I don't want to upset her. I run inside and shake them a little.

'Yasmine is here! Yasmine is here! Quick!'

Amira jumps up but Ali opens his eyes slowly and then closes them.

'Quick Ali! Before Yasmine leaves!'

'Why is she leaving?'

'I don't know, I just don't want her to leave again!'

'Okay, go Adam, I'll wake Ali up and come.'

'Quick!'

I run out and look at the spot Yasmine was sitting in and find her there. I breathe out slowly and quickly walk to her.

'Do we have enough water for me to wash?'

'Mmm…' Khalid stumbles for an answer. I don't know if we do so I don't say anything.

'Yes we have enough, you can use the water I'm warming up now.' Tariq says.

'Thank you, I'll take a bath then.'

'I'll put the water into the bathtub when it's ready.'

'Enta Malak!'

'Am I an angel too Yasmine?'

'Of course you are!' she laughs and I smile and lie back on the sofa.

Baba was right when he said that after he dreamed of her she would come back.

Ali and Amira come out as Yasmine is walking towards her room. They both hug her and kiss her then at the same time stare at her head.

'I'm pregnant Yasmine!'

'What? Really! Wow!'

'I can't wait!'

'How long has it been?'

'I have no idea, but it feels long.'

I wonder if Yasmine believes Amira because her voice sounds different.

'I'm going to call him Khalid.'

'Aren't you a lucky one?' Yasmine looks back at Khalid.

Khalid winks at her. I love it when we are all together. That's all I can think about. Yasmine is finally back! I have someone to talk to!

Yasmine goes into her room and Tariq pours some more

water to warm up. Amira and Ali come to sit in the sitting room and start talking. Their voices now sound the same. Like they're one person. I don't know why.

I sit outside Yasmine's room and wait for her to come out.

I wait for so long for Yasmine to come out and start getting bored. Why isn't she coming out? I want her to take a bath quickly and come and see my paintings.

'Yasmine, when are you coming out?'

'Why Adam?'

'The water is ready and then I want to show you my paintings.'

'Okay Adam I'm coming.'

'What are you doing?'

'I told you I'm coming Habibi.'

I don't say anything else and just wait for her. I start counting silently, once I get to 57 she comes out and smiles.

'I'll see your paintings in a bit Habibi, I am going to have a bath.'

'Don't take long Yasmine.'

'I won't.'

I go to my room and lie down on my bed and call for Liquorice around the room. I don't see her around and look under the bed. She loves hiding there. I lean down and snap my fingers for her to come out. She comes out and I pull her up.

'Yasmine is back Liquorice! You haven't met her before but she's really nice. She's my favourite person in the world! Are you excited to meet her?'

Liquorice licks her paws. She is so cute. I like the warm feeling with her on my belly. When she purrs my stomach vibrates and it tickles me. It feels funny.

I close my eyes for a bit to rest until Yasmine comes out of the bathroom and wake up to a scream. It seems like that's my daily alarm now. What could it be? Is Yasmine being taken away again? I will not let it happen again!

I come out of my room and follow the scream. It is coming out of the bathroom.

'What is wrong Yasmine?' I shout.

'It's not me,' Yasmine says as she comes up behind me. I sigh deeply. I am glad it's not Yasmine.

'It's Amira,' Yasmine says.

I knock on the door three times but she continues to scream and doesn't say anything.

'Let's just go in!' Yasmine says. I move back because I can't go into the bathroom without being told to come in.

'Move, I'll open the door!' Yasmine opens it and I stand behind her.

Amira is sitting on the floor with blood on her hands and her thighs. Why is she bleeding? Did she scratch herself?

Yasmine covers her mouth in shock like she knows what is going on.

'Khalid Habibi! Khalid!' Amira screams and hits her face with her hands. The blood spreads on her face.

'Yasmine, why is she calling Khalid Habibi?'

'Quickly go get me some of the towels in my cupboard!'

'What is happening Yasmine?'

'I said quick!'

I run out of the bathroom and to Yasmine's room. When I get back Yasmine is holding Amira's head on her chest and Amira is crying and shouting. Yasmine grabs the towels from my hand and tells me to get out and lock the door. I want to know what's going on but I'm scared Yasmine is going to shout at me again. Ali comes up and asks me what's wrong. I tell him what I saw and he sits down on the ground outside the bathroom. What does he know that I don't?

'What does that mean Ali?'

'It means she lost her baby.'

'How? So she was actually pregnant? But she wasn't fat.'

'You don't know how people lose babies?'

'No…'

Ali explains everything to me but I'm still confused. So she had a baby and didn't at the same time? I didn't know babies could die in people's stomachs. I don't even know how she knew she was pregnant as she was still skinny. All of this is confusing and making my head hurt. I knock on the door three times and Amira shouts so we just wait outside. Doesn't she need to go to the hospital? What if she dies from bleeding too much? Yasmine is a nurse so she should know what to do, I think.

Ali and I sit outside for ages biting on our nails. I am so hungry and the dirt on my nails has a salty flavour so I keep on eating it to satisfy myself. I wonder if anybody else does it. I look over at Ali but he isn't doing the same thing. He is just looking into the distance. Yasmine at last opens the door holding Amira who is sweating.

'Yasmine, we have honey.'

'Where?'

'Behind the toilet.'

'Why didn't you tell me earlier? Go get it for me. And Ali go call Tariq.'

We both quickly move and Tariq comes and asks what's going on. It doesn't look like Amira can hear us any more. Her eyes are still open but they look white, like she isn't even with us. I want to tell Yasmine that Amira looks really sick and she needs to go to the hospital but whenever I start saying something Khalid or Yasmine interrupt and speak to each other.

'Can't you do something here? The hospitals are really

busy! It's risky Yasmine.'

'Just carry her and let's go, we are wasting time, I did all I can but she's still bleeding. I think she is in too much shock.'

'Okay!'

Tariq carries Amira over his shoulder slowly and Yasmine runs to her room and comes back wearing a scarf. I follow them out.

'Adam stay home.'

'I want to come Yasmine, I don't want to stay alone.'

Yasmine puffs in and out deeply and holds my hand.

We walk fast to the hospital. It's not that far. When we get there memories from Isa's day rush into my mind and hit me like a hammer on the head. I can see birds flying around my head like in cartoons.

No matter where we go in this city there are always screams and pools of blood on every corner. Every person's blood is a different colour. I stare at a woman whose leg is chopped off who is being carried by a man. The blood dripping from her leg is red with yellow dots. It looks so disgusting but when we pass her the smell isn't that strong.

Yasmine hates it when I stare at people and she pinches me to stop staring. It hurts. I look down and try not to look around or then I'll stare. When we get inside Yasmine speaks to a woman running around in a white coat and she tells us to follow her.

'There are many people injured, I don't know what we can do for your cousin.'

'Please, she just lost her baby, you should know how shocked she is.'

'Other people have been losing their limbs and eyes and ears.'

'Please doctor.'

'Bring her in,' she sighs.

We follow the doctor inside but she tells us to wait outside, only Yasmine is allowed to go in.

Tariq pulls me back and we stand against the wall and wait. People are constantly running around the hospital carrying people or pushing them in wheelchairs.

There is a family of five being pushed in a metal bed with wheels at the bottom. They only covered their bodies and their heads are out. The two boys look like the father and the girl looks like her mother. They have stickers on their foreheads with numbers '1, 2, 3, 4, 5.' They look alive, their eyes are closed but their faces look healthy. I think they have just died now. They all have smiles on their faces. It can't be. I close my eyes and open them again quickly before they pass by me and their smiles are still there. Maybe they're happy to die. They died all together, they don't have to miss each other.

'Why do they have numbers on their foreheads Tariq?'

'The hospital is overcrowded, they need to keep track.'

'Does it happen in every war?'

'I don't know Habibi.'

Everything seems so different here even though it's just down the road from us. There are boys that look younger than me running around with a white doctor's coat on. How does that make sense? I am sure they are young and not just short.

'Tariq, did you see that?' I look at him and point at the young boy pushing an old man in a wheelchair who is bleeding from his right eye.

'They need people, doctors die every day.'

'How do they know what to do?'

'They learn quickly!'

'Can I do it Tariq?'

'NO!'

I look around and don't say another word. Does Tariq like me? He doesn't let me do anything. Why are other kids helping out but I can't? I don't know how to do anything but if they can learn then I can too. But I don't want to be a doctor anyway I want to be a painter.

Yasmine comes out holding onto Amira. Tariq runs to her and carries her on his back. Nobody says anything and we slowly walk out. Everyone's eyes are on us as we walk through blood and tears.

Amira doesn't even look like she is breathing. She is limp on Tariq's back. I try to stare at her closely to see if she is breathing. I think I can see her back move up and down slightly but I can't really tell.

'Is Amira okay?'

'Yes Adam, don't worry.'

'Is she breathing?'

'Yes, where did you get the honey from?'

'It's Amira's, she said it was for her baby.'

Yasmine doesn't reply so I look at her. Her face looks like a puzzle, it's scrunched up and her tears are rolling down through the creases trying to find a way to a smooth surface. It looks like a pinball game. She wipes her tears and looks at me.

'Why are you crying Yasmine?'

'For life…'

'What does that mean?'

'You always know how to make me stop crying,' she says as she laughs.

'Why Yasmine? Why are you crying for life?'

'Because there's no feeling like losing a child.'

'I didn't know she was pregnant Yasmine. I thought she was just saying it.'

'She really was Habibi.'

She wipes her tears again and tells me to run to the door and open it so they can follow. We are not home yet but close enough for me to run and have some fun. I run fast and feel the air hit my face over and over again. It's like someone is slapping me. I like the feeling, it's waking me up.

I open the door and go inside. I keep it open for them and look for Ali. He is still sitting outside the bathroom in the same position. Why has Ali changed so much? He is no fun any more. At least I have Liquorice now.

Tariq lies Amira down and she starts whispering Khalid's name and crying.

'Let's leave her to rest a bit.'

'Yasmine do you want to see my paintings now?'

'Okay, come on, let's have a look.'

I am so excited to show Yasmine my paintings. I skip to my room and start whistling. I wonder why when someone's happy they whistle, skip, jump or move around. I have never seen a happy person just sit in the same place and not do anything. It's like happiness is something we need to shake out of our system straightaway by doing something. I sound clever in my mind but I wonder if I would sound as good if I said it out loud.

I start showing Yasmine my paintings from when she left but she doesn't say anything and keeps her eyes on the painting on the canvas.

'Is that blood Adam?' Yasmine points and her fingers are shaking.

'Yes, does it look good?'

'Where did you get it from?' Her voice is cold. Ice cubes come out of her mouth. It makes me shiver.

'From outside Yasmine.'

'You're gathering other people's blood Adam? Are you crazy?' She shouts really loud: so loud that I have to cover my ears before the ice goes into them.

'Adam! Are you crazy?' Yasmine pulls her hand up and before I can pull my hands down from my ears she slaps my cheek very hard. I hear the sound of her hand on my face echo. My whole body suddenly turns purple and for the first time I feel the way I see Yasmine. Bruised. My mind is like a war zone. I hear bombs go off and see explosions. I move back and fall to the ground and rock myself violently waiting for the war to stop. I HATE WARS. I start crying. The more I cry the quieter the war zone gets. The bombings and explosions lessen and then disappear. I look up and can see Yasmine's mouth moving through my tears. Even though my mind has calmed down I still block out her voice. She puts her hand on my arm and I move back quickly. I don't want her to touch me. I don't know what to do with myself. My mind is shutting down on me. I'm desperate for an answer, for something to make me come back to reality. I am losing the battle. I can feel my eyesight dimming and my heart beating faster. My tears are hot on my face. So hot. It feels like my head is being dipped into hot water. Liquorice comes and rubs her fur on my leg. I can't hear her purring but I know she is. Can she feel that I am upset? I want to run away. The pain on my cheek is stinging me. I can feel the shape of Yasmine's hand. It has made an outline of pain. Liquorice starts walking away and I crawl after her slowly, I don't want her to leave me, I don't want to be left alone with Yasmine.

I run after Liquorice and can hear Yasmine calling out to me. I don't want to answer though. The front door is open and Liquorice runs out.

'No Liquorice! Come back!'

Yasmine says my name. Is Liquorice ignoring me like I am ignoring Yasmine? But I didn't do anything wrong to her. I run after Liquorice and don't look back. I don't know if Yasmine is following me or not. I run so fast.

Liquorice hasn't stopped running. It's like she wants to get away from everything. I run after her and try to forget what happened. I would have had nowhere to go if Liquorice hadn't run out. I am thankful to her.

'Liquorice!'

I see big men in the distance walking down the street. I run faster after Liquorice but I have no energy. I can feel the bones in my right knee pressing on each other. It hurts. I stop and massage my knee because I can't move with the pain. I look up and see one of the men pick up Liquorice and start stroking her. She is not squirming in his hand so I guess he is a good guy. I reach her at last and start panting. If I look back I am sure it won't look like I ran a lot but I still can't stop panting.

'Can I please have my cat back?' I open my arms so the guy can give me Liquorice.

He laughs in my face and some spit lands on my eye. I wipe it off and smell it. It smells like blood.

'This cat is mine now.'

'But she lives with me.'

'What are you? Stupid? She. Is. My. Cat. Now!'

My heart hurts me when he speaks to me like that. Why is he being horrible to me? Have I ever done anything to harm him? Why would he want to take away my Liquorice? I don't even know him. I start to repeatedly click my fingers and tap on my hip. I'm confused. The other men around him don't say a word but I can feel their eyes on me. They're piercing through my head like they're trying to read my mind.

'Walk on boy!'

I start humming loudly so I don't hear what he's saying. I want to drown out everything. This feeling of unease is building up, I try to contain it but it gathers in my mouth, urging me to spit it out. I just want Liquorice back. Liquorice squirms. I think she can read my mind.

'What is wrong with this boy? Does he not know who I am?' The guy looks back at the others. They don't even flinch. Their eyes are still set on me. I want to go home. I'm scared. But I don't want to go anywhere without Liquorice.

'I'll teach you a lesson for getting in my way. I don't have time for stupid boys like you,' he says and looks back at his men.

I quickly jump to pull Liquorice out of his hands and end up pulling her tail. She screeches. I'm sorry Liquorice; I didn't mean to hurt you.

The guy looks into my eyes and I can see evil in him. He has seen a lot of blood. I think he wants to see a lot more blood. I thought he was good at first. I want to go home. I don't care that Yasmine slapped me any more. I just want this horrible feeling to go away.

'Are you going to hurt me?' My voice shakes.

The man laughs again. Why does he keep on laughing? It's rude to laugh at someone who is asking you a question.

'I guess you're catching on,' he sneers.

My mind is popping words like popcorn. I keep staring at the man but the moment I remember to say something it pops; my heart is clenching.

'Liqu...' I whisper but the popping sound in my mind gets louder and I can't finish my sentence. The guy looks down at me, right into my eyes. I close my eyes and put my hands behind my back and scratch them. I wish I didn't bite my nails. I don't like strangers. I want to run away. I want to run away. I keep repeating it in my mind but my legs aren't moving. I am stuck. Voices are reaching my ears but they pop the moment they enter my ear. My mind feels like hot oil. I open my eyes slowly and see the guy throw Liquorice at me. I quickly open my arms but don't catch her in time. Her claws hold onto my leg and pierce through my skin like a knife. I scream from the pain. I can run away now. What am I waiting for? Run! My mind isn't listening to me! I stomp my feet and start running around but I can't run away.

The men all start laughing at me. My face is going red and I feel like my cheeks are going to explode.

'He's asking for it isn't he?' the main guy says and walks towards me slowly like he wants to scare me. I freeze and stare at his feet while rubbing my fingers against each other. I think he wants to help me. I smile a little before he spits at me.

'Yasmine!' I shout and start crying. My voice echoes in my ears and reminds me of the cry of a horse. Whenever I hear someone shouting in pain it reminds me of an animal. Are we all animals when in pain?

'You know what we do to little boys like you?'

I can feel Liquorice scratching at my leg but I can't look down at her. I feel like a statue. The man pushes me down to the ground and I scratch the palm of my hand on a stone. I look down at my hand and twitch my finger. He grabs a gun out of his pocket and points it at me. Why is he pointing a gun at me? I... I'm confused... my head... my head hurts... I pick up the stone under my hand and throw it at him. I never knew I could do such a thing but I can't even think. It's like my hand has a mind of its own.

'Ya Kalb!' the man shouts and I hear the shot of a gun. I didn't know a bullet could travel this fast. The moment I hear the gunshot I feel a burning sensation in my hand. I look at it and see two of my fingers blown off on the ground. My hand is pouring with blood. I scream so loud and cry while screaming. This is the feeling I was talking about before death. The guy is rubbing his eye where my stone hit him. His eyebrow is bleeding and he is spreading the blood all over his face without realising. One of his men is trying to help him but the others don't even flinch. I look around looking for Liquorice and don't find her in front of me. Liquorice. I see her sitting in the corner looking towards me. She looks scared.

'Liquorice come here.' I close my eyes and scream for mama.

The pain in my hand is making me shake and feel dizzy. I keep my eyes closed so I don't have to look down at the blood. I hold onto my hand tighter so I can stop the pain from spreading down my body and then hear the guy speak again.

'I'll show you what it means to mess around with Khanjar!'

I have heard that name before... I have heard that name before. He's a bad guy.

I open my eyes and see him point the gun closer to my face and I say the prayer in my heart. I'm sorry I ran away Yasmine. Where are you?

Two of the men standing behind him suddenly fall to the ground after loud sounds of shooting. I put my wrists on my ears so I don't have to hear the bad sounds. My hand is dripping blood down on my ear. I hate the hot sticky feeling but I want to cover my ears. I look up and see the three men pointing their guns at someone on top of me. I lean down and rock myself while covering my ears. I keep my eyes open. I reach out one hand to my fingers and try sticking them back onto my hand. They're not sticking back! They're not sticking back!

'Are you okay?' A man leans next to me and I start rocking

myself harder and making a sound from my throat to make him go away.

He picks me up and I kick and spit on his back.

'Stop it!'

I ignore him and keep doing it till he puts me down.

'You're fine now, those bastards are being dealt with by my men.'

I just want him to leave me alone.

'Liquoric…'

'Huh?'

I look behind him and see Liquorice coming towards me. I start crying and get up slowly and run before the guy holds me again. I can see Liquorice running after me so I run faster.

Chapter Eighteen

LAVENDER

I WAKE UP to my floor shaking. It feels like it is going to split and suck me in. I jump up quickly and run out of the room. I see Yasmine and Khalid standing outside their doors in their pyjamas. I think they feel it too.

'Yasmine, I'm scared.'

'Don't worry Habibi, it should stop soon.'

I run to her and we wait for the shaking to finish. It feels like we are on a roller coaster that has a problem with it. It is shaking and my heart is constantly falling to the ground and jumping into my throat within seconds. My whole body feels the tremors. We start to hear bombs and can see explosions from the sitting room window. I have never seen so many bombs at once. The bombing seems far away.

'Yasmine let's wake everybody and run to the cupboard room.'

'Okay, you go wake Baba up and I'll wake up the rest.'

I run to Baba's room and jump on the bed and start telling him to wake up quickly. His eyes are still half closed when he starts speaking to himself.

'Don't kill me please, I have a family, I have a wife!'

'Baba! Wake up!'

Baba jumps up and wipes the drool from his mouth.

'What is it?' he slurs.

'There are bombs outside, we need to hide!'

I try to help Baba up when Ali and Amira come in and start

going to the other room.

'Quick Baba!'

Baba starts walking faster but he is still very slow. The cupboard isn't far from the bed but it feels like we have been walking for five whole minutes. I don't know if that's true or if I'm just nervous. Yasmine and the boys still haven't come. I'm really scared.

'I need to go to the toilet.'

'Not now Baba, we don't have time.'

Baba makes a face and we quickly go into the room. I hope we are protected here.

'Yasmine!' I shout from the top of my lungs.

'Coming!'

We sit inside and start praying. The bombs start to get louder and the shaking more violent. I hold onto Baba's arm and squeeze it. I have never liked roller coasters and now I am living on one. My heart is beating fast. I want to vomit from the fear.

'Yasmine quick!'

I close my eyes and try to think about the girl with the chocolate eyes. Whenever I think about her I feel better. But this time my heart is pounding too fast and I can hear it loudly. I can't keep my mind off it. Yasmine comes in with Khalid and Tariq and we close the door quickly. We can hear the bombings and feel the impact on the ground. I cuddle next to Yasmine and feel her breathing in and out. Khalid doesn't say a word: he just looks down at his lap. I look down at my hand and fiddle with the bandage Yasmine put on it for me. My hand sometimes hurts me when I remember what happened but I try to forget. Yasmine said I was lucky to be alive so I shouldn't complain about my hand. I am so lucky it isn't my painting hand. Baba is breathing in and out heavily. There is a weird sound coming out of him like something is stuck in his throat. Nobody seems to mind the sound but the room is too silent and Baba's breathing isn't in the same rhythm with my mind. I want him to stop but I can't stop him from breathing. Now that I think about the small space we have and how many people are all squashed sharing the same air I start to get sick. I want to get out. The more I think about it the more I feel like the walls are closing in on me. No! I need space. Give me space!

'Adam, stop fidgeting!'

I open my eyes and realise that I was hitting Yasmine by accident.

'How long do we have to stay here Yasmine?'

'Please don't start with your questions Adam.'

I just want to know how long we are staying here, my chest is tightening up and I don't think we have been here for more than ten minutes. The ground shakes again and we hear a bomb go off. It sounds like it is just outside our door. Could it really be? I really want to go out and see what is happening but I don't want to get hurt.

'Did you hear that Yasmine?'

'Yes, keep praying…'

Tariq starts praying out loud and we all repeat after him except for Baba who is making his own prayers.

Another loud bomb goes off and the ground shakes. It feels like there are falling angels. Dust starts falling from the ceiling and I start wondering if we are going to survive. I want to ask Yasmine so many questions but my heart is shaking out of fear. There is another shake and bricks fall down around us. One falls down on Ali's leg and he starts screaming. Amira and Yasmine turn to him and try to tend to his wound. His scream sounds like a whale's cry and with the echoes of this small space I feel like I am drowning in hopelessness. I feel my body give up to death. Dust keeps falling down and whenever I look up I get some in my eyes and mouth. I start rubbing my eyes in pain and spitting the dust out. My eyes are burning and they feel red. I don't need to look in the mirror to know that. Bomb after bomb goes off and I stop counting because I feel the look of death on me. There's no space to breathe and there's blood under me from Ali's leg. The biggest bomb of all hits and shakes us all and we all duck down as the bricks fall one by one. That's it. I know it's the end. As every brick falls, it feels like I am being stoned with coal pieces. I can feel my back itching from the blood trickling down. Then everything stops. No more screams from outside, no more bricks falling on us and no more shattering bombs. We all lift our heads slowly and look up. I'm alive! We are alive! We all have blood on us. I can't see myself but I can feel the hot sticky feeling on my back. It feels like a snake is slithering down my body. It makes me shiver.

Yasmine says she thinks it's safe to get out but I'm not sure. Tariq slowly pushes the door open. We can't see his head any more so I guess he is looking around.

'Oh my God! Oh Lord!' Khalid starts calling out for God. What happened? Are dead bodies surrounding us? Yasmine helps Khalid up and goes up herself. I go up next because I can't breathe any more. I need fresh air. When I reach the top I see Yasmine on the floor in Baba's room with her hands slapping her head and yelling God's name. She is crying like the women I saw in the hospital.

I look up and see Baba's bed in place but nothing else is. I can see Yasmine's room from here. The walls have collapsed and everything is gone. Our house is in ruins. Our house is gone. My eyes dart around trying to figure out where to begin. Is there any way we can get out of here? It looks like we are stuck between rubble and heavy bricks. I can see one of my paintings amongst the dust, bricks and cracked plates. I climb over some bricks and try to pull it out delicately but it's gone. My painting is gone. You can't even see the colours any more: it's all grey. I run around trying to reach my room and get my paintings. I need to find them, I can't go anywhere without them. Yasmine calls me back telling me it's not safe but my paintings are more important. I can see my easel broken in the dust and rubble. Navy-blue spiders start climbing my heart again. I feel the anger boil inside me. I pick up the pieces of the easel but there's no hope. I go around and pick my paintings out of all the mess. I have to save them. I find my painting kit lying by one of the books that Isa gave me. I pick the book up. Its pages are partially ripped out and it looks like an elephant stepped on it. All the pages are flat out like a fan. I can't even read the title any more. Why did they have to do this to us? Where else are we going to go? I pick up all the remains of my paint and paintings and all the brushes I can find. The blood I collected is spilt over my duvet. I have no bed to sleep on now, no cover from the cold, no food, no water, no hope and my healing fingers start to bleed again.

We all sit on the rubble and rock ourselves back and forth. Everyone is following a rhythm of their own, but we are all sharing the same pain and fate.

★

The city is in ruins, we are now stripped of everything and the only things surrounding us are Pillars of Faith. Yasmine said that to me. Every night we look for abandoned places to sleep in and rest our heads. When the bomb hit I found Liquorice after hours of searching. I am happy I didn't lose her. Sometimes she sleeps on my stomach and sometimes I lie on hers. She doesn't say anything. Everyone's face looks like they have rubbed themselves in dust and dirt. We have no clean speck on our bodies. Our clothes are ripped and we have no others and we walk the streets every day looking for help. I have no shoes on and the soles of my feet are starting to crack. It really hurts when we walk for a long time looking for a new place to stay. Yasmine says we have to be careful where we go. She said some places are filled with people from the free army and some places belong to the government army. People have already taken the rest of the places that were free. Before yesterday we asked a family if we could stay with them. Yasmine told them we have young ones and old ones who can't walk any more and I think that's what made them say yes. We had to share the same covers with them that they found in the bins. I wanted to itch all night. I couldn't sleep. I kept playing scenarios in my head from books I've read. I wanted to get up and paint but I had nowhere to paint. We were all rolled up under one cover like sardines. If someone had come in and seen us they might even have thought we were dead. Nobody moved and hardly anybody breathed.

There is no more colour in Aleppo. Everything is grey, even we are. Everybody looks like they are dragging every limb of theirs with as much strength as possible and still we are having so much difficulty. Especially Baba, I think he has forgotten everything. He doesn't even know we are in a war. He thinks we are travelling to see his mother. Whenever I ask Yasmine a question about Baba she gets annoyed. She ends up shouting at me and telling me that he lost his memory. I don't think he remembers who I am. I don't know how he can forget me. The only name he keeps on repeating is mama's name to Yasmine. He doesn't even notice the rest of us. His eyes are certainly cloudy, it's not just something I think I am seeing. We are walking down the road far from home. We left days ago and every day we walk for a bit. I don't even know if we are still in Aleppo, I think we are though. The ground is really hot today. It's really sunny and sweaty. We have no water and the sun is hitting us right on our heads. We have no shelter. I can't even open my eyes properly; the sun is really powerful. The soles on my feet are burning because they are cracked and the heat on the ground isn't helping. We walk and I bite all my nails off and chew on them until I get all the taste and swallow them. I am so hungry.

Liquorice runs in front of me but I don't have the energy to run after her.

'Liquorice… please!'

I try to run after her but nothing in my body is helping me. I have no energy. Liquorice turns a corner and I have no choice but to push my legs that extra mile and run after her, I don't want to lose her.

'Liquorice!'

I look back at my family whose shoulders hang down as they drag their feet. Khalid is literally dragging his feet on the ground. I look down and he has blood on his toes. I don't know if I should tell him or not, I don't want to scare him. Tariq is carrying Baba because Baba can't walk any more and Yasmine and Amira are holding onto each other. Ali and I are the only ones who are kind of okay. I turn the corner to find Liquorice and see her rummaging through a bin. My heart skips a beat out of joy and all the grey I am surrounded by slowly turns into pink. There's hope.

'Quick guys, there's a bin here!'

I laugh at how everyone's face turns pink as well. I can even see a slight smile on Yasmine's face. I am so grateful to Liquo-rice. Thank you God for helping us out. I wait for Tariq to put Baba down on the ground so he can help me tip the whole bin up. Liquorice finds a lot of bones and cakes and cheese. How can people throw these away? How do people even have food? How can they afford it? I ask Yasmine and she tells me it's probably from Damascus and it's the soldier's food. When she says that she realises we might be sitting in an area where government soldiers are around. It's not safe. She tells us to collect all the food and carry it in a bag we found inside the bin and walk somewhere else. We all walk quickly this time. I feel happy again, maybe there is hope. Thank you God.

★

We all sit down and start eating and even laughing. We have the energy for it now. I always wondered how people lived during a war when I used to watch TV and how they used to laugh, weren't they too depressed? Now I understand, there's always a reason to laugh.

Yasmine is starting to look ruby. I can see the pink becom-ing darker and turning into ruby, which makes me very happy. The colour is very faint but I can see it. Everyone's eyes look like they are starting to close and mine are too. Eating for the first time after so long makes you want to go to sleep. This time we are sleeping happy, not sleeping because we need to curb our hunger. It feels really good. I start humming a Chopin tune in my mind. I don't know the name of the song but mama always used to listen to it when she was happy. It's been a while since I thought of mama because I have had no energy to even think, I have just been dragging my body. The melody I'm humming is starting to sound like a buzzing in my mind because I am too tired so I just close my eyes and let sleep take me to a happy place.

I wake up to the loud sound of a man speaking through a speaker that is used at the top of a mosque where they usually call out for a prayer. What is he saying?

I rub my eyes and look around. The sun starts to go down a little but it's still there. Everyone else starts to get up and listen to what is being said. This is unusual, what is going on? My legs have pins and needles and I slowly get up and shake them off. I have marks on my arms from the stones that were poking into my skin.

'Ahh it hurts,' I say as I rub my skin and kiss it so I can make myself feel better.

'Shh Adam, let's hear what they're saying,' Tariq whispers.

We all look up as if the sound is coming from the sky and listen quietly. There's something peaceful about looking up at the sky and hearing a loud voice giving you a message of hope. I want to paint the sky.

The speaker was saying something about Turkish aid but I stopped listening once I thought about painting the sky. I start to take my painting things I rescued from the bag but Yasmine stops me.

'What are you doing?'

'I'm going to paint the sky.'

'Did you not hear what they said Habibi?'

'No Yasmine.'

'We need to walk back before others get there, there's help that came for us, we will have food and shelter at last Adam!'

'Really Yasmine? Really? Let's run then!'

She laughs and holds my hand and we start running. The others are running behind us. I look back and can see Tariq behind us all trying to run with Baba on his back. Is this really the end? Are we safe now? I pray to God that we are saved. I don't want to walk on the hot ground any more and eat from bins. I wonder where they will take us. We get to the place where they told us to go and we already find a queue of people. How did they get here so fast? I guess they were closer. There are three red-and-white vans and there are men giving out things from inside. They're giving a box to everyone but I don't know what is inside it. The men look red. They're speaking a different language to us. I wish I understood what they were saying. I wish I understood all languages. I used to daydream that I would hear people speaking different languages and I would understand and they would be shocked. But nobody speaks anything but Arabic around here. Khalid said that in Damascus people speak other languages. I want to go there. We are nearly at the front of the van. There are six people in front of us now. I can't wait to get to the front and see what is in the box. It feels like it's Eid. Who are these people helping us? They don't speak the same language even though they kind of look like us. Are they good people? They must be good if they're helping us. No one else is.

I hear them say a word in Arabic that means 'in God's will'. But it sounds different when they say it. Do they know Arabic?

We are at the front of the line now and the man gives Yasmine a box and then gives a box to me. Then he starts smiling and saying things to me that I don't understand. I look to the side to see if Yasmine knows what to do. She just says 'thank you' in Arabic and walks away. I really wish I knew what he was saying.

Yasmine holds onto my arm really tightly. She isn't looking at me though, she's looking at a guy walking towards us.

Is he going to hurt her? I won't let anyone hurt Yasmine any more.

'What's wrong Yasmine?'

Yasmine doesn't reply and holds me tighter. The guy is next to us now and says 'hi' to her. Yasmine doesn't reply, she just stares at him. What's going on?

'Wisam…'

He laughs and puts his hand on her shoulder.

'How have you been?'

Yasmine lets go of my arm and her face goes so red like she is going to pour strawberry juice. The guy is looking at her the way Baba used to look at mama. There's something familiar about him. Is he the guy I read about in the diary?

'I… I'm good…'

'I never stopped thinking about you…'

'Neither did I!' Yasmine jumps and speaks fast. I have never seen her act this way. I think she realises she spoke too fast because she moves back a little and looks down.

'I hope you come to Turkey with me…'

'Are you…'

'I work with them. I'm in and out of Syria constantly nowadays.'

'We are going to Damascus God willing.'

'You are?'

'Yes…' Both them are fiddling with their hands in the same way.

'Yasmine is he the man you love?' I ask her.

Yasmine turns to me shocked.

'How… How do you…?'

Wisam laughs and I tell her I read her diary. She goes really red again and pinches my arm but it's not like the way she always does. I don't mind her pinching it like this; it doesn't hurt and it feels playful.

'Can I… Can I come look for you when I come back?'

'Yes!' Yasmine jumps in again.

I think she is too excited.

Wisam leans in and whispers something into her ear and Yasmine giggles. I want to know what he said.

'What did he say Yasmine?'

Yasmine doesn't answer and she stares at him as he walks away. He turns around and waves at her and she waves back. She doesn't say anything for a long time. Her eyes look far away.

Yasmine and I wait for the others to get their boxes and queue in another line where they have forms for us to fill in. I don't know what it is about but we queue so we can ask. I really want to open the boxes but Yasmine tells me to wait. We get to the front and ask a Syrian man what the forms are for and he tells us they have spaces for people to go to Turkey but they are only going to take the people in need so everyone has to fill in a form with their age and information. Yasmine fills it out for everybody and we wait at the side and open our boxes.

'Yasmine, is Turkey nice?'

'It's just like Syria Habibi, just a different language.'

'Is it safe Yasmine?'

'Very safe.'

'What if they don't pick us?'

'Aunt Suha invited us over anyway, we will head to Damascus, it's safe there.'

'I want to go to Damascus too.'

Yasmine smiles and tells me to open my box. I slowly open it because I don't want to ruin the excitement. On the top there is a plastic bag with a tent with instructions inside. I have always wanted to go camping. At least now I have a tent and we don't have to sleep in the open air. Under it there are thin blankets made from a weird material I have never felt before. We have bottles of water and food and bread and shampoo. I am so happy now. This is the best present ever! I want to start fixing my tent.

The Syrian man calls for everyone's attention and starts calling out names for people to walk in front and get into the van. The family in front of us starts crying because only two of them got in. The mother is screaming and crying and her daughter is pulling her into the van.

'I'll see you soon,' she calls out to her children. The vans start filling up quickly and none of us have been called. I don't think there is any more space for all of us. I don't want us to be separated. The man starts apologising for the lack of seats and a woman comes running up to him, begging him to let her and her family through. She is on her knees kissing his feet. The guy tries to move her away gently and asks for her name. She tells him her name and he says she is not on the list. She falls to the ground again and begs him. He calls for the Turkish people to help and they slowly carry her away. I feel sorry for her.

The man suddenly calls Baba's name and I wait for him to call all of us but he doesn't. Only Baba gets to go through. Tariq puts Baba down now for the first time and stretches.

'Baba did you hear that?' Yasmine leans down and asks him. Her voice sounds like vanilla ice cream. Yasmine is not sad any more.

'What?'

'You're going to be safe again and we will follow you later.'

'Okay.'

I expected Baba to say more but it must be because he isn't feeling well.

'Yasmine, are we going to leave Baba alone?'

'It breaks my heart but we can't carry him the whole way.'

'But he's Baba.'

'I know Habibi, but we have to, they didn't call our names.'

I blow Baba a kiss on the forehead and hand and smile at him. I also blow him a kiss on the bags under his eyes and make a small prayer. I pray that I see him again soon so he will remember who I am.

'Excuse me, is he coming?' the Syrian man comes up to us and asks. Yasmine says 'yes' and the two Turkish guys behind come with a wheelchair and pick Baba up. They start pushing him away. No, I don't want them to take Baba. My heart becomes black the moment he turns around and they push him away. He is my father, he is meant to stay with me.

'No Baba, come back!' I run to him and try to stop them. Yasmine and Tariq run after me and try to stop me. Tariq carries me and tells them to take Baba away. I kick and hit Tariq to let me go but he doesn't. Upside down on Tariq's back, I watch the vans drive away with Baba. The moment they leave I stop doing everything and just give up. My heart hurts me. Baba didn't even say goodbye because he doesn't know what is happening. I wish he had waved. Liquorice squirms in Ali's arms and runs to me.

Chapter Nineteen

MAGENTA

WE'VE BEEN WALKING for 11 sunsets and dawns. My feet have split and bled so many times. The blood is dry now because we slept for the night inside another ruined building. I found it this time. I want to be happy about that but I can't. All colour is gone in my life. I see nothing but grey. Even when I paint my surroundings the only colour I ever need to use is grey. We all sleep inside our tents whenever we find a place that isn't too exposed. I don't close my tent when I sleep. I feel too suffocated. When I am isolated I start to imagine bad things coming out to hurt me. Like snakes and spiders and monsters. The only way I go to sleep every night is by reciting the Quran in my heart. If I don't my mind starts wandering off to far away places and I can't sleep from fear and nostalgia. I told Yasmine what I think about and she said I was nostalgic. That's how I learnt the word. I like the way it sounds. It has three syllables and I like all words with three syllables, like fortunate and lunatic and subsequent. I used to search the Internet for words with three syllables. They always sound the best. I get out of my tent once I notice some light outside and go to my box and take a sip of my water. I have been taking a sip every day just to wet my throat but not finish it any time soon. I don't know when I will be able to drink water next if I finish it all. I have been tempted so many times to just drink it all, my throat itches for it, but I put it in the box and close it before I do something I regret. Every day we walk till we can't any more and most of us vomit and cry from the pain. Yesterday it was Amira and I who vomited and I was crying for us to stop walking and just rest somewhere. Before yesterday it was Ali and Amira. Amira talks to herself most of the way. She laughs and cries and shouts to herself. I don't know who she thinks she is speaking to. But sometimes she turns to us and asks us if we heard what the other person said because she didn't hear it. When she cries it's usually about losing her baby and she sits on the ground and doesn't move. We have to wait until she is calm again for us to walk. Yasmine just wants to get to Damascus as soon as possible. She says we will be safe there. I can't wait. I wish there was an easier way to get there. Yasmine gets up and starts waking everybody up now.

'Come on, we need to get to Damascus!'

'How long do we have left Yasmine?'

'I don't know Adam, long…'

'I just want to be there.'

'We all do Habibi. God willing we'll get there soon.'

We all get up and pack our things and start walking while pushing our boxes in front of us. The sun isn't too strong today. I look up at the sky and don't have to squint my eyes too much. We have just entered a new town. It looks really small because I can see the end of the houses, after that the street is empty just like the street we just came from. We walk in and I pray someone from this town will give us some food. I think this is more a village than a town. We walk past three kids running around and throwing stones at each other. It looks like they're having fun but I have never heard of this game before. This makes me think of my friend Nabil and the games we used to play together. Those were really fun.

The kids are laughing while playing so it must be fun. I want to join them now.

'Can I play with the kids Yasmine?'

'Don't be silly Adam! You're not a kid!'

I don't say anything and walk on. I am bored of walking. Yasmine knocks on the first house we reach and an old woman answers the door.

'Yes sister?' Everyone calls each other sister and brother here.

'We have been walking all the way from Aleppo and we are hungry and tired, do you think we can rest here for a bit?'

The woman looks at all of us and counts us.

'With pleasure sister but I don't have enough food for all of you, I have children to feed.'

'I understand, anything will do, we aren't asking for much.'

For the first time since Baba left us I see colour in a person. She is pink. I feel happy that there is still colour in Syria.

'Come in sister.'

We all go in and sit in the sitting room. The TV is on and they are watching an old Syrian drama that mama used to watch. The woman comes back from the kitchen and gives us all water. She looks at Amira and asks if she is okay.

'Your face is green.'

'I lost my baby.'

The woman's face turns green too and she doesn't say anything. She sits next to Yasmine on the sofa and starts telling her about her husband who died in Aleppo. She talks for 20 minutes. Tariq and Khalid are asleep and Amira is playing with Ali's hair with him on her lap. Liquorice is being a good girl and is just lying on my lap. She must be tired. The woman gets up and goes to the kitchen again. Yasmine and I look at each other and laugh quietly. My heart feels like honey is melting inside it. We are safe in a house and Yasmine is laughing.

THE BOY FROM ALEPPO WHO PAINTED THE WAR

'How much can someone talk?' Yasmine whispers.

'Did you listen to everything?'

'No, I lost her at her son wanting to be a doctor and he is only five years old!'

'I didn't even hear that bit!'

Both of us laugh again and the woman comes back in and I go back to being silent. I can't speak to people I meet for the first time. The two little girls that were playing outside are now bringing in two plates of food. The smell fills my mouth with water. I try to remember the last time I ate fresh food but I can't remember. My mind makes a map and I try to trace everything back but all I can think about is that there is food in front of me. I am happy that everyone has their own plate of food otherwise I wouldn't be able to eat. Yasmine wakes Khalid and Tariq up and we all start eating. As I start to get full I look around and can see colour again in everybody's faces. I want to thank this woman for bringing colour back into our lives. I finish eating quickly and take my painting kit out of the bag.

The woman is sitting down watching TV. The moment I start painting she stares at me.

'He paints all the time,' Yasmine explains to her. The woman doesn't stop staring though. I can't paint with someone staring at me. I want to paint this scene because it looks like a broken rainbow but the woman is disturbing me. I don't know what to do. I turn to the side and start painting again. I paint quickly before everyone finishes their food. I get them all in the painting! I look at it and smile, it looks perfect. I want to show it to Baba.

We leave the house and Yasmine and Amira kiss the woman six times on each cheek and pray for her safety and for God to protect her children. I don't know why women do that. They are not kissing each other's cheeks with their mouths yet they make the kissing sound. It's annoying to watch.

We walk on now and I have so much energy I put my box down and start running.

'Don't waste your energy Adam! We have a long way!' Yasmine shouts.

'Do you know the way Yasmine?' I shout back.

'Yes I do.'

I get back to my box and start walking with all of them now. I am panting from running up and down but it feels good. I have a lot of energy. I have colours buzzing inside me.

A bus drives up and passes us and the people inside are all staring at us. Tariq runs after it and bangs on the side of it. The bus stops and Tariq gets on to speak to the driver. We run to catch up. Tariq then pops his head out of the door and gestures for us to come. We all run. I pick Liquorice up and hide her in the box so they don't take her away from me. Today is starting off very good. I am excited about sitting down on a bus and not having to walk. The driver lets us get on without having to pay. I don't know what Tariq told him but I am glad the guy is kind enough to let us on. There are four spaces at the back where Yasmine, Amira, Ali and I sit and Khalid and Tariq sit in the middle, where they find a seat each. I am so excited. I take Liquorice out of the box and put her on my lap. She is very quiet so it's easy to take her to places. I start jumping up and down on my seat and singing. Yasmine laughs and starts singing with me. This is the best day ever.

A grumpy man sitting in front of us turns around and tells us to be quiet. His mouth and nose are scrunched up like a bulldog. Yasmine and I look at each other and laugh quietly. I look outside the window and notice how everything is green around us. There are only trees and grass all around. I wonder where we are. I don't even know where this bus is going.

'Do you know where the bus is going Yasmine?'

'I don't know, Tariq must know.'

'Can I ask him?'

'Just rest Habibi, we'll ask later.'

I rest my head on the window and feel the bumps and shakes of the bus. It feels like it's turning my brain into scrambled eggs. I can't sleep like this. I continue to stare out of the window. I notice several tents in the middle of nowhere by the trees and two women are standing outside them talking. Did they move there or are they walking to Damascus like us?

I see police cars and men holding big guns in front of us. They are wearing the green army uniform.

'Look, look Yasmine!'

'Oh no!… God help us, don't say a thing Adam, pretend you're asleep!'

The bus stops and I close my eyes and lie back. My heart is beating fast and loud. What if they hear it? It reminds me of the story 'The Tell-Tale Heart' by Edgar Allan Poe. When I first read it I couldn't finish it all because I was too scared and then when I finished it I loved it. What if my heart tells on me too? I shut my eyes tight and try to block out my thoughts. I can hear a man speaking at the front. His voice sounds like a soldier. They have different voices like they have been voice trained. His footsteps are heavy and sound like they have a mind of their own. I start to imagine the conversations he would have with his legs if they had a mind of their own.

'Go right, leg!'

'No, I don't want to!'

'Damn it, go right I said!'

'You can't control me!'

Then he starts punching his legs and realises that he likes the pain. I want to laugh to myself because the scene is funny but I try my best to hold it in. His footsteps get closer and heavier.

'Sir, your ID?'

My heart drops. Is he speaking to me? I have no ID. Should I open my eyes?

'Sir, your ID please?' he repeats louder. I open my eyes slowly and swallow the saliva building in my mouth. I try to control myself; I don't want them to take me to jail. I open my eyes and find the soldier three seats in front of me. I breathe out really loudly. The soldier looks at me for a split second and back at the guy. I hold tightly onto Yasmine's skirt.

'I don't have my ID,' the guy says. His voice is shaking.

'Please come with us.'

'Please don't take me, I have a family, please.'

'Sir, please come quietly with us.'

He pulls him up from his seat and ties his hands behind his back.

'Please leave my husband alone! Please!' The woman next to him shouts and leans towards the soldier.

'Sit down,' the soldier shouts at her. The whole bus is silent.

The woman screams and begs and runs after them to the door but they push her in and close the door. She lies on the floor at the front of the bus crying.

'Please someone help my husband! Please!'

Nobody says anything, they all look down.

I stand up a little to see the husband outside.

'Sit down Adam!' Yasmine hisses. I slowly sit down but I can still see them. I put my feet under my legs to boost me up. They push the guy against the bus and I feel the bus move a lit-

THE BOY FROM ALEPPO WHO PAINTED THE WAR

tle. I can see the man's lips moving but I don't know what he is saying. The bus starts to move but I keep my eye on the man. Is he not coming back with us? Are they really taking him?

'Yasmine…' Before I get to ask her my question we hear a gunshot and everyone turns around. The man is now on the ground with blood pouring out of his head. Yasmine tries to pull me down and cover my eyes but I have already seen him. I saw him fall to the ground. I saw them kill him. The wife is screaming and banging on the window.

'Are you okay Adam?'

I can hear Yasmine asking me if I'm okay but I can't answer. Why are soldiers killing people? They should be protecting people. Who are we even in a war against? Ourselves?

'Why do we have a war Yasmine?'

'I wish I knew,' she says.

'But who is fighting against who?'

'The government against the free fighters.'

'But we are one country Yasmine, why would they do that? Why would the government kill Syrians? What about the national anthem? We are meant to be together.'

'If only everybody thought like that. Politics are complicated Habibi.'

'I don't like politics. They confuse me. Why do people lie?'

'For greed…'

'But we are not greedy Yasmine so why are we in the war?'

'We can't do anything about that, don't worry Habibi, we'll get to Damascus and be safe for a while.'

'How long is a while?'

'As long as possible Adam.'

★

I wake up to Yasmine whispering in my ear.

'Wake up Habibi, this is the last stop.'

'Are we in Damascus?' I jump up.

'Not yet, but we are closer now.' I get up and put Liquorice back in the box and leave the bus. I watch the bus drive away and wish it could take us all the way to Damascus.

'Is everyone ready to walk?' Yasmine shouts.

We start walking. It is starting to get dark, the sun is setting. I think about the food we had at the woman's house and get hungry again. I look back at the road we came down and realise how far we are from home. I have never been this far away from it and for this long. I wonder if we will ever have a new home.

'Look there's a town! I can see lights!' Tariq shouts.

'Can we rest there?'

'Of course! Come on let's get going.'

We all walk faster. I hope there are nice people there who will look after us again. I feel bad that we have to ask people for help because I don't like to. This actually looks like a town, not a village. There are people walking down the streets. I notice some buildings that have collapsed and some blood trails on the ground. It looks like Aleppo before our house got bombed.

'Yasmine can you please tie my hair back again?' Khalid asks. We all have long hair now because we haven't cut it in ages. We all tie it back because it gets annoying but Khalid can't, he always asks Yasmine. Before he used to be shy to ask but now it's fine. I always ask Khalid if he needs any help because I know that living without hands must be annoying. He always smiles when I ask him so I always do. Liquorice runs ahead of me and makes a weird noise I haven't heard before. I notice another cat approaching her and they start talking together in cat language. I hope she is telling the other cat that she's happy with me. A man runs up to us and picks up the other cat.

'There you are, now stop running away, we are all hungry.'

The cat squirms in his hands and Liquorice hisses. When the man spoke he had bad breath that reached me. There's something wrong about him.

'You're lucky you've got your meal too, many families are looking for something.' He looks down at Liquorice. I don't understand what he is saying.

'Excuse me?' Tariq asks.

'Huh?'

'What do you mean we have our meal?'

'The cat.'

'The cat? We don't eat cats!'

I pick Liquorice up and stroke her in my arms. This man is going to steal my cat.

'Did you not hear? We have no food so the sheikhs allowed us to start eating cats so we don't starve to death.'

I really don't like this man. No one is going to eat my cat.

'Thank you,' Tariq says and the man walks off.

'Tariq how can people eat cats?'

'Well we are not in a normal situation, people starve.'

'No, no! No one is going to eat Liquorice!'

'Okay don't worry, calm down maybe we can find another cat.'

I can't believe Tariq is saying that.

'Adam don't give me that face, there is no food, no food anywhere!'

'We ate food at the woman's house.'

'That was probably cat meat too actually...'

No, no, I didn't eat a cat! My heart starts to hurt me, I feel sick. Green smoke forms a cloud around my heart, it's pushing it down.

We set our tents in the town and I hold onto Liquorice the whole time in case someone takes her. There are other tents around so it doesn't feel too lonely. We set our tents next to a family who start speaking to us. The woman is speaking to Yasmine and the man to Khalid. The rest of us sit around and just listen. I hear the lady tell Yasmine that she takes her children to school every morning even though they don't have a house. It got bombed just like ours. How come we don't have school? I wish we did. A woman with hair that looks like she got an electric shock is holding a dirty pillow and talking to it. I keep staring at her and she looks at me and starts shouting. I hold onto Yasmine who tells me not to look at her.

'She lost her son when they came walking in a crowd from Aleppo,' the woman explains. 'She thinks the pillow is her son now.'

'Poor woman,' Yasmine says and tells me it's okay.

I go into my tent and close it to paint. I can hear voices outside so I don't mind closing it. My paper is nearly finished. I don't know what I will do when it finishes. I used both sides of every page and I have two left. I start painting the tents and the kids running around and then remember I left Liquorice outside. I quickly open the zip and look around. I just left her outside my tent, where did she go?

'Yasmine... Yasmine! Where's Liquorice?'

'I don't know, I haven't seen her.'

'They're going to eat her Yasmine! Don't let them eat her!'

'Who will?'

'The people who took her!' I run around looking and calling out for her but I don't see her anywhere! I see a black bag next to the bins and my heart tells me it's Liquorice. I go up to the bag and realise it is just a bag and I throw it on the floor.

'Liquorice, come back to me!'

I hear a scratching sound coming from the bins and my heart opens up like a flower because I know it's her. I know I have found Liquorice. She loves bins. I tip the bin up and Liquorice jumps on one of the bags. I laugh and pick her up and stroke her. Thank God she is alive. She smells like rubbish. She squirms out of my hands and jumps into the bin bags again and finds her food. I squat down beside the bin and play with the rocks on the floor until she finishes eating.

'I found her Yasmine!'

'I knew you would Habibi!'

'Goodnight.'

'Goodnight.'

I go into my tent again and continue painting, with Liquorice on my lap this time. I add my tent to the picture and paint myself with Liquorice so it looks like someone else has painted us all.

Chapter Twenty

CHESTNUT

'HELP! HELP! People of Syria, help!' I rub my eyes quickly and behind the zipped tent I see shadows of people walking around slowly with their hands out and their clothes ripped up and dangling. They look like the shadows of zombies walking around the city. I am scared to unzip my tent. Liquorice is still asleep on my stomach so I pick her up and gently put her down and unzip the tent. I say my prayers while doing so. Nobody is around. Where did they all go? I am scared. None of their tents are up, did they all leave me? I walk on and see people walking around with blood on their bodies, moaning and screaming. I think another bomb went off. Wherever we go we are followed by disaster. We have no luck.

'Yasmine! Yasmine!' I see Yasmine kneeling down on the floor wiping blood off someone.

'Go back!'

'What happened?'

'Just go back!' Yasmine shouts at me. The man she's wiping the blood from screeches like the tyres of a car in an accident. What is happening? What did I miss? I didn't even hear anything while I was asleep. I see a man lying on the ground with his head split open and his brain coming out. I stop and cover my mouth in shock. I have never seen anything like this. I have seen blood every day for a long time but I have never seen a brain. I close my eyes and run even though I can't see where I am running. I can feel myself getting sick. How did that happen? How did his brain come out? I wonder if he will have flies all over him later when they smell the pool of blood. It looked thick and deep. I stop and open my eyes because I can feel the vomit coming out. I have no time to move, I vomit straightaway. There was nothing under me; I vomited on the ground thank God.

I get up and walk on to look for everybody else. I find a shell covered in blood on the floor and lean down to pick it up. The moment I pick it up I throw it back down and scrunch my face in disgust. It felt soft and gooey. What is it? I go to it and lean down and stare. The shape looks familiar. I am sure I have seen something like this before but I have never felt anything like that. It's an ear! It's an ear! Oh my God! Does it belong to the man with his brain on the ground? I want to walk back to check if he has his ear but I am scared of feeling sick again. I clench my heart and grab the ear again. It feels just as disgusting as the first time but I hold my breath and wipe the blood on my trousers. It looks beautiful. I didn't know an ear could be this beautiful. I put it in my pocket and walk on.

I see Ali running around with clothes dripping blood.

'Adam! I'm scared!' Ali comes up to me holding the clothes in a disgusted way.

'Let's go to my tent!'

'People need our help!'

A woman running to my right is carrying a young girl. The girl's whole body is brown and white like she has been burnt. How did this happen? There is no blood on her, just burns all over her body. One of her shoes falls off while she is being carried away. It's a white shoe with a flower on the side. There is no blood on it. She doesn't say a single word or even moan in pain.

'Let's go Adam, I'm scared!'

'Where are you going to put those?' I point at the clothes in his hands.

'I don't know!' He puts them down by the white shoe and we run to my tent.

'What happened Ali?'

'There was a bomb in the morning at the school, but it wasn't a normal bomb, the people have burn marks all over their bodies.'

'What bomb could it be then?'

'I don't know, we all tried to help.'

'Nobody woke me up!'

'We all woke up at the same time and rushed to help.'

'Why is this happening wherever we go?'

'I don't know, I'm scared, I can't wait to get to Damascus!'

'Neither can I, I hate the war!'

Ali lies down on his side and closes his eyes. He is purple. I turn the page around and start painting him. If anything happens I hope someone finds these pictures and sees everything we went through.

Ali suddenly wakes up.

'Let's run away?'

'Huh?'

'Let's run away, find a bus and let it take us to Damascus. I don't want to stay here. I am having nightmares. I don't want to die, I miss my family and I dream about them every day, I'm scared.'

I don't know what to say. I'm not good with telling people what they should do or dealing with emotions.

'Can I paint you?'

'Okay.'

'Go back to sleep.'

'I'm scared.'

'Just close your eyes.'

I paint Ali but I make one eye very big and sketch the white shoe and bloody white clothes in his eye. The other eye is closed. I think this is my best painting.

'You can open your eyes.'

'I'm fine now, I'm thinking of something good...'

'What are you thinking about?'

'Damascus, I heard they have a lot of swings and slides.'

'I heard they have water parks like we see on TV.'

'Let's go together!'

We both smile and I tell him he's my best friend now.

Yasmine comes into the tent with blood on her face and her clothes.

'Do any of you have water?'

'I do Yasmine.'

'Can I have some?'

'You can have all of it, it's your turn to drink today.'

She drinks it all quickly like she has a sea monster in her throat who is thirsty for the water.

'Don't move boys, we'll be back and we'll move. We are close to Damascus. Just another few days.'

'Really Yasmine?'

'Really Adam.'

'I want to eat a lot of food there.'

'I will make sure you do Habibi, now I have to go nurse the injured people.'

She runs out and I lie down opposite Ali and take the ear out. It is now clean, I think the blood rubbed off in my pocket. There is still dry blood where the ear was cut off but it isn't a lot. I pull it up to my mouth and start whispering about what I dream of doing in Damascus.

★

We leave the city by evening; the sun is starting to set. Everybody looks like they are going to drop on the ground. They are walking like the zombies I saw this morning. I can't wait to get out of this city. I didn't like it the moment I saw the man chasing after the cat. I am glad I have Liquorice with me so nobody can eat her. I have slept all day so I don't want to sleep yet. I am just hungry and thirsty. I start painting in my mind while walking so I don't have to see the war around me. I think of the Nutella-eyed girl and wonder if she is still alive. I hope she is, I want to see her again one day. I paint her eyes in my mind but I can't continue because mama's eyes keep coming into my mind too. Why do mama's eyes always come up when I think of the Nutella-eyed girl?

I have so much to ask and say but Yasmine is holding my hand so tight that it scares me. I don't know where we are going, but I know it's not good. When Yasmine is with me I can smile even when I'm scared. I smile even though I don't have a reason to. Smiling is charity, so I keep smiling till I can't keep hold of my questions.

'Where… are we going Yasmine?'

I look up at Yasmine but can only see the sun shining in my face. I cough and try to get rid of the dirt in my throat. I see Yasmine's eyes look down at me through the sun. It looks like the sun has eyes. It's looking down at us.

'Far away from here Habibi.'

We pass by a river and find boats tied to a dock. I have always wanted to ride a boat.

'Wait here,' Khalid says and runs towards the boats. Tariq runs after him. I wonder what they're thinking.

'Are you okay Yasmine?'

'I can't wait to sleep!'

'I don't want to sleep yet.'

'You haven't been working all day.'

'I know I haven't Yasmine.'

She doesn't say anything and turns back around. I don't know why she is upset. I didn't do anything.

Tariq and Khalid come back with huge smiles on their faces and tell us to follow them.

'Where are we going Khalid?'

'Just follow...'

We go to the biggest boat on the dock and they tell us to get on. Yasmine laughs and asks if we are actually doing this. She is happy again. She is happy and sad and angry at the same time.

Tariq pushes the door open with his back and it opens quickly and we all go in. The boat has beds in it and a kitchen and a bathroom. I can't believe what I am seeing. My heart is filled with rainbows. I jump up and down and clap my hands and look at Yasmine and give her a huge smile. I am so happy.

'Thank you Tariq!'

'No Habibi, thank God!'

'Thank you God!'

I jump on a bed and roll around on it.

'We have beds!'

'I'm sleeping here!' Tariq says pointing at one quickly.

'I am sleeping here!' Khalid points at the other one and laughs.

'I already rolled on this bed, it's mine!' I jump in.

Everybody laughs and I get up and run to the bathroom. I actually have a bathroom to go to! I don't need bushes and leaves, I don't need to hide and be scared of insects! Thank you

God. 'There's a shower!' I say loudly and everybody turns and has the same colour pink.

After everybody showers we sit in the middle with the lights on and play I spy. There is actual light. I am so happy. I don't want to leave this place.

'Are we going to leave tomorrow or are we going to stay Yasmine?'

'We will leave.'

'Why? It's perfect!' Tariq jumps in.

'Damascus is safer, we are in the middle of nowhere and this isn't our boat.'

Nobody says anything to Yasmine. We all have to listen to her.

'We are close to Damascus right?'

'Yes, very…'

'Where's the map Yasmine?'

'In my box, I'm tired, I'm going to sleep.'

'Do you have to?'

'Yes I do Habibi, I'll see you in the morning.'

I look at Amira lying down on the ground and notice something wrong with her. Her face looks scrunched up like a piece of paper. Is she in pain?

'What's wrong Amira?'

She looks at me and her eyes look yellow.

'Nothing.'

She is holding her stomach really tight. Does she still think she is pregnant?

I notice dry blood on her fingers.

I walk towards her and sit by her. She doesn't look my way.

'Amira, you're bleeding!'

She looks at me and lifts one of her hands up and pushes

me away.

Everybody looks at us now and Ali jumps up and comes to us.

'Amira, did you get hurt?' Ali asks.

'My baby is begging me to take him out.'

'What do you mean?'

'I need to take my baby out!'

'Amira you don't have a baby!' I shout. I don't know what else to say. I can see more blood coming out of her stomach. I think she stabbed herself.

'Did you stab yourself?'

'I wanted to take my baby out!' she shouts and tries to get up. She pushes herself up but her body won't let her move.

'Stay down Amira!' I run to the bathroom to get some tissues and notice scissors on the sink with blood on them. Everything makes sense now. I run to Amira and put the tissue on her stomach and see it soak up in seconds. I think it's very deep. I can't see under her shirt but the bleeding is a lot. There is a door in the middle of the boat and Yasmine is on the other side sleeping. I open the door quickly and wake Yasmine up. Her eyes are half closed and she looks upset.

'Amira is bleeding!'

'Not again!'

'She stabbed herself.'

'What?' Now she jumps up.

Yasmine never gets to rest, I feel sorry for her but none of us know what to do. Khalid and Tariq are sitting outside the boat. I don't know what they're doing.

'Amira what did you do?'

Amira looks up at Yasmine and doesn't say anything. Her face is green and purple. The colours together make me feel like snakes are slithering inside of me. I shiver from how disgusting it is.

'Boys get me water and tissues.'

We get up and get them and Amira starts screaming. What is Yasmine doing to her? Is Amira going to be okay?

'Here you go Yasmine.'

Yasmine now starts cleaning the wound under Amira's shirt and I can see how deep it is. Why doesn't Amira understand that she's not pregnant?

'I don't know, I don't know! I have no equipment!'

'Who are you talking to Yasmine?' I ask.

'Myself! Myself! All of you drive me crazy! Problem after problem!'

I didn't do anything to upset Yasmine, why am I everyone?

'She's bleeding a lot,' Ali says. Khalid and Tariq walk in and ask what's wrong. Nobody answers so I tell them what happened.

'Oh Lord!'

'Is Amira going to be okay?'

'I don't know Adam, what she did isn't simple.'

'But she is going to be okay right?'

'Adam, you're always asking the same questions!' Khalid gets annoyed and I start spitting on the floor.

'No Adam!'

I continue spitting because I don't like people shouting.

'Adam, calm down Habibi.' Khalid leans down to me.

I don't want him to shout at me so I spit to show him I am angry.

'Adam we discussed spitting a long time ago and you stopped, don't get back into it.'

'I want to go home!'

'Shut up both of you! The girl is dying. What do I do?'

'I can't deal with blood,' Khalid and Tariq both say at the same time. Yasmine gives them a dirty look like she wants to swallow them with her eyes.

Amira shouts God's name and starts crying.

'Take my baby out, I don't mind dying,' she sobs.

'Habibi, I am doing my best, you are bleeding too much and I have nothing and we are in the middle of nowhere.'

'Can you save my baby?'

'I will, you just rest!'

Amira closes her eyes and she is smiling. I know that Yasmine is lying to her but I don't know why. My head starts hurting me like someone is knocking inside. I close my eyes and bite on my tongue so hard it hurts. I go to the bathroom and take out the ear in my pocket and speak to it about Amira. Is she going away from us too? I find soap on the sink and pick it up and smear it on the wall and play around with it. It smells nice, like flowers are growing inside. I hum a song that Baba used to sing in the morning over breakfast. I still think about him leaving us all the time. I wonder if he is still with us or went to mama? I don't know who he loves more. He has been calling out mama's name a lot lately so it scares me that he wants to go to her. I smear the soap harder on the walls.

'Adam get out of there, I need to use the bathroom!' Tariq knocks on the door.

'One second.'

I put the ear back in my pocket and get out of the bathroom. Tariq goes in and as I walk away he comes out again and shouts my name. Pigeons come out of his mouth. I don't like pigeons, which means I won't like what he is going to say.

'Did you do this Adam?'

'Do what?'

'Put the soap on the wall!'

I did it because it was fun. I don't want to get into trouble for it. I put my head down and don't say anything.

'Go in and clean it up.'

'How?'

'You figure it out!'

I start banging my feet on the floor and shouting.

'Adam stop! Don't try that with me!'

I don't say anything and continue to bang my feet. I don't like this.

'STOP IT!' Yasmine shouts and I freeze in place. My heart stops. I am scared of Yasmine.

'She's dying and you're crying! How many things can I deal with at once?'

'I'm dying?' Amira whispers.

'Close your eyes Habibi, you're not feeling well.'

'I feel like my baby is slowly coming out! I am having cramps.'

Yasmine's face looks hopeless. If Yasmine loses hope we won't stand together. She is our glue.

'Shall I push harder?' Amira breathes heavily. This is all confusing. The colour in her face is fading away like a shaved lemon.

'Just relax, your baby will come out on its own.'

I get up and walk off of the boat. Everyone is shouting, upset and angry with me. I want to jump into the water. I just showered and smell nice and I think the water is dirty but I want to feel free. I want to feel free. I jump into the water with my clothes on and feel my body shrink from the cold. I laugh and jump up and down in the water. The boat moves up and down slowly because there is movement inside. I lie on my back in the water and watch the boat go up and down. I wish I could live here. After the war I want to come back and live here. I flap my hands up and down in the water and start putting it in my mouth and spitting it out. I love being in the water.

'Adam come back in! It's dark,' Ali calls out for me.

'I don't want to!'

'Yasmine told me to tell you!'

I quickly climb the ladder, get dressed and follow Ali.

'Are you still going to Damascus?' Ali asks me.

'Of course, are you?'

'I don't know, I like it here.'

We walk in and see Amira breathing really hard and sweating. Her face is see-through. You can see her veins and the blood pumping under her skin.

'Pray Amira, pray, don't give up!' Yasmine is holding her hand. Khalid is blowing onto her face.

'Adam please get me water from the sink,' Yasmine asks. I am soaking wet but she doesn't say anything. Did she not notice or does she not care any more? I fill a cup with water and give it to her. She puts her hand inside and sprinkles the water on Amira's forehead. She looks up at me and tells me to take my shirt off.

'Why do you want my shirt Yasmine?'

'For Amira.'

I take my shirt off and Yasmine squeezes it and puts it on Amira's forehead. Amira is still bleeding. I don't know how long it's been but that's a huge loss of blood.

'Can I go to sleep Yasmine?'

Yasmine doesn't look at me so I just go to the other side of the boat, take my trousers off and hang them to dry. I hide and wear a towel around my waist and go under the covers. This feels so good. I can hear a lot of noises so I cover my ears with the pillow and think of running around in a park. I want to run until I can't breathe any more. I run in my thoughts until I fall asleep.

★

I wake up to no noise from outside or from inside. No one is awake. I open the door into the other room and see everyone sleeping on the floor. Why are they sleeping all together? I lean down over each of them to make sure they're breathing. I start with Yasmine first. Amira is in the middle of them with her hands on her stomach and a bloody cloth on her stomach. Is she feeling better now? I try to notice her breathing patterns but I see her chest move up and down once and that's all. As I was about to touch her to try to wake her up Ali's eyes open and he jumps up.

'You scared me!'

'Sorry, I wanted to see if everyone is alive.'

'We all are!'

'I can't see Amira breathing…'

Ali looks down at Amira and puts his hand on her heart.

'I can feel something but I don't know if it's good.'

'What shall we do?'

'Amira… Amira…' Ali whispers into her ears. I slowly poke her three times and feel my fingers start to twitch so move away from her. I can't see her breathing at all.

'Do you think she is dead Ali?'

'I don't know.' His face looks sad.

'I don't understand how she is here but she is not at the same time.'

'Death is weird…'

'Maybe if we shake her we can wake her up?'

Ali and I both start shaking her and calling her name. Her hands slide to the side and there's a darker circle of blood on the cloth where her hands were. It doesn't look nice. I can imagine maggots coming out of her stomach and eating away at the blood. I close my eyes and shake my head.

'What is it Adam?'

I don't reply and keep shaking my head till the thought leaves my mind. I bite down really hard and grind my teeth together. The sound annoys Ali but I can't stop. Everyone else starts getting up and I move back to sit in the corner. I don't want anyone to touch me.

'Adam?' Yasmine's voice sounds like she swallowed a frog.

I slightly smile at her then close my eyes and rock myself. Mama used to put a lot of scents and candles around me so I could relax. I wish I could do that again. It helped me forget the bullies at school. I think it would also help me forget how many people have died in front of me. I want to delete every memory from the war. I want to start again. I don't even know what day or year we are in. How long has it been? Years? Months? Days? I don't even know any more. My mind thinks of all these things really fast and then everything stops midway and there's a beautiful image in my mind of Amira's face when she first came to visit us. She looked like a princess. I want to paint her. I start in my mind because I have no paper. Or maybe I can paint on one of the rocks outside in the harbour. I get up and run outside. I can hear them shouting my name but I don't reply. I collect some rocks and come back. Everyone is sitting around a white cloth and praying. Apart from Amira... Is that Amira? Khalid is praying loudly and everybody else's lips are moving but I hear no sound from them. I feel my body start shaking and I start screaming

Isa's name and cry. My body starts collapsing on me and my screams gets louder. I can't see or hear anyone any more. I am alone in a white box because I don't want to see any more. I want to be blind.

Chapter Twenty-One

CARMINE

I CAN'T HEAR ANYTHING and I don't know where I am. I try to open my eyes but can only see the strong sun shining. I feel like I am riding on a camel's hump. I can't see what is happening. I move my hand around and feel hair. I move my hand quickly and try to move away. I don't know what I am doing.

'Yasmine!'

'Shh calm down!' I don't recognise the voice. Am I kidnapped? No God, please!

'Yasmine! Help me!' I shout.

'I'm here Adam, what's the matter?'

'I can't see Yasmine, I can't see, where am I?'

I feel someone put me down on the ground, put their hands around my head and pull something off and I can see again. I look around and feel good again. I'm alive! I haven't been kidnapped!

'Did you not recognise my voice Adam?' Khalid laughs.

I look at him. Now I recognise his voice but before I couldn't. I don't know why.

'Where was I?

'We are walking, Khalid was carrying you on his back.'

I didn't know Khalid could carry me, I thought he couldn't do anything without his hands. Tariq usually carries me.

'Where's Tariq?' I look around and only see Ali, Yasmine and Khalid.

'Where's Tariq?' I ask again.

'He's coming, we just went ahead of him, he met some friends.'

I look back and don't see anyone, we are on an empty street.

'He's not behind us,' I say.

'I just told you he's coming, we are near Damascus,' Yasmine says. I listen to her and don't say anything. I look back once more and hope to see Tariq walking up to us, but he isn't.

'Come on, let's walk.'

I have a good feeling bubbling inside me. We are near Damascus and we are going to be safe again. I might even see mama again because Aunt Suha is mama's twin and everybody says she looks like mama but I don't think so but maybe now she does. The skin on my feet is hard and cracked. It looks like mama's before she left. I asked mama why her feet were like that and she said it was because she worked hard. I prayed that her feet would get better, I can't remember if they did because I didn't take notice before she left us. She was too sick and her feet were covered with blankets. Mama left all of a sudden one day, I was at school and I came back and Yasmine told me she left. I didn't believe her and started breaking and kicking things because I was angry and I had a black hole in my chest. I wanted to break my ribcage and fill the black hole. It hurt a lot and I didn't know what to do with it. Why can't I see mama again? But now I've buried the black hole and I don't let it come back. I didn't know how close the cities were in Syria until we walked all this way. I can tell people I had an adventure and had to walk all the way from Aleppo to Damascus. I don't think they would believe me but it's true. We enter a city that says 'Welcome' and I smile at the sign. It is a kind sign.

'Yasmine are we really close?'

'Really close…'

'Yes! I am happy Yasmine.'

Yasmine smiles but it doesn't spread across her face. I don't want to rest in this town, I want to go straight to Damascus, I am really excited.

'Are we going to stop again?'

'Not in this town, the next one.'

'Do we have to stop? Can we go to Damascus straightaway?'

'Everyone will be tired by the time we get there.'

'Did you hear that Ali?' I run to him 'We are going to be in Damascus tomorrow!'

'I can't wait!'

'Neither can I! Do you think we can stay there forever and never see the war again?'

'I don't know, I hope so.'

Ali doesn't speak like 16 any more. He used to laugh and run around at school and everybody used to want to speak to him. People used to call him cool. I don't know how that makes sense. Cool means he was icy but I didn't see him as icy, I saw him as fun and I wanted to be his friend. I put my hand in my pocket and feel the ear in there. I want to pull it out and speak to it about how excited I am but I am scared that someone will see it and take it off me. I don't know whose ear it is but imagine if they can actually hear everything I am telling them but they don't know where the voice is coming from? I laugh to myself then look around to see if anyone noticed. I hear beeping coming from a car behind us. We move out of the way but the car doesn't stop beeping.

'Want a ride?' a man shouts sticking his head out of the window. The car looks small. I don't know how we are all going to fit in there.

'We're fine thanks,' Yasmine says as she waves her hand and walks on. Why is she saying no? I want to get into the car.

'Why Yasmine?'

'We can't get into a stranger's car!'

Yasmine's right but I hate walking now. It's so boring and no one is talking.

'When is Tariq coming back?'

'Soon…' Yasmine doesn't even look at me. How does she know he's coming back soon?

The car beeps again and comes closer this time. I notice Yasmine's shoulders sloping and her neck looks like it is about to break off. It's like she is holding an invisible heavy child on her shoulders. Baba used to carry me on his shoulders when I was four years old. I remember that clearly, I was flapping my hands up and down and I wanted to speak but I couldn't.

'Get in the car, we are heading down.'

'No thank you,' I tell them.

'I said get in!'

Khalid turns around and tells them to leave us alone. They laugh at Khalid and stop the car. Two men come out and smile while walking towards us. What do they want? I have no money to give them like in the movies.

'You don't want to get in?'

None of us answer.

'Oh come on! We're joking, we're not going to fight!' They start laughing and slapping their hands together in a high five. Their chests suddenly sink in and they look skinny. They don't look scary any more. What do they want?

'Come on! Did you not recognise me Khalid? I recognised you just from your walk from behind.'

'Do I know you?'

'Seriously? You haven't changed! Apart from… Anyway it's

Walid!' The man speaking looks down at Khalid's hands and this makes me angry. I don't want them to bully my brother the way people bullied me at school. I'm not going to use my anger on them because mama said I should never fight.

'Walid? Seriously?' Khalid has a huge smile on his face now.

'Yes!' Walid comes towards Khalid and gives him a hug. I hear their chests slap together. It is a big hug.

'How have you been man?'

'Come, I'll tell you in the car.'

Khalid tells us to all get into the car even though I don't see much space.

'Give me that box, I'll put it in the back,' one of Khalid's friends says. I don't want to give him my paintings. I look at Khalid and try to send him messages without saying anything.

'Come on Adam…'

'Can I hold it?'

'There's no space.'

I hold tighter onto my box and stomp my feet, I don't want to give it to them.

'How about you put it in the back yourself?' Khalid asks me.

I can do that because then I'll know where I put it and can take it out later.

I walk to the boot and put my box in the right corner.

Yasmine, Ali and Khalid and I are squashed in the back of the car. Liquorice is with us too. I feel like they're stealing the air I'm breathing. I breathe in and out deeply so I don't suffocate.

'Stop doing that,' Yasmine whispers to me and pinches my leg.

'I can't breathe.'

'Yes you can.'

I want to tell her again that I can't breathe but she'll just get angry.

The two men start talking to Khalid about things I don't understand.

'We've been having meetings without you, we were wondering where you had gone.'

'Our house got bombed…'

'I'm sorry to hear that. We are brothers, you could have come to us.'

Khalid doesn't say anything.

'Where are you headed then?'

'Damascus,' Khalid replies.

'Ah of course, everyone is trying to get there.'

'You going there?'

'No, but we won't drop you too far from there. We can't go there with all this ammunition.'

'What does ammunition mean?' I ask Yasmine. She elbows me on the side of my stomach and tells me to stay quiet.

One of the men looks back at me after I ask the question and smiles. I don't like him. He looks like he is hiding something behind his eyes.

It feels like the car is going to break down any minute. We have been driving down a straight road for so long I didn't even know if we were really moving any more until I felt the bumps on the road. Every now and then it sounds like the bottom of the car is scratching the ground. It makes a horrible sound, which makes my teeth feel sensitive. I hate it. One of the guys puts the radio on and there's a song on that I love. I always want to clap my hands and jump up and down whenever I hear it. I start smiling and clapping my hands. I can't jump up and down in here though because there's no space.

'Turn it down, I'm trying to sleep,' the other guy says.

I can hardly hear anything anyway so I stop clapping. I continue the song in my mind though.

'What about this intervention crap? What do you think of it?' Khalid's friend asks him.

'Mmm, I don't know, I don't talk about politics any more.'

'Why? That's ridiculous, that's all people talk about nowadays!'

'Has anybody from your family died?'

'No, thank God they're all in hiding.'

'That's why you're still interested in politics and I'm not.'

'Come on, don't take everything to heart, we'll get our country back. We've got a plan, I tell you!'

'What's the plan? Are we all going to die by the end of it? Is this what our country deserves?'

'You've changed so much.'

'I've opened my eyes, I don't want to fight anyone any more, I just want my family and I to live peacefully…'

'Do you have anyone is Damascus? Because they won't let you go in otherwise.'

'Yes, we have family.'

'Well I hope you get what you want. I just don't see things turning out well so we need to fight. They will keep on killing us otherwise!'

'Since when do we kill family and say otherwise they'll kill us?'

'I don't even trust my own family.'

'Well that's why your eyes won't open.'

'The army won't stop killing us, if we don't fight back we will all be the meat in their soup.'

Khalid doesn't reply and I think about what he means by meat in their soup. Will they eat us?

Yasmine is sleeping so I close my eyes to sleep too. I have nothing else to do.

★

'Are we going to sleep here?'

'It's dark, we can't walk now.'

We are very close to Damascus. I can see the lights in the distance now. I am so excited. I can't wait. We are going to be safe at last. Liquorice looks pink with happiness too.

'Is Tariq coming?'

'Yes Habibi,' says Yasmine.

'Where is he?'

Yasmine pulls me closer to her and plays with my hair.

'Look Yasmine, I can see a TV through the window!'

We stop outside the window and look in. I miss watching TV. There's a group of soldiers that each put a hand to their head and start marching and singing.

'What do you think they're singing Ali?'

'The national anthem, that's what it looks like.'

'Really? Let's sing!'

Ali and I walk towards the window and start singing our national anthem like we used to at school and watch the TV with the soldiers marching and then it changes into kids like us singing. I look over at Yasmine and she has her eyes closed and there are tears coming down her face. I stop singing to go and see what's wrong but she opens her eyes and tells me to carry on so I do. I feel my heart open up and my throat tighten. I can feel tears building up. I clear my throat and carry on singing then Ali and I bang one foot down at the same time at the end. We look at each other and laugh. I wipe away the tear coming down and run to Yasmine.

'Did you like it Yasmine?'

'I loved it!'

'Why are you crying?'

'Because the last time I sang that national anthem I was so proud.'

'The last time I sang it was at school Yasmine.'

'Yes I know Habibi.'

'I don't think I can sleep tonight, I am so excited!'

'Me too Habibi, I can't wait for us to be safe again.'

'Shall we set out tents here?'

'Let's walk a little into the centre.'

Khalid walks in front of us because he can't carry anything and is looking for a place for us to rest for the night. There's an old woman sitting down and crying on the side of the road. Her thick glasses make her tears look huge.

'Why is she crying?'

'I don't know everything Habibi.'

Khalid stops and we start setting up our tents. I try to set mine up as quickly as I can so I can run around and have fun.

I am tired now. I said I wouldn't sleep but I have run around a lot so I am tired. I pick some rocks so I can paint on them.

'I found some friends, come play with us Adam,' Ali calls out to me.

I have just run around and I don't want to meet new people so I look away and take my painting kit out.

'He's weird,' one of the girls says. Ali doesn't reply.

'Do you want to come with us to school tomorrow Ali?' someone asks him.

'Sure! Can I bring my friend with me?'

'The one painting on something weird?'

'He's painting on a rock.'

'Why? I knew he was weird!'

'He's not, he just likes painting!'

'Whatever, bring him if you want.'

They all run and play. I like Ali. No one has ever defended me when people called me weird before.

'Yasmine can you please open your tent?'

'Why?'

'Because I am scared of being alone.'

'Where's Khalid?'

'In his tent as well.'

Yasmine opens her tent and sits up and prays on beads. I haven't seen them in ages. Where was she hiding them? Baba used to always use them to praise God. I wish I hadn't remembered Baba because now I don't feel happy. I want to paint Aleppo the way it looked before we left.

'What are you painting?'

'Aleppo.'

'Really?'

'The way I saw it when we were walking out.'

'It wasn't pretty!'

'I don't paint pretty things Yasmine.'

Yasmine laughs and Ali comes running back.

'Are you sure you don't want to play with us? We are playing hide-and-seek!'

'I am sitting with Yasmine.'

'If I stay here do you want to play with me?'

'Okay then, I can paint after we play.'

'What do you want to play?'

'Do you want to play the countries game?'

'Sure. Do you want to join us Yasmine?' Ali asks.

'Why not!'

We start playing and then I hear a weird hissing sound that I recognise from cartoons.

'Can you hear that?' I ask.

'I can!' Ali says and puts his hand behind his ear to try to listen out.

'It sounds familiar.'

Yasmine says that at the same time as there is a loud bang and then suddenly I can't even see in front of me any more. There is a thick cloud of smoke and I want to yell out for Yasmine but I can't breathe. I cough and cough trying to find some air to breathe but I can't. I close my eyes and try to scream but I just cough instead. My chest feels like it's filled with smoke. I feel a hand on me and open my eyes to see Yasmine. I want to smile but I cough out some more and see blood on my hands. I move away from Yasmine and start coughing even more and shaking. I can't stop shaking. I fall to the ground and Yasmine falls after me. I don't know if she is shaking too. My eyes start to close and I can't open them. My breathing is deep and I am forcing myself to breathe in and out. I want to tell Yasmine the answer to the country she was stuck on but I feel myself going to sleep. I hear Yasmine's voice and even though her face is close to mine her voice seems so far away. Yasmine speak louder. Yasmine I'm just going to sleep for a bit but when I wake up I'll finish my painting and call it 'The Boy From Aleppo Who Painted the War'. I know you'll like this one Yasmine. I feel a warm river of blood flow through my nose. It makes me even sleepier so I sleep.

Chapter Twenty-Two

CLOUDY WHITE

I OPEN MY EYES to blurred lines. I feel like I have been dreaming my whole life. I rub my eyes but I see the same thing: blurs. I touch the air in front of me to make sure nothing is there. My eyes hurt and my head pounds like an elephant is knocking on my brain. What is happening?

'Yasmine…' I whisper. I clear my throat and try to speak louder but it's still a whisper. I have lost my voice. My head starts to get dizzy and I quickly lean down and start vomiting. My vision starts to clear up a little and I remember Baba telling me to see with my vision and not my eyes so I try to think about his voice so I can feel better. I see people lying around, almost as if everyone just decided to go to sleep. Some roll on the ground and are whispering things I can't hear. They look like cockroaches after being sprayed with poison. I look around and find Yasmine to my right. I crawl to her and put my ear to her chest. I can't feel anything. I can hear a low rumbling sound like she is trying to breathe but she can't. I don't even know if it's coming from her or someone else. I'm in so much pain. I can barely move and everything hurts. I cry while trying to move. I just want this to end.

'Yasmine! Yasmine!' I bang on her chest and shake her. She moves to my shaking but she doesn't open her eyes or respond. I don't have any strength to shake her any harder so I keep doing it the same way.

'Yasmine, please wake up!'

I start crying and with my tears and limited vision I can't even see Yasmine's face any more. I repeat Yasmine's name and shake her until my hands hurt me and I cry loudly. I keep trying until I start coughing painfully, I can hear the pain in my own tears but I can't speak loud enough for Yasmine to hear it. I put my head on her chest and then get up and grab her clothes in my hands and punch her chest. Yasmine please don't die. Yasmine we are so close. We can see Damascus from here. The same feeling that made me sleepy starts coming down my nose again. I lift my head up and touch it. The warm thick texture brings back too many memories that I can't put together. They are scattered all over my brain and it feels like I have electricity burning away in my mind.

'Yasmine! Breathe!' I shout with everything in me and hit her chest as hard as I can. I feel something but I am not sure if I am right. I hit her again as hard as I can and hear her trying to gasp for air. Yes! Yes Yasmine! Breathe. I remember seeing this on TV but I don't know what I'm doing, that doesn't matter now, nothing matters, just come back Yasmine! She gasps again and I wipe my tears and close my eyes. I have to do this. I have to do this. I hold my breath and hold Yasmine's face in my hands. She can't leave me. She is my only sister and she looks like mama. I put her head on my lap and open her mouth. I close my eyes really tight again and ignore the colours leaping into my mind and the images that make my heart shake. I put my mouth onto Yasmine's and hold my breath tighter before fear comes leaping onto me. I blow and blow and blow into Yasmine's mouth and for a minute let go of all the colours and images that have always held me back.

'Yasmine!'

Her eyes roll under her eyelids and open a little. Yes! Yes! I love you Yasmine! Please don't leave me. I am always scared without you.

Yasmine starts coughing and her arms shake. I hold them down for her and sit her up. Her body feels heavy as if she has eaten rocks. Her body isn't helping me. It pushes me back. I give her one big push and rest her head on my shoulder.

'Yasmine, you're alive.'

Yasmine coughs more and starts scratching her skin.

'It hurts…' she whispers and coughs more.

'We are so close to Damascus, you'll be okay.'

I sit down in front of her and put her arms around my neck and try to stand up slowly.

'Yasmine please try to get up, I feel weak.'

She doesn't say anything but I can feel her try to push her body up. I push her up a little more and get up. I try to forget how heavy she is and walk slowly.

'We are going to Damascus Yasmine. Aunt Suha is waiting for us, we promised we would be there.'

'Adam…'

'Yes Yasmine!'

Yasmine's head falls on my shoulder and she doesn't say anything. I think she is tired.

I walk past the bodies lying down like they will never get up again. I would usually be so sad Liquorice is gone but all I can think about is Yasmine and my brothers. War means losing what you love. Peace is what you have left when the war is over. I look back and try to look for the boys but I can't see clearly. I can hardly see in front of me. Everything is a blur and the bodies and houses look like ghosts. But I can see the lights of Damascus. I can see the lights…

Chapter Twenty-Three

ROSE

I CAN'T EXPLAIN HOW we got here but I know God was with us. I am sitting in the bathtub with tiny bottles of oil. Mama used to put the same ones around me to help me to relax. The smell makes me want to melt under the water. I duck my head under and start crying. I feel like I'm drowning. I miss everyone. There are so many holes in my heart. I can't fill them up. I only have Yasmine left now. I miss the thought of mama smiling at me while I painted. She said I reminded her of herself when I got absorbed in painting. I miss the look on Baba's face as he unlocked the door to find me waiting for him every day after work. I miss watching my brothers argue and tease each other and how they'd tell me to go away when I would ask too many questions. It's been so long since I've recalled these memories. I wipe my tears but I can't stop this constant waterfall. I remember crying this much when mama left. Yasmine is the closest I have to mama but she's not her. I get out of the bathroom and walk around Aunt Suha's apartment to try and distract myself from all these thoughts. I find a painting set left by her on the shelf near the window: a brush in a cup with paint bottles nearby. I take one of the brushes out and just stare at every hair, every colour stain, which hasn't been washed off properly. Purple is Yasmine's anger when I do something wrong. Blue is Khalid's sadness when he came back home without any hands. Grey is Baba when he kept asking for mama and white... white is Isa's death.

Why is this happening, why, why, why? Please stop, please let this all end, I want my family back. I just want to see them all again. I want to taste mama's food. I want to play with Liquorice. I just want to go back home now! I feel dizzy. My head really hurts and my chest feels heavy. I can barely see in front of me but I feel sleepy. I go to the room Yasmine is in and I lie on the floor, I'll just rest until she gets up. I stare at the clock on the wall, it's 3:30 p.m. I'll wake up in an hour. I close my eyes and smile. I let go of all my colours and thoughts and look up at a white sky. I can at last see the sun through the clouds of smoke that used to cover me. I can taste the colour green in my mouth.

'Adam. My sweet Adam. I have missed you so much Habibi.'

'I missed you so much too mama. The world is such a scary place without you.'

I hug mama tightly and cry my heart out.

'I know Habibi, I know, I'm here now.'

Chapter Twenty-Four

APRICOT YASMINE

'ADAM! ADAM!' What in the world is going on? 'Adam Habibi!' Adam is shaking on the ground like a fish out of the water.

'Auntie! Auntie! I need your help! Auntie!'

I get up quickly and try to run to Adam but trip over the covers around me. My body still feels weak and I can hardly pick myself up. I drag myself once more and lift Adam's head up and kiss him. Adam Habibi, I'm here for you.

'Wake up Adam!'

He starts to violently shake and foam runs out of his mouth.

'Auntie! Quick! Bring a wet towel and bowl of water!'

'What is it Yasmine?' Auntie runs into the room 'Oh my God! Okay I'll bring everything!'

'Quick!'

I turn him to the side and tear off the lower part of my skirt, roll it up and put it on my lap to lift his head up higher. I start to cry while holding his head close to me, every tear landing on his delicate face.

'Please Adam, please hang in there, please Adam, my God, please hold on! Everything will be okay, we'll go home together again, I'll watch you paint, I'll make you food, I'll play with you again. Please Adam!'

I can't stop crying, I would never forgive myself if I lost him, I can't lose him, I promised mama. I promised Baba. I promised myself.

I look up at the clock on the wall: it's 3:31 p.m. If he doesn't stop after a minute I'm going to have to call the ambulance. The last time Adam had a seizure was when mama died, I guess he has the same kind of burden on his shoulders now. Aunt Suha comes in and times a minute. She splashes water on his face and prays under her breath. It's moments like these that I realise that Adam is just like my own child. Even if I don't have the chance to have a baby of my own, having Adam is a blessing.

Adam's breathing suddenly stops and he lies still. What is happening? My heart drops to my feet. A laugh comes out of me from shock. No, is this some kind of joke? I freeze in place. Aunt Suha is shaking him and looking at me but I can't react. I can't. Have I lost all feeling?

'Yasmine! He's breathing! It's low but he's breathing!' I snap out of it quickly and hold him tight. I wipe away the foam from his mouth and kiss him over and over again. Aunt Suha laughs through her tears.

Adam opens his eyes and just lies in my arms. For the first time he doesn't move away from human contact. I smile at him and he smiles back. I start laughing and can't stop. Why not? I am happy with Adam and we are safe. I'm in a happy place. I laugh on and on until Aunt Suha joins me. I look down at Adam and can see him trying to smile.

*

All the tears in my body have dried and I can't think of anything that will ever make me cry. I'm a new person now. I'm watering the plants in the sitting room while Adam watches TV and Aunt Suha takes a nap. I feel serene. The doorbell rings and Adam jumps up.

'I don't think we should answer, it's not our house.'

'But… the doorbell rang Yasmine.'

'I know Habibi, just wait,' Yasmine says. The doorbell rings again and Aunt Suha shifts on the sofa. I guess I should open it before it wakes her up.

'Let's tiptoe to the door,' I whisper to Adam.

'Why?'

'Because it's more fun!'

I open the door and freeze in place. Despite all the shocks I have been through this one has probably the strongest effect on my heart. I feel like every cell in my body is trying to react in a different way and they can't decide what to do.

'Yasmine, it's that guy you like.'

'Wisa… How…'

'May I come in?'

'Of course!'

I can't believe my eyes. I want to say so much. I want to cry and laugh at the same time. I guess I still do have tears in my body.

'I had to go through a lot to find you,' he says as he smiles.

Ahhh that smile, so familiar. I can close my eyes and fall into it.

'Do you think we can fix things?'

'Yes!' My mouth spits the word out. I didn't even take a second to think about it.

Wisam and Adam laugh at me. Two of my favourite men are here. I wish the others were too.

'Who is it?' Aunt Suha shouts.

I don't know what to say. Who is he to me?

'A visitor for Yasmine,' he answers for me.

Aunt Suha comes wobbling into the hallway with her hand on her back.

'He's... He's...'

'The guy you told me about?'

'Yes.'

There's an awkward silence as we all stand in the hallway not knowing what to do.

'Do come in,' Aunt Suha tells him.

He's just as handsome as always. I really missed him.

'I came to ask you for Yasmine's hand in marriage.'

What? What? All of a sudden?

'Well, her father isn't here and she lost the rest of her family so I don't know what to say.'

'I know where her father is...'

'You do?' I jump in.

'I made sure I told my colleagues in Turkey to look out for him. He's in safe hands God willing.'

I can't stop smiling.

'Yasmine, is there an invisible clown pulling at your mouth?' Adam asks. I know he's being serious but we all laugh and again Adam breaks the ice. He's my angel.

'Do you want to see your father again?' Wisam gets off the sofa and squats on his knees in front of Adam.

'You mean Baba? He didn't say goodbye to me.'

'I'll take that as a yes.'

'Take what as a yes?'

Wisam looks at me confused.

'You'll get used to him I promise,' I say as I wink at him.

He winks back and I forget my past, present and future and just replay his wink in my mind.

I look back at Adam who begins to paint. He picks the colour red and starts to fill in the sketch of Baba's face. He is smiling in the picture and there are no bags under his eyes. Our house in Aleppo is in the background. There is no grey colour in sight.

I smile and a tear rolls down my cheek. My innocent Adam. My boy from Aleppo who painted the war.

Acknowledgments

For their support and belief in me, many thanks to my loving parents. Without your wisdom I wouldn't be half way here.

To my Song, thank you for your love, patience and the many hours you have spent working with me. I will always be grateful for everything you've done.

A huge thank you to my wonderful friends Iulia Avram, Tone Troen and Tharmim Azzid for their constant humour, and good-hearted nature. You always knew how to lift my spirits.

Last but not least, I would like to express my gratitude to Todd Swift for believing in me and showing me a great deal of understanding. You helped me believe in myself.

Notes On Arabic Words

Adhan — Call to prayer
Baklawa — Sweet pastry
Eid — An Islamic festival
Enta Malak — You're an angel
Habibi — My love
Khalas — That's it / end of conversation
Khanjar — Sword
Labna — Strained yoghurt
Makkah — Mecca
Miswak — Teeth cleaning twig / Islamic toothbrush
Ota — Cat
PBUH — Peace be upon him
Prophet Suleiman — Prophet Solomon
Sahlab — Hot milk and Salep dessert
Sheikhs — Islamic scholars
Surat Al-Fatiha — First verse from the Quran
Wudhu — Ablution before prayer
Yalla — Come on
Ya Kalb — You dog - derogatory term